When Kemoc, brother of witches and son of an Earth-man, rode out with his weird allies to pursue the conquest of the lost lands of the East, it was to prove the test of his whole purpose for existence.

For there was one among that mixed cavalcade of warriors who was not of them—whose form concealed a different and far more alien menace than any they expected to encounter. That alien in disguise bore Kemoc a very special enmity.

It would take Kemoc the very limit of his inborn war-lock talents just to survive the rigors of a war against unknown monsters in an unconquered land——let alone to meet the unsuspected onslaught that rode at his very side.

⑤

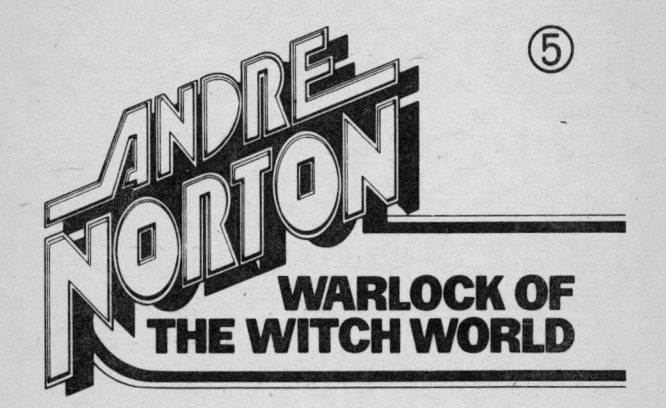

ANDRE NORTON

WARLOCK OF THE WITCH WORLD

ACE FANTASY BOOKS
NEW YORK

WARLOCK OF THE WITCH WORLD

An Ace Fantasy Book/published by arrangement with
the author

PRINTING HISTORY
Ninth printing / April 1983

ISBN: 0-441-87326-X

Ace Fantasy Books are published by Charter Communications, Inc.,
200 Madison Avenue, New York, N.Y. 10016.
PRINTED IN THE UNITED STATES OF AMERICA

I

It has been an oft-told story of our birthing that our mother, the Lady Jaelithe (she who put aside her witchhood in Estcarp to wed the outland warrior, Simon Tregarth), did demand of some Power she served certain gifts for us, whom she bore in great and painful travail. That she named my brother Kyllan, warrior, my sister Kaththea, witch (or one to control powers), and asked for me, wisdom. But it has been that my wisdom consists in knowing that I know very little, though the thirst for learning has ever been in me. Only, in spite of all my striving, I have done no more than nibble at the edges of knowledge's rich cake, liplicked the goblet rim of true wisdom. But perhaps to know one's limitations is, in itself, a kind of sagecraft.

In the beginning, when we were children, I did not lack fellowship, for we three, born at one birth (which in Estcarp was something hitherto unknown) were also one in spirit. Kyllan was formed for action, Kaththea for feeling, and I—supposedly—for thought. We worked together smoothly, and the bond between us was tight, as if it were wrought of flesh as well as of spirit. Then came that bleak day when Kaththea was rift from us by the Wise Women who kept the rule of the land. And for a period we lost her.

Still, in a war a man can lose himself, or be able to put aside one set of fears for another, living from each sun's rising to its setting, each dusk to dawn. And that we were forced to do. For Kyllan and I rode with the Borderers who kept a thin line of ever-ready defense between Estcarp and the darksome menace of Karsten.

1

Then luck deserted me in a single swing of a short sword, and I was swept from usefulness into that human wastage resulting from the chances of war. Yet, for this once, I welcomed such a respite, painful as it was for my body. For from it came the freeing of our sister from the bondage of the Witches.

Though my right hand was maimed, my warrior life apparently past, I waited hardly past the outward healing of my wound before I went to Lormt. For during my days in the mountains I had stumbled upon a curious piece of knowledge. Which was this—though those of Estcarp knew the south of their long enemy Karsten, and the north of Arizon, greedy too for their downfall, the western seas where their long-time allies, the Sulcar seamen, cut wave and harried shores halfway around our world, yet of the east was no mention among them. It was as if the world ended at a chain of mountains we could see on clear days. And in the minds of those with whom we rode there was, I came to be sure, a block against that direction, so for them the east did not exist.

Lormt was very old, even for Estcarp which has a history so buried in the dust of years that no modern searching can disinter its beginnings. Once perhaps it was a town, though for what purpose one should be set in that bleak country I could not guess. Now it is only a moldering handful of buildings, surrounded by crumbling ruins. But in it there are records of the Old Race, long forgotten; though there are those who tunnel molewise among them, copying and recopying what seems to them worth the preserving, the choice of what to save, theirs alone. When, perhaps in the next cupboard may lie, in near tattered scraps, something far more worth renewing.

There I sought out an answer to this mystery of the unknown east. For Kyllan and I had not surrendered (though outwardly those about us might have believed that we did) our hope of bringing Kaththea forth and reuniting our company of three. But to escape the wrath of the Council we needed a refuge—and this eastern mystery might offer such.

So in Lormt I found two tasks to occupy me through the months; one the searching of ancient manuscripts; the other of learning to be a warrior once again, though now my left hand must curve to the sword hilt. For in the twilight world in which we lived, when the sun of Estcarp was red on the horizon, half-slipped into the dark of night, no man could ride unarmed.

I discovered enough to make me sure that in the east did indeed lie our salvation—or at least a chance of escaping the wrath of the witches. Also, I became once more a warrior—of sorts.

The final blow, decided upon by the Council, to finish Karsten, gave us our chance. While the Witches drew all power to their bidding—to stir the mountains of the south as a cook would stir a pudding in the kettle—Kyllan and I met once more at Etsford, which had been home to us. And we rode together through a night of turmoil, to bring our sister out of the trap which had held her so long.

Then did we go east, to find Escore, that riven land from which the Old Race had come in the far, far past, where the powers of both good and ill had been unleashed to walk as they would, wearing strange guises. We strove with those powers, separately and together. Kyllan, having used part of his gift on our behalf, laid himself open to the possession of one of these forces, and, while the cost to him was high in peril and pain, it

3

brought us to the People of Green Silences and into their sanctuary.

They were not wholly of our blood. Even as we were not wholly of the Old Race, sharing the inheritance from our father who had come from another space and time. Though they had in them some of the Old Race, yet for the rest they were older still, being akin to the land in a way which those of my blood are not. But then, in Escore there are many legends we had heard in our childhood which lived to walk, burrow, fly.

Then a geas was laid on Kyllan, by what Power we had no telling. And under it he went back across the mountains to Estcarp. From him spread a kind of need— I do not know the proper words for its description— which settled into some of the Old Race, who had been driven out of Karsten during the Kolder War and since had been a restless, homeless people. When he came back to us, they followed him.

Not only fighting men came so, but also their women and children, bringing all that they could to enable them to set up households in this new land. The Men of the Green Silences under Dahaun, their Lady (she who had succored Kyllan during his great peril), and Ethutur, their warlord, aided them over the cliffs and brought them to the safe Valley.

So much have I wrote in this chronicle, and perhaps it repeats what is already a too familiar tale. But it has been set upon me to add this to the record begun by Kyllan. This is my portion of the story, which stands a little apart from the history of the Great War, though it was a rightful place in that, since it helped in bringing about the final victory.

Rightfully, my adventure begins in the Valley—which was a lightsome place in which the heart could rejoice.

Through the years the ones who dwelt there had set such Symbols and bonds about it that it remained free of all evil—a place in which a man could take his ease. I knew those Symbols from my studies at Lormt and I thought them high protection.

Peaceful as it was in the Valley, we could not give ourselves to rest there, for about us the whole of Escore was astir. Long ago this land had been riven time and time again with wars as great as those which now gnawed our homeland in the west. Here men and women had sought knowledge, and then passed beyond the bonds set by prudence for such seeking. There arose those who sought power for the sake of power alone; and from that always issues the Shadow which is darker than any night. There was a drawing apart and some of the Old Race retreated over the mountains, wrecking behind them all roads, closing their minds to the past.

Then the remnants warred, titanic and awful force against force, blasting and blighting. Some, such as the Green People, who abode still by laws, drew back into the places of wilderness. And to them came others—a handful of humans of good will; others who were the result of early experimentation by the dabblers in strange knowledge, yet were not evil, nor had been used for evil purposes.

But all these were too few and too weak to challenge the Great Ones, drunk with their controls of energies beyond our comprehending. So they lay very low and waited for the storms to sweep and ebb. Some of the Dark Ones destroyed each other in those blasting struggles. Others withdrew through Gates they had opened that led to other times and spaces—even as that gate through which my father had come into Estcarp. But all of their striving left behind pools of ancient evil, servants

5

who were freed or abandoned. It was unknown, too, whether or not they might choose to return if something chanced to summon them.

When we first came into Escore, Kaththea had drawn upon her witch learning to save and aid us. In so doing she had broken the false calm which had long abode here. Things awoke and gathered, and the land was troubled, so that the Green People believed we were on the eve of new war. But this time we must fight or be utterly ground into powder between the millstones of the Dark.

Now came an in-gathering of all who were of the light, that we might plan against aroused evil. Ethutur had called this Council and we sat there, a strange mixture of peoples—or should I say, living creatures; for some in that assembly were not men at all—neither were they beasts.

Ethutur spoke for the Green People. To his right was a Renthan, who could and did bear men on occasion on his back, yet spoke with a voice when there was need, and captained a band of wily fighters—and that was Shapurn. On a large rock squatted a jewel-scaled lizard who used its front feet as hands and now fingered in its claws a cord on which were knotted at irregular intervals silver beads, as if these were reminders of points to be made in any discussion.

Beyond the lizard's rock was a helmed man whose like I had seen many times, and to his right and left sat a man and woman in stately cloaks-of-ceremony. This was Lord Hervon, who had come from the holding Kyllan had found in the hills, the Lady Christwitha, and his Leader-of-forces, Godgar. Then there were Kyllan and Kaththea and Dahaun. Perched on another rock—thus giving him more presence in a company which towered above him physically—was Farfar the Flannan, with feathered, human shaped body, spreading bird wings, clawed feet. The Flannan was there for reasons of prestige only, since his people lacked the concentration to be reckoned among a fighting force, although they made good messengers.

On the other side were the newcomers. There was another bird-like form, but it had the head of a lizard, narrow, toothed of jaw, covered with red scales which glittered in the sun, in bright contrast to its blue-gray feathers. From time to time it spread its wings uneasily, darting the head from side to side, eyeing the company with sharp measurement. This was a Vrang from the Heights and Dahaun had greeted it with ceremony as "Vorlong, the Wing Beater."

Beyond that strange ally was more human appearing company, four of them. These were, we had been told before their arrival, descendants of the Old Race who had fled long ago into the hills and managed there to exist and carve out some small pockets of safety. Chief among them was a tall man with the dark, familiar features of the true blood. He had the seeming of a young man, but that could be deceptive, since the Old Race show no signs of aging until a few weeks before death—if any of them live to grow old, which in the past years few have. He was both comely and courtly of manner.

And I hated him.

Bound together as we three had been, in the past we had never reached out beyond for companionship. After Kaththea had been torn from us, still had Kyllan and I been so allied. Even so, there had been comrades in arms which had our liking, and some we viewed with distaste. But never in the past had I known such strong emotion as speared me through—save when I had cut down some Karsten raider. Yet then my hated had been more for what the foe represented than the man himself. Whereas this Dinzil out of the Heights I hated bitterly, coldly, and the reason I did not know. In fact, I was so startled by the emotion which filled me when Dahaun introduced us that I hesitated over the greeting words.

And it seemed to me in that moment that he knew what I felt and was amused—as one would be amused at some act of a child. Yet I was not a child, as Dinzil would speedily discover if the need arose.

If the need arose . . . I realized it was not hatred alone which shook me whenever I looked upon that smooth, handsome face, but also apprehension . . . as if, at any moment, this lord of the peaks would suddenly change from what he was to something very dangerous to us all. Still, reason told me, the Green People had welcomed him in friendship, regarded his arrival as a stroke of good fortune. Since they knew all the dangers of this land, surely they would not freely open their gates to one who carried with him the taint of evil.

Kaththea had insisted when we first crossed the fields and woods of Escore that she could smell out pockets of old dark magic as an ill stench. My nose did not so mark Dinzil. Yet inside of me some guardian stood to arms whenever I looked upon him.

He spoke well at our council, with good sense and showing a knowledge of warfare. Those other lords and warriors with him would now and then offer some comment which laid plain to us a past in which Dinzil had been the backbone of their country.

Ethutur brought out maps which were cunningly fashioned of dried leaves, the ribs and markings on them serving for points and divisions. These we passed from hand to hand while the Green People and the men from the Heights supplied pertinent comments, as did also the nonhumans. Vorlong was very emphatic in his warning of a certain line of hills which bore, he croaked in barely understandable speech, three circles of standing stones containing something so deadly that even to fly above them brought death. We marked out those danger spots which were known until all present recognized them.

I was smoothing out one of those maps when I felt a queer drawing. My scar-twisted right hand—of it I was seldom aware nowadays, since it had ceased to pain me and I had as much use of it as I could reestablish with exercise—drew my eyes from the lines on the gray-brown surface of the map. I studied it, puzzled, and then glanced up.

Dinzil—he was looking at my hand. Looking and smiling a small smile, but one which brought a flush to my face. I wanted to snatch my hand away, hide it behind me. Why? It was scarred in honorable war, not from any shameful thing. Yet shame spread from that scar merely because Dinzil regarded it so—as if anything which marred the symmetry of one's flesh was a deformity one should conceal from the world.

Then his eyes arose from my hand to meet mine, and again I thought I read amusement in them—the kind of amusement some men find in the misshapen. And he knew that I knew—yet that only added to his amusement.

I must warn them, I thought feverishly. *Kyllan—Kaththea*— Surely they could share my apprehension and vague suspicion of this man. Let us but get to ourselves again and I would bring them into my mind so they could be on their guard. On guard against what? And why? To that I had no answer.

My eyes went once more to the map. And now, with a kind of defiance, I used my ridged hand with its two

9

stiffened fingers, to smooth it. In me anger was cold and deadly.

Ethutur spoke at last. "It is then decided that we send out the summons to the Krogan, the Thas—"

"Do not count upon them too much, my lord." That was Dinzil. "They are still neutral, yes. But it may well be their desire to remain so."

I heard an impatient exclamation from Dahaun. "If they believe that when battle is once enjoined they can be so, then they are fools!"

"In our eyes, perhaps," Dinzil answered her. "We look upon one side of a shield, my lady. They may not yet look upon the other. But neither do they wish to make such a choice at another's bidding. Knowing the Krogan at least, for we of the Heights have had some dealings with them in the past, we are also aware that if they are pushed they snap at the pusher. Therefore, approach them we must, but let it be done with no pressure. Give them time after the warn-sword is passed to hold their own council. Above all, do not show them an angry face if they say you nay. For this will not be a short struggle we now enter upon, but a long one. Those who stand uncommitted at its beginning, may be drawn in before its ending. If we would have them join behind our war horns, then leave them to their choices in their own time."

I saw Ethutur nod agreement, as did the others. We could not raise contrary voices, since this was their land and they knew it. But I thought it was never wise to war in a country where there are those uncommitted to either side, for a neutral can turn enemy suddenly and find an unprotected flank to attack.

"We send out the warn-sword to the Krogan, the Thas —the moss-ones?" Ethutur ended on a questioning note.

Dahaun laughed. "The moss-ones? Perhaps—if any

can find them. But they follow too much their own ways. Those we can count upon wholly stand here and now—is that what you would tell us, Lord Dinzil?"

He shrugged. "Who am I to call the roll of those who walk apart from my own men, Lady? It is but proper caution to awake, or summon, naught but those we have had dealings with in the past. Change and counterchange have wrought deeply here. Perhaps even long ago friends are not now to be trusted. Yes, I would say that what army we can trust to the blooding stand now within this safe Valley of yours—or shall when we marshal all our forces. The hills shall be horned. To the low country, yours the summons."

I had not dared to call mind to mind in that assembly, so I was impatient for its breaking. As yet we had but small idea of what powers or gifts those about us had—so I would not so summon my kin. Thus it was much later that I tried to get speech with them apart. I had the first luck with Kyllan as he rode with Horvan to seek a camping place for the ones from over-mountain. But first I was beside Godgar, falling into talk concerning the border war. We found we had once served in the same section of knife-edged ridges, but at different times.

His type I knew well. They are born to war, sometimes having the spark of leadership in them. But more often they are content to come to the horn as shield men under a commander they respect. Such are the hard and un-breakable core of any good force, unhappy in peace, feeling perhaps unconsciously that their reason for life vanishes when the sword remains too long in the scabbard. He rode now as one who sniffs a scent upon the air, glancing from side to side, marking out the country for his memory as a scout, alert to all the tides of war.

Horvan found land to his liking and set about putting

up tent shelters, though in the valley so mild was the air that one could well lay in the open with comfort. At last I was free to ride with Kyllan, and, avoiding mind touch here, I spoke to him of Dinzil.

I had spoken for some moments before I was aware of Kyllan's frown. I stopped, to look at him sharply. Then I did use the mind touch.

To discover with surprise—confusion—because I found something which at first I could not identify and then met—for the first time in our close-knit lives— refusal to believe! It was a shock, for Kyllan believed that I was now one looking for shadows under an open sun, trying to make trouble—

"No—not that!" His protest was quick as he followed my thought in turn. "But—what do you hold against this man? Save a feeling? If he wishes us ill—how could he pass the Symbols which seal the Valley? I do not think this place goes undefended against any who walk cloaked in the Great Shadow."

But how wrong he was—though we were not aware of it then.

What did I have to offer in proof of the rightness of my feeling? A look in a man's eyes? That feeling alone— yet such emotions were also our defenses here.

Kyllan nodded; his amazement was beginning to fade. But I closed my mind to him. I was like a child who has trustingly set hand to a coal, admiring its light without knowing of the danger. And then, burned, I regarded the world with newly awakened suspicion.

"I am warned," my brother assured me. But I felt he did not think it a true warning.

That night they had a feast—although not a joyful one, since the reason for the gathering was so grave. But they held to the bonds of high ceremony; perhaps because in such forms there was a kind of security. I had not spoken with Kaththea as I wished; I had waited too long, shaken after my attempt with Kyllan. Now it rested as a burden on me that she sat beside Dinzil at the board and he smiled much upon her. She smiled or laughed in return when he spoke.

"Are you always so silent, warrior with a stern face?"

I turned to look at Dahaun, she who can change at will to seem any fair one a man holds in mind. Now she was raven of hair with a faint touch of rose in her ivory cheeks. But in the sunset her hair had been copper-gold, her skin golden also. What would it be like, I wondered, to be so many in one?

"Do you dream now, Kemoc of the wise head?" she challenged and I came out of my bemusement.

"No good dream if I do, Lady."

The light challenge vanished; her eyes dropped from mine to the cup she held in her two hands. She moved it slightly and the purple liquid within it flowed from side to side.

"Look not in any foretelling mirror this night, Kemoc. Yet you have more than the shadow of a dream over you, to my thinking."

"I do."

Now why had I said that? Always had I kept my own counsel, or our own counsel, for we three-who-were-one shared. But was that still so? I looked again to my sister, who laughed with Dinzil, and to Kyllan, who was talking eagerly with Ethutur and Hervon as if he were a link between the two of them.

"Branch, hold not to the leaves," said Dahaun softly. "There comes a time when those must loose for the wind to bear them away. But new leaves grow in turn—"

I caught her meaning and flushed. That she and Kyllan had an understanding between them I had known for weeks. Nor had it hurt me that this was so. That there might come a day when Kaththea would step into a road wherein she would walk with another, that I also accepted. I did not resent it that Kaththea laughed this night and was more maiden than witch and sister. But I resented whom she laughed with!

"Kemoc—"

I glanced again to Dahaun and found her staring at me.

"Kemoc—what is it?"

"Lady—" I held her eyes but I did not try to reach her mind. "Look well to your walls. I am afraid."

"Of Dinzil? That he may take from you that which you have cherished?"

"Of Dinzil—what he may be."

She sipped from her cup, still watching me over its rim. "So, I shall look, warrior. I was ill-spoken, ill-thought, to put it to you as I did. This is no jealousy of close kin eating at you. You dislike him for himself. Why?"

"I do not know—I only feel."

Dahaun put down her cup. "And feelings can speak more truthfully than tongues. Be certain I shall watch— in more ways than one."

"For that I thank you, Lady," I said low-voiced.

"Ride hence with foreboding this much lightened, Kemoc," she replied. "And good luck ride with you, to right, to left, at your back—"

"But not before?" I raised my own cup to salute her.

"Ah, but you carry a sword before you, Kemoc."

Thus did Dahaun know what lay in my mind, and she believed. Yet still did I face the morning to come with a

14

chill in me. For I was the one selected to ride to summon the Krogan, and Dinzil showed no sign of leaving the Valley himself.

II

It was decided that the Green People, and we who were joined with them, must pass the warn-sword through the lowlands to such allies as they might deem possible of influencing. With Dahaun, Kyllan would ride to the Thas, that underground dwelling people of whom we had yet caught no sight. They were of the dusk and the night, though not one with the Shadow as far as was known. Ethutur and I would go to the Krogan, those who made the lakes, rivers, waterways of Escore their own. It was thought that the very sight of us from Estcarp might add to the serious meaning of our summoning.

We went forth in the early morning while Kyllan and Dahaun must wait for night and the placing of torches as a summons in a waste place. So they watched us go. Horses we no longer had; instead I bestrode one of Shapurn's people and Ethutur rode Shapurn himself. Large, or a hand's breadth larger than the cross-mountain mounts, these were, sleek of hide of a rich, roan red, with creamy underbody. Their tails were a fluff of cream they kept clamped tight against their haunches as they cantered, a tuft which was matched by a similar puff on the tops of their heads, beneath which a long, red horn slanted up and back in a graceful curve.

They wore no reins nor bridles, for they were not our

servants, but rather fellow ambassadors who were gracious enough to lend us their strength to speed our journeying. And, with keener senses than ours, they were our scouts, alert to all dangers.

Ethutur wore the green of the Valley men, their most potent weapon, the force lash, clipped to his belt. But I went in leather and mail of Estcarp. It seemed a heavy weight across my shoulders, one which I had not noted for a long time. But my helm, with its throat veil of fine chain weaving, I carried in my hand, baring my head to the soft dawn wind.

Though it had been autumn, close to the time of frosts, when we had come to Escore, yet it would seem that summer lingered longer here. We saw touches of yellow and red in leaf and bush as we passed—still, the wind was softer, the chill of early morning quickly gone.

"Be not deceived," Ethutur said now. Though little or no emotion ever broke the handsome perfection of his expression, yet now there was warning in his eyes. As in all the males of his race he showed the horns, ivory-white among the curls above his forehead. To a lesser degree he shared Dahaun's ability to change his coloring. Now in this early light his curls were dark, his face pale. But as the first sun reached to touch him, it was red locks and brown skin I saw.

"Be not deceived," he repeated. "There are traps upon traps, and the bait for some is very fair."

"As I have seen," I assured him.

Shapurn pulled a little ahead, turning from the road which led into the Valley. My mount followed his leader without any order I knew of passing between them. At first it seemed that we were going back up into the Heights, but having climbed for a short space, again we were on a downward slope. Narrow as this passage was, there were traces that this had once been a road of sorts. Blocks of stone protruded from the soil as broad steps which our four footed companions took cautiously.

We came into a second valley, much choked with a growth of dark leafed vegetation which was either stunted tree or tall bush. From this loomed masses of ancient masonry, tumbled and broken, but still with a semblance of walls.

Ethutur nodded to it. "HaHarc—"

"Which being?" I prompted when he said no more.

"A safe place once."

"Overrun by the Shadow?"

He shook his head. "The hills danced and it fell. But they danced to a strange piping that night. Let us hope that that secret is indeed lost to those we front now."

"How much of such knowledge does remain?" I asked, already sure men might only guess.

"Who knows? Many of the Great Ones destroyed themselves when they fought. Others went out through their gates to find new tests, new victories—or defeats— elsewhere. Some are so withdrawn from our kind now that what happens here holds no meaning for them. It is our hope that we face not the Great Ones of old, but those who were their lesser shield men, whom they long ago left behind. But never forget that those are formidable enough."

Having seen some, I was not likely to.

Our faint and ancient road took us through the edge of the tumbled ruins. They were well earth-buried, and trees had rooted themselves among those stones and died in turn. Time had lain long here since HaHarc had been shaken to its ending.

Then Shapurn turned left, again following the traces of an old way. We rode from the mouth of that haunted valley into a tall, grassed plain. Now the sun was well up and warm. Ethutur threw back his cloak. Resting across his thighs was the warn-sword—not fashioned of any steel but of white wood, with intricately carved runes running the length of its broad and edgeless blade. About its haft and guard were, twined and tied in fantastic knots, cords of red and green.

We were well out into the open when Shapurn threw high his head and halted, my own mount following his example. The nose flaps of the Renthan were spread wide; he turned his head from side to side in a slow sweep, questing for scent.

He spoke to our minds. "Gray Ones—"

I stared over the grass which rippled under the touch of the wind. It was tall enough to provide hiding for a creeping man. Since Kaththea and I had fled before a wild pack of mixed monstrosities, I had learned to distrust all landscape, no matter how innocent seeming.

"How do they cast?" Ethutur's thought and mine were almost the same.

"They prowl; they seek—"

"Us?"

Shapurn inhaled the breeze. "Not so. They are bellylean; they hunt to fill themselves. Ah—they have started meat! Now they yammer on its trail."

Faintly I could hear it, too, a distant howl. Having been so hunted, I knew pity for the game they now ran. Ethutur showed a small trace of frown, a break in the usual calm of his face.

"Too close," he said aloud. "We must ride the borders more often." His hand went to the whipstock at his belt. But he did not draw that weapon. For as long as he carried the warn-sword he was barred from that by custom.

18

Shapurn broke into a trot, a pace my mount easily matched, crossing the open end of the plain with a speed not even one of the famed Torgian mounts of Estcarp could better. Then we were in a defile where bushes grew a thick curtain on either side of the way. There was a thin thread of stream curling a snake-path through sand and gravel, as if it were the ghost of a torrent which ran there at other seasons. I caught a glint from a pocket of pebbles, a flashing which could not be denied. Without thinking I swung down to pluck out of that drab nest a blue-green stone. It was one of those esteemed by the Valley people. Its like was set in the gemmed wristlets and belt Ethutur wore. Although this was rough and uncut, still it caught the sun and flashed sea fire in my palm.

Ethutur turned impatiently to look back, but when he saw what I held he gave an exclamation of surprise and pleasure.

"So! By so much does Fortune smile on us, Kemoc. It is a promise that ill does not intrude too far into this country—since such loses all fire when the Shadow touches them. A gift to you from this land, and may it be of profit." He raised his right hand from the hilt of the warnsword and made a gesture which I recognized from the crypts of Lormt to be one of well wishing.

It would seem that my finding of the jewel had heartened my companion, for now he began to talk. I listened, for all that he had to say concerning this country and its in-dwellers was of importance.

The Krogan, to whom we were bound, were another race born of early experiments on the part of the Great Ones. Initially of humankind, volunteers from among the experimenters, they had been mutated and altered to become water dwellers, though they could also exist for varying periods of time outside their aquatic world. However, during the devastation of Escore, they had withdrawn into those depths for safety, and now were seldom seen ashore. They sometimes inhabited islands in lakes, and came now and then on the banks of streams.

They had never been hostile to the Green People. In fact, in the past, they had sometimes united with them. Ethutur spoke of a time when they had loosed a flood for the taking of a particularly noxious nest of evil things which had holed up where riders from the Valley could not rout them. Ethutur now had hopes of binding them officially to our company. Hitherto any alliance had been loose and temporary. They would make excellent scouts, he pointed out, for water ran everywhere in this land; where it flowed, either the Krogan or the stream dwellers that served them could venture with ease.

As he talked we came out of the stream cut into a wide, marshy space. But the land had the look of drought. Marsh reeds and growth were sere and brown. Farther beyond were small hillocks in pools of water and those were still green. Farther the morass advanced until it touched a lake.

In spite of the sun over our heads a mist hovered over that lake. I thought I could see what might be islands, yet there was a wavering which was bewildering to the mind and made me uneasy. I remembered the Tor Fen of Estcarp in which dwelt that strange race which had held my father captive during the Kolder War. That, too, was a place of like mystery, and none ventured therein without the permission of its people . . . though that was seldom gotten.

The Renthan brought us to the edge of this bog. Ethutur slid from Shapurn's back and I also dismounted. The Green war-leader steadied the warn-sword across his left arm and raised his right hand to his mouth. Making a hollow trumpet of its flesh and bones he sent forth a call which rose and fell, then rose again with an inquiry in the sound.

We waited. I saw naught save the passing of large water insects which either flew above the reeds or ran across the surface of the pools, as if water under their feet was solid. There were no birds, nor even the tracks of any animal in the mud, which was long-dried and crumbling into a thick yellow dust about our boots.

Three times Ethutur called; each time we waited for an answer which did not come. Just as a shade of frown had earlier crossed his face, so did I now detect impatience there. But if he inwardly seethed at this delay, he gave no other sign of it.

Neither did he retreat from there. I began to wonder how long we would continue to stand, awaiting the capricious pleasure of what dwellers did make this swamp-lake their home.

It was not a sound which alerted me to their coming after his third summons, rather a troubling or stirring of the air. I have felt a similar thing at times with my mother and Kaththea. It is as if a creature with great confidence moves to some purpose. Now I glanced at Ethutur, content to take my cue from him. There was power here.

My companion held up the warn-sword to face the strip of bog and the lake it guarded. In the sun the red and green cords were brilliant, so dazzling they might have been woven of molten jewels. He did not call again, but only stood, holding out his credentials as envoy.

Beyond, where still living reeds curtained the edge of the lake, was movement which came from no passing wind. Out of the water arose, to stand knee deep in the flood, two figures.

As they came to us, moving swiftly and with ease through mud, pool, and reed thicket, I saw that they were manlike. They possessed legs and feet, save that those feet were webbed and wedge-form in shape. Their arms and hands were a match for my own, but the skin covering the flesh and firm bones was pallid under the sun and glistened when the light struck it.

Their heads were very human, too. But their hair was short and sleeked tight to their skulls and it was only a shade or two darker than their skin. On either side of their throats were circular spots which marked gills, now closed in the air.

They wore scanty waistcloths made of a scaled substance rippling with jeweled coloring. To the belts, which held those, were attached large shells which appeared to serve as pouches. In their web-fingered hands were staffs. Half the length was green and richly carved, the rest black and keen-pointed, to give one the impression of a wicked and deadly weapon. The Krogan carried those point down, to assure us of good intentions.

When they at last came to stand before us I saw that, human as they appeared from a distance, those eyes turned unblinkingly upon us were not man's eyes. There were no whites, only a deep green expanse from lid to lid—as the eyes of a snow cat.

"Ethutur." Instead of any greeting, the foremost of the two just repeated my companion's name.

"Orias?" His return was in a note of inquiry. Then he moved the warn-sword a fraction and again the color of its binding glowed brilliantly.

The Krogan stared at us and the sword. Then the leader beckoned. Gingerly we followed them back through the mud holes, jumping from tussock to tussock of coarse growth wherever that was possible. There was the smell of rotting stuff, which is normal in such places, and slime clung to our boots after only a few steps. But our guides appeared to be able to move through all this without carrying any smears.

We reached the edge of the lake and I wondered if they expected us now to wade in. But a shallow shadow shot from one of those barely seen islands, heading toward us. It turned out to be a boat, made of the skin of some type of water dweller pulled tight over a frame of bones cut and fitted together. Embarking in it was something of a feat. The Renthan did not even attempt that, but took to the water as did our guides and the Krogan who had towed the boat, the three water people pulling the craft after them.

As we approached the island I noted that unlike the unwholesome shore, it was ringed with a wide, silvery beach of clean sand. The stench of the bog was gone. Vegetation grew back of that sand, unlike I had seen elsewhere. The shoots rose well into the air and were soft plumes, such as the Sulcar traders sometimes brought from overseas. They did not have a green shade, but more of a muted silver tone, and here and there a frond had green or dull yellow flowers in lines along the upper portions of the main branches.

The beach itself was divided into neatly geometric patterns by the setting out of large shells and pale colored rocks. Among these ran path-roads bordered with stake fences, ankle high, fashioned of bleached driftwood.

Our Krogan guides started along one of these roads and Ethutur and I fell in behind them. As we passed the marked parts of the beach, I saw that in those were small baskets and mats woven in delicate patterns. But of those to whom these belonged there was then no sign. We came into the shade of the plume trees and I smelled the perfume of the flowers. Also I caught glimpses of those we must have disturbed on the beach. More men, like unto our guides, and with them the women of their race. The hair of the latter flowed free save for bands of shells or reeds interwoven with flowers. They had garments of a softer substance than the scaled material, caught with shell clasps on their shoulders, confined with ornamented belts at their waists. Those robes were softly green, or yellow, or pink-gray. But we saw little of them, for they kept back among their farther trees.

When we came into the open again it was to front an outcrop of rock which perhaps once had been natural. But since it had been wrought upon by master carvers. Monsters with eyes of shell or dull gems leered and menaced. Some were more amusing than threatening with their grotesque grins. Two such guarded a flat shelf which served the Krogan chief for a chair-of-state.

He did not rise to greet us, and across his knees lay a spear staff similar to those his guards carried. His hand rested ready upon it and he did not reverse the point as we came to face him.

Ethutur drove the warn-sword point down into the soft sand earth, dropping his hand from its hilt when it stood firmly upright.

"Orias!" he said.

The Krogan leader was much like the two who had brought us here, except that a dark seam of some old scar ran along the side of his face from temple to jaw on the left, drawing down a little on the eye corner, so the lid remained almost closed.

"I see you, Ethutur. Why do I see you?" His voice was thin and, in my ears, toneless.

"Because of this—" Ethutur's fingers just touched the hilt of the warn-sword. "We would talk."

"Of a carrying of spears, and a beating of drums, and a killing," the Krogan interrupted him. "Stirred up by outlanders . . ." Now he turned his head so that he surveyed me squarely with his good eye. "They have awakened that which slept, these outlanders. Why do you take up their cause, Ethutur? Have you not past hard-won victories to nurse for your kind?"

"Victories won long ago do not mean that a man may hang his weapons to rust in the roof tree and never have need to draw them again," returned Ethutur levelly. "There are forces astir—no matter how awakened. The day draws near when men must hear the beating of the drums whether or no they would thrust fingers in their ears against such summoning. The men of the Heights, the Vrong, the Renthan, the Flamman, we of the Green Silences, those from overmountain, drink brother-drink now and close ranks. For in union we have a chance. While such begins to stir as promises no safety in sky, on land—" he paused and then added, "—or in water!"

"No one picks up the warn-sword in haste." I thought Orias used words to cloak thoughts. I did not try mind touch; it promised danger. The Krogan continued, "Nor does one man's answer cover that for all the water folk. We take counsel. You are free to remain on the visitor's isle."

Ethutur bowed his head. But he did not touch the sword, leaving it point-planted where it was. Back they took us through the plume wood and into the boat, drawing us to another island. Here was vegetation, but that of normal growth. There was a paved space of rock slabs and a hollow for a fire, with a pile of drift nearby. Ethutur and I brought out our supplies and ate. Afterward I

25

wandered back to the shore and stared across at that silvery island. But the haze which might be born of some wizardry blurred its details. I believed I saw Krogan come out of the lake and return into it. But no one came near our island, or, if they did, we were not aware of it.

Ethutur would make no guess as to how Orias' council would decide. Several times he remarked that the Krogan were a law unto themselves, and, as Dinzil had warned, could not be influenced by outsiders. When he mentioned Dinzil my forebodings, which I had managed to push into the back of my mind, awoke. Deliberately I set about learning what I could concerning the war leader from the Heights.

He was of the Old Race, truly human as far as the Green People knew. His reputation in the field was firmly established. It seemed that he controlled powers of his own, having had for tutor in his childhood one of the few remaining wonder workers who had set a limit on his own studies and used what he learned for the preservation of the small portion of Escore into which he had fled. So high was Dinzil in Ethutur's respect that I did not venture to mention my own doubts; for what was feeling against such proofs?

There came no signal from the other isle. We ate again and rolled in our blankets for sleep. But with sleep there came to me such a dream of evil as brought me sitting up, cold and shivering, wet drops running down my cheeks to drip from my chin. I had had such a dream before Kaththea had been rift from us—so had I awakened then, unable to remember what I had dreamed, yet knowing it to be evil indeed.

I could not sleep again, nor could I disturb Ethutur with my restlessness. What I wanted most of all was to leave this island, strike out for the Valley to see for myself that no ill had chanced to those two who were the other parts of me. Greatly daring, I stole away from the campsite and went down to the shore, facing as I hoped in the direction of the Valley—though in this place I could not truly be sure of north, south, east or west.

Then I put my head in my hands, and I sent forth the call. For I *must* know. When there was no answer, I put to the full strength of my will and sent again.

Faint, very faint, came the answer. Kaththea . . . alarmed for me. Quickly I let her know that the danger was not mine, but that I feared for her or Kyllan. Then she replied that all was safe, that it must be some evil in the land between us. But she urged to cut the bond, lest it be seized upon by an ill force and used to seek me out. So sharp was she I did as she bade. But I was not satisfied; it was as if, though she reported all aright, it would not be so for long.

"Who are you, to call upon the spirit of another?"

I was so startled by that query out of the night that my sword flashed in the moonlight even as I turned. Then I dropped it, point to the ground, and watched her come into the open, her webbed feet noiseless on the sand. The waters of the lake had made her garment like unto a second skin, and she seemed very small and frail, her pallor a part of the moonlight. She brushed back wet strands of hair and tightened the shell band which held it out of her eyes.

"Why do you call?" As Orais, her voice lacked timbre, was soft and monotonous.

Though I am not one who naturally tells all to strangers, yet at that moment I spoke the truth.

"I dreamed evilly, as I have beforetimes in warning. I

sought those I had reason to be concerned about, my sister and brother."

"I am Orsya, and you?" She did not comment upon my words; it was as if she needed at once some identification.

"Kemoc—Kemoc Tregarth out of Estcarp," I told her.

"Kemoc," she repeated. "Ah, yes, you are one of the outlanders who have come to make trouble. . . ."

"We did not come to make it," I corrected her. Somehow it was necessary to assure her of that. "We were fleeing trouble of our own, and we came over the mountains, not knowing what lay here. We meant no more than to find a refuge."

"Yet you have wrought disturbances." She picked up a pebble and tossed it into the lake. It splashed and ripples sped across the surface. "You have done things which could awake old evils. You would draw in the Krogan."

"Not I alone," I protested. "We shall stand together, all of us!"

"I do not think that Orias and the others will agree. No." She shook her head. Her hair, which seemed to dry very quickly in the open air, fanned out in a silver net about her. "You have had your journey here for naught, outlander."

Then she took a skip, a leap, and the water closed about her.

But she had the right of it. When we were ferried back to the plumed island in the morning the warn-sword was as Ethutur had planted it, untouched, bearing no added cords of agreement. Nor was Orias there. We faced an empty throne and the feeling that it was better for us to be gone from territory where we were not wanted.

III

"What do we now?" I asked when the silent Krogan had brought us back to the swamp shore and were gone again into the lake before we could voice any farewell.

"Naught," Ethutur replied. "They have decided to remain neutral. I fear they will not find that so easy." He spoke absently and I saw that he watched the hills about us with a scout's eye.

I followed his gaze. There was nothing to see, or was there? The sun shown as it had the morning before, and the country appeared empty. Then I saw a black speck wing across the sky and behind it another.

"Mount!" Ethutur's voice was urgent. "The Rus fly. Indeed there must be a beating of the borders now!"

Shapurn and Shil, who trotted under my weight, picked a careful way along that nearly dry stream bed. But they were swifter than in their coming. I drew a deep breath. The corrupt miasma of the swamp still clung. I glanced at my boots to see if the slime spotted them, though we had wiped ourselves with withered grass.

No such traces on me, yet that breath of rottenness grew stronger as we rode. I watched the rises which fenced this water way. A man who has gone often to war, such as we knew along the border, develops senses of warning. The sun was hot and strong, yet a shadow stretched to touch us. I set my helm on my head in spite of the heat, threw the ends of its mail scarf about my throat. Also I loosened the sword which was a weight against my thigh.

29

Ever it seemed to me that that stench grew stronger, brought to us with every small puff of wind which found its way into that narrow ravine. No longer did Ethutur carry the warn-sword before him. Rather it was fastened to his belt, since his mission as envoy was done; he freed the stock of his force whip, holding it ready in his hand. It was as if an enemy massed unseen upon the heights above us.

Yet there was nothing we could see: Only the smell and the warning within us. I marveled at the speed with which the Renthan bore us through that place which was a natural trap. Yet one part of my mind wondered why the trap was not sprung. The enemy were throwing away an advantage they might not find so easily again.

"Why?"

I saw Ethutur's lips fold tight and then he answered my unfinished question:

"Those who watch have not the strength to pull us down. But the Rus fly for reinforcements. If we can reach the open plain—"

We did that, coming to where the grass rippled grain-ripe and tall. But the plains were not empty. I saw those who gathered to dispute our passage. Some were old enemies I had fronted before. There were those unholy mixtures of men and beast who raised brindled, wolfish muzzles to catch our scent and had pricked ears to hear. About them the grass moved and I thought of the Rasti which could be in hiding there. Ethutur cracked his force whip, and the fire of its strike upon the earth was a flash bright enough to be seen even in the sunlight, leaving smoldering stubble behind.

I longed for the dart gun which had been mine over mountains. We had brought such weapons with us in flight, but long since their ammunition had been spent, which left them useless tubes. Now I had to wait until the enemy was sword-length for fighting.

The Gray Ones and their unseen allies—if the rippling covered the movements of the Rasti—did not attack. They had a deep respect for the force lash. But they circled about as at a distance. Their circle now lay between us to the entrance of the HaHarc road.

"They must not three time us!" Ethutur cried. Again my studies at Lormt came to my aid. If the enemy could put that running circle about us and hold it for a thrice running of all who made it a barrier, then they could put a will-lock on us—even though they did not venture to attack openly the prisoners within it.

Shapurn and Shil ran. Again, as I settled my body to the rise and fall of those mighty muscles under me, I thought that no horse of Estcarp could match these. At the same time, though I am not learned in the Mysteries, I shouted aloud certain *words* from very ancient texts.

And as I did so, I was startled and almost stricken dumb. For—this I swear, though a man who has not seen such may disbelieve me—I *saw* those words as well as heard them! They were flaming fire arrows and they went before, as darts might have been shot from that weapon I no longer had. I will swear again that I saw them strike the ground where the Gray Ones ran and that light burst upon impact, even as the fire which came from Ethutur's lash.

There was sound, too; more than the mouthing I made, claps loud and clear. Then I heard a shrill, high screeching overhead as Ethutur called out something I did not understand. His head went back as one who searches danger in the sky. Then his lash curled up and that shrill, ear-tormenting screeching was cut in mid-note. From the sky fell something which struck the ground before us, and exploded in a puff of dark smoke which choked us with its foulness as, a moment later, Shapurn and Shil, unable to avoid it, rushed on through.

But of any body which might lie there, I saw no sign. Only the smoke and smell before we burst into the clean air.

Now I heard the howling of the Gray Ones and a squealing from the grass, which, once heard, could not be forgotten. Rasti ran here, right enough. They came upon us in a wave and Shapurn and Shil stamped and danced in fury, while Ethutur's lash cut again and again, firing the grass to clear us a path. We met the Gray Ones at the mouth of the HaHarc road and there we fought them. My blade cut flesh, jarred upon bone, and Shil screamed as raking claws and gnashing teeth tore his hide. Once more I hurled at them those *words* and saw them flinch from what became darts of flaming energy.

Then there came a *sound*, and before that all the other clamor of our fight was nothing. For it was a blow which appeared to fall upon us all equally. I clung, weak and deafened, to my seat on Shil's back. Dimly I saw Ethutur's arm drop limply to his side, the force lash dead, only the stock gripped in his fingers. But I also saw the Gray Ones reel back, the hand-paws pressed to their ears, their heads twisting to and fro as if in agony.

For how long we were so stricken I do not know. But at length my mind cleared and I felt Shil trembling under me. The Renthan took one step and then another, and I raised to see that he was following, as he had throughout that journey, his war chief Shapurn, and that other one was walking, one step at a time, down the road to Ha-Harc. On his back Ethutur sat with drooping head, as one who rode in a daze.

I wanted to turn my head and see if the enemy padded behind us. But trying, I found I could not. It was not that I was too weak; it was rather in some way all my muscles had been locked. When at last I was able to look behind I saw no sign of any pursuers. That stench which had been with us since we had left the lake was also gone. But there was another odor heavy on the air, a metallic scent I could not set name to.

When we were among the ruins Ethutur straightened and looked over his shoulder to meet my eyes. He was very pale, but there was a set to his features I had not seen before.

"Do not so again!" His words were an order.

"I do not know what—"

"You evoked ancient powers back there and were *answered*. Do not bring your witchcraft here, outlander. I had not believed that you might also evoke forces—"

"Nor did I," I answered truthfully. "And I do not know why I did what I did. I am no witch, but a warrior."

I could not quite believe in what had passed, even though I had been a part of it. For we were so confirmed in the belief, we of Estcarp, that only the Wise Women could control the unseen, or communicate with it, that this was unnatural. Although it was true that my father had certain gifts, which even the Witches had not been able to deny. With my mother, the Lady Jaelithe, he had shared strengths which were not of hand and body, but of mind and will.

But me, I wanted no more of this. For I had wisdom enough to know that experimenting with such matters, when one is untaught in the proper safeguards, is rank folly, liable to harm not only he who rashly tries it, but those about him. Ethutur could be sure I would not do so. Still I remembered that *sound*, which I could find no words to describe, and I wondered what it was and from whence it had come.

It seemed to be effective in protecting our back trail, for, though we took every precaution and backtracked to be sure, we had no pursuers. At last Ethutur was satisfied and we went up that stair road which led out of HaHarc to come again to the boundaries of the Valley.

As we rode between the carven stones, which had on them protective words, Ethutur paused now and then and made certain signs to each. Some I knew; others were strange to me. But I knew that he was relocking the guards of the Valley, alerting them. We came at last to the greatest of all, which was Euthayan. Deep graven it was, and inlaid in those cuts was a thread of green. Then did the warlord of the Valley turn to me with his second order:

"Go, lay your hands to that, your bare hands!"

I knew a small stir of anger, for his suspicion was plain. He believed that I was, or had become, that which the Valley dared no longer shelter for the good of those who dwelt there. But I did as he bade, slipped from Shil's sweaty back, went to lay my bare palms flat against that symbol which was so much a part of Power that no evil might look upon it, let alone touch it.

I was startled as my fingers touched cool stone, rough and gritty with windblown dust when first I set them upon that surface, yet under their tips there came a change. I saw, or seemed to see, those inlaid traces of green become brighter, while the stone grew warm. But I was not blasted, nor did any warning come—only the brightening of the green and the gentle warmth. I held my hands so and looked to Ethutur.

"Are you now satisfied that you do not harbor a traitor?" I asked.

But he was watching the stone and there was puzzlement in his eyes. He raised his hand and rubbed across them as if to clear away a mist. And he said:

"I do not know what we harbor in you, Kemoc. But it would seem that you do our company no ill. This I had to know." There was a note of apology in his voice.

"As your right." It was, of course, in spite of the smart to my pride. As warlord he had no right to bring into the Valley any weak link which might open it to the Great Shadow. And what did he know of we three from Estcarp, save what we have done since coming to Escore?

It was late afternoon when we came down to those houses of living vine and roofs of green-blue feathers. Along the way we picked up a company of Ethutur's men. But I did not see any of the hill men who had come with Dinzil. That gave me a feeling of relief.

When we swung off the Renthan in the open space where we had taken counsel earlier, we found a varied company awaiting us. Their faces were sober, their mood one of impatience. It was Dahaun who spoke first.

"There was—she seemed almost at a loss for words— "a Great Troubling. What happened? Or do you know?"

"Ask of Kemoc," Ethutur returned shortly and their attention fastened upon me. Kyllan looked surprised but Kaththea, at his side, was frowning slightly.

"I do not know," I told them. "We were about to be thrice-ringed by Gray Ones, together with Rasti. All I did, and why I cannot tell you, was speak words I had learned at Lormt. And then—then—

"You were *answered*." It was Kaththea who spoke. "Unwise, unwise to meddle when you are not trained in the Mysteries."

For the first time in my life I met in her—not the incredulity which Kyllan had earlier shown—but a turning from me, a closing of doors. Behind was some emotion I could not read. Was it that her long years of Witch training had set into her the belief they all shared, that no man was to usurp their dealing with the Invisible? If so, it was so unlike the Kaththea I knew that I could not accept it. Yet withdraw she had and I was too hurt to pursue her, or even question. I would not put it to the proof. Sometimes we cling to uncertainty, dreading fact.

I spoke then to Dahaun, rather than to my sister. "Be sure that I shall not try it again. I do not even know why I did it then."

She took a step forward and laid her hands on my shoulders. Then, as I was the taller, she looked up to meet my eyes. But she used words, not the mind touch, to answer me, because, I am sure, she wanted all those others to hear her.

"What lies within a man, strength, will, or gift, rises to the surface when need calls. That you were *answered* is a shock, for it was our belief that the Great Ones had sped from us long ago. But now you have taught us that they are not to be disregarded, and that is well worth our knowing. It is in my mind that you have done us a single service this day."

Her words appeared to ease the tension. Now Kyllan raised the question of how our mission to the Krogan fared. He frowned when he heard it was a failure. Then the war leader asked in turn concerning the Thas and Dahaun replied:

"They did not even come to answer the torch signal. So we can continue to guess whether their absence means neutrality, or whether they have allied themselves elsewhere."

"But there is other news," Kyllan offered. "The sentinels from the peaks have signaled that another party

36

from overmountain comes into the foothills."

"Then they must be met with a guard to bring them here," Ethutur said, "It is my belief that the country is roused and the lesser ones of the shadow will do all they can to prevent our mustering of any force."

As I went to bathe in one of the renewing pools of the Green People, to put on the lighter clothing they wore, I still looked for Dinzil or any of his following. Kyllan came to sit upon a bench, watching me draw on breeches, latch the golden clasps of the jerkin across my breast.

Finally I brought my thought into the open. "I do not see Dinzil."

"He rode out before dawn. There is much to be done in raising the Heights. What of these Krogan?"

It seemed to me that Kyllan skirted the subject of Dinzil, was too quick to change the subject. But I followed his lead and told him all I had observed of the water people.

"Would they matter to us greatly?"

"Ethutur says they have ways of penetrating wherever there is water, they, or the creatures who give them allegiance. I saw no weapons except their spears. Yet those looked deadly. Who can say that they do not have other arms which were not shown? Ethutur believes they are still neutral. He accepted their decision without argument."

That had puzzled me, for my reading of him was that he had too much force of character to accept rebuffs tamely.

"He was bound by custom," Kyllan said. "There has been no compelling, nor pleading, between race and race after they fled into refuges. They have been content to go their own roads apart."

"Custom cannot save any of us now," I countered

"Which way did Dinzil ride?" Deliberately I came back to my own questioning. "Kyllan—you know how it has been with us always. Would I push this uneasiness if I were not convinced that it holds some danger for us three?"

He looked me eye to eye as Dahaun had done earlier, and we mind touched; I opened to him all my worries.

"I believe that you believe, brother."

"But—you do not?"

"Enough so that I shall hold watch and ward if he returns. But—this I must say to you, Kemoc—do not flutter those flags of war before our sister, not when they are to raise hosts to face in that direction!"

My hands tightened until my stiff fingers pointed palely.

"It is like that then." I did not ask a question; I stated a fact.

"She has clearly shown her liking. She will read ill will into any contrary urging, not against him, but against the one giving the warning. She has . . . changed." There was uncertainty in him also, a kind of bewilderment which was less than that pang I felt when she had closed her mind to me an hour earlier, yet which carried some of the same hurt.

"She is a maid, unwed. We knew that sometime she would look upon some man with eyes she did not turn to us. That we could face . . . but this man—no!" I said that as one swearing an oath. I knew that Kyllan heard it so, but he shook his head slowly.

"Over this we may have no control. He is a man esteemed, and he pleases her; that is to be seen by the least observant. Against that, you offer but a feeling of wrongness, which she and others may read as jealousy. You must have more proof."

He spoke the truth, but sometimes the truth is black hearing. So did it seem to me now. Again Kyllan picked up my thought.

"It is hard to believe that you summoned one of the Great Ones and was *answered*. We were schooled that such is impossible save for an adept. No man of Estcarp ever trod that path, so you can see that Kaththea finds it hard to accept. How *did* you do it?"

"I tell you, I do not know. Ethutur warned of thrice-ringing; we were riding to cut through before that happened." I spoke of seeing the words as fiery darts. And then that *sound* which had blasted at us all.

"Our mother asked wisdom for your share when she called our futures," he said thoughtfully when I was done. "It would seem that you *do* have some power. . . ."

I shook my head. "There is a vast difference between learning and wisdom, brother. Do not confuse the two. I called upon learning then, and without thinking. Perhaps that was folly—"

"Not altogether. It saved you; did it not? And, as Dahaun has said, it made known to us that certain forces are still at work here, powers long thought gone." He spread out his hands and regarded them thoughtfully. "For most of my life I had been at war. But before it was with steel and weapons known to me. This is a different war, and I am no worker of power—save that which lies within my own mind and body."

"Nor shall I be, henceforth!"

He shook his head. "Vow no vows upon that subject, Kemoc. We do not read the future—nor, I believe, would we really want to if we could. For I do not think it is in us to change what will come to pass. You shall do that which is set before you for the doing, as shall I, and every living thing within Escore. We shall go down to defeat, or ride to victory in the end, each playing his own ordained part."

I broke through his somber words. "You said that once you dreamed of this land at peace once more, and of holdings of our folk well planted here. Do you not remember?"

"Dreams are not the truth. Did you not dream a darker dream only a night ago?"

"Kaththea told you?"

"Yes. She believed it to be a seeking sent by some black power, a try at influencing you."

"And you?"

Kyllan got to his feet. "It can be that you are both right: That you had a forewarning; that it was twisted by some power. This is no country in which to dream. And no country to allow some comrades to ride into, unwarned, unarmed . . ."

So we went forth again in the dawn, Kyllan, I, Godgar and Horvan, and three of Ethutur's men, together with Dahaun. We rode to the mountains over which those we sought must come. Above our heads quested both Flannan and those birds who were the messengers and scouts for Dahaun. Their reports were of a land aroused. We caught sight of sentinels on high places. Some of them had the seeming of men, and some were clearly monsters. Whether they constituted the enemy now in force, or whether they answered to stronger leaders, being only hands, feet, eyes and ears for yet more powerful adversaries, we did not know.

We made detours around some places. There was a grove by the river which Dahaun made a wide arc to avoid, pausing to face it, her fingers in a vee before her mouth as she spat between them to right and left. Yet to my eyes it was a grove as fair as any in the Valley and I felt no uneasiness when I looked upon it. Varied and hidden indeed were the many traps for the innocent and unwary in Escore.

Two days it took us, even with the speed of the Renthans, to reach the place where we left the animals and climbed by foot to aid those of Estcarp. But that climb was not as demanding as it had been when we came into this land, for exploration along the mountain walls had found shorter and easier paths.

Those who came, moved apparently by that inner compulsion which Kyllan had sown unwittingly in Estcarp, were men from Borderer companies, among them those I knew, having served with them in the scouts. They rubbed their eyes a little dazedly, as men will when awakening from deep sleep, as they reached us. Then they shouted greetings and came eagerly to us, hands outstretched, not with the anger outlaws might expect.

Once more the past caught up with us—a past which seemed so far removed. We heard the news out of Estcarp that the Council, so weakened by the effort of churning the mountains against Karsten, held now only part power. For many had died in that battle, and Koris of Gorm, my father's long comrade, was now virtually the ruler. He was in the process of tightening control over what might otherwise have fallen into complete chaos.

These Borderers were of a patrol sent out to track us, for Koris stood to us as a father, and his wife, the Lady Loyse, was more mother than she who had had too many duties to claim that role with us. Thus, if we wished, we might return—our outlawry done. But Kyllan and I knew that we had left that road and there was no turning back.

41

The patrol had met with a household kin to Hervon's and the planted desire to ride east had spread to them. Now they listened in wonder to the tale Kyllan told, but for them there was no return either. Chance had served us very well in sending these war-tried men to join our ragged standards.

IV

We came down into the lower lands with all the speed we could muster. There the Renthan and those from the Valley awaited us. It had been bright sunlight when we had begun that descent. But when we reached the meeting place clouds were gathering. Dahaun gave slight greeting to those from Estcarp—rather she turned her head from right to left, surveying the country. About her flew, constantly coming and going, her winged messengers.

In part Kyllan and I felt, too, a lowering of spirit and a chill which was not born of the cloud sky nor the rising winds. It was a foreboding which was folly to dismiss.

But those who had come overmountain were wearied, and among them were women and children for whom the climb and descent had been a trial of strength. We should camp soon.

"We must ride!" Dahaun's gesture brought up the Renthan. "This is no place in which to face the dark and that which may prowl there this night."

"And *what* may prowl?" demanded Kyllan.

"I do not know, for such lies now unseen to the eyes of my feathered ones. Yet that it comes, I have no doubt."

Nor did we. Even those from Estcarp, who had none of the gift, glanced now and then over their shoulders, and made a wall about their women folk. And I saw that the Borderers went helmed, their mail scarves fastened high.

"These cannot make the Valley without a rest," I warned Dahaun.

She nodded. "There is a place, not as far as I would like, but better than here."

She led us. Under the clouds, she was all sable and silver, no longer red and gold. We shared our mounts, taking up women and children with us for that riding. A little maid, her hair close braided beneath a scarlet hood, her gloved hands holding tightly to my sword belt, went with me on Shil.

"Please, lord, where do we ride?" Her voice was a clear pipe.

"To where the lady leads us." I gave her the truth. "This is her country and she knows it well. I am Kemoc Tregarth, and who are you?"

"Loelle, of the House of Mohakar, Lord Kemoc. Why do those birds fly with the lady? Ah, that is no bird, it—it is a little man!"

One of the Flannan beat wings, hovering shoulder high beside Dahaun, while she turned her head to look at him.

"A Flannan, Loelle. Have you not heard tales of them?"

I felt her grip grow tighter. "But those—those are tales, Lord Kemoc! Nurse Grenwel said they were but stories, not the truth!"

"In Escore, Loelle, many old stories are true. Now, hold tight—"

We had come to a level space and the Renthan burst into speed to shame any horse out of Estcarp, Dahaun setting the pace. That brooding menace I had felt in the foothills was almost tangible as the clouds gathered, twilight dark, over us.

Through that gloom were glimmers of light, reminding me of the ghostly "candles" we had seen on tree and bush that night when the Witches of Estcarp had readied their power for the mountain twisting. Pale, hardly to be distinguished from the general gloom, these clung to a rock, a bush, a twisted tree. Looking upon them, I knew that I did not want to see them any closer.

Once more the land began to rise, and on the crown of a small hill stood some stones. Not gray, but blue in hue, and they glowed. Once before had we refuged with such stones, when Kaththea and I had fled after Kyllan had disappeared, taking sanctuary in a place where a great altar of such blue had been our guard.

To this place Dahaun brought us. This was no standing circle of pillars about an altar stone, but rather scattered blocks, as if a building, once there, had been shattered into rubble. But the blue glow welcomed us and we slid down from the Renthan with a sense of freedom from that which had followed us from the mountain's foot.

Dahaun broke a branch from a bush which grew among the stones, and, holding that in her hand, she walked down the hill, to beat the leafy end against the ground. So she encircled the entire hill, appearing to draw some unseen protective barrier about it. Then, as she came back to us, she stopped now and again to pull leaves and twigs from plants.

When the Green Lady was back among us she had her cloak gathered to form a shallow bag and in that was her herb harvest. There had been a fire kindled in a sheltered spot between two stones and she stood by that, tossing into it first a pinch of this, and then three or four leaves of that. Smoke puffed out, bringing an aromatic scent. This Dahaun fanned so that it wreathed among our company.

As the smoke cleared and I could see better again, I noted the darkness had grown. In that unnatural twilight the "candles" were brighter. But the light burning in them did not spread far. It also seemed to me that there was movement beyond the hill, a stirring which could only be half seen, to vanish if one looked straightly at the suspected spot.

"Against what do we bare swords here, Kemoc?" It was Rothorf of Dolmain who came up beside me as I watched that interweaving which seemed so sinister.

"Strange things." I gave him the best answer that I could. He was one of the half-blood ones found among the Borderers. His mother had been of the Karsten refuges. Rescued by Sulcar seamen, she had later married into that seaborne race. But it was a mixture which had not proved too happy. When her sea lord had fallen in one of the raids along the coast of Alizor, she had returned to her own people. Her son had the frame of the bull-shouldered sea rovers and their fair hair, so that always among the Old Race he was marked. Inwardly he was of his mother's people, having no wish for the sea, but a love for the hills. Thus he had come to the Borderers and we had been blooded together in a raid before we were truly men.

"It is true then; this is a land bewitched." He asked no question, but made an observation.

"Yes. But once it was a fair land. By our efforts it may so be again. Yet it will be a long time—"

"Before we cleanse it?" he finished for me. "What manner of enemy do we front?" There was a briskness in that which returned me to the old days when Rothorf had looked upon maps in the hills and then waited for the orders to move out.

Uneasiness moved in me. These old comrades (drawn from a war, it was true, but a war which seemed simple beside the complexities which faced us here), would they be as children blundering among the dangers they could not foresee? What had we done to them? Kyllan, when he had returned from that geas sending into Estcarp, had reasoned so: that he was drawing after him those of his blood, perhaps untimely to their deaths. Now I knew what he had felt then.

"All manner, Rothorf, and some of which we have no knowledge." I spoke then of the Gray Ones and the Rasti, but also of such deceits as the Keplian-stallion which had nearly borne Kyllan to his death, and of the traps which awaited the over-curious and under-cautious. He listened to me gravely, not questioning anything I said, though much of it must have sounded wild.

"A place where legends walk," he commented at last. "It would seem we should search our memories of childhood tales to be warned. How far is it to this safe Valley of the Green Folk?"

"Another day's journey. We muster there."

"To attack where?"

I shook my head. "That we do not know. They still wish to bring to our warn-horn any uncommitted forces left."

We posted guards as the night drew in, the clouds bringing it early to us. No rain fell from them, though they looked heavy-bellied, as if they carried pent within them some tempest. I saw flashes of light about the hills, as bright and crackling as the force whips of the Green People, but knew them to be lightning, foretelling the storm which sullenly refused to break.

Kyllan was no more inclined to sleep than I and we paced around the ruins among which our people sheltered as if we walked sentry beats on the walls of Es City, constantly alert to the least suspicion of change beyond the perimeter Dahaun had drawn.

The Lady of Green Silences remained by the fire, having about her all the women and children, creating for them a pocket of safe feeling in which we caught glimpses of smiling faces and from which we heard soft laughter. I saw Loelle on Dahaun's lap, staring up into her face and listening to what she said as a thirsty child might drink crystal water from a bubbling spring.

There was such a spring among the ruins, fed into a very old and silted basin. It might have been the remains of a fountain which no longer proudly played, defeated by time.

We had shared out journey rations earlier. At last those about the fire rolled in cloaks and slept. Still the storm did not break, yet the threat held above us. Godgar tramped to where I stood behind an earth-buried rock staring down the slope. The gray candles grew more confusing to the eyes and I tried not to look at them. Yet still they drew my attention, and I found myself engaged in a small struggle not to stare at them.

"There is something brewing this night," Hervon's man told me, his voice harsh and heavy. "It is not the storm. This place may be good for defense, but I do not like to be driven to making a defense."

"Neither could we ride on through the dark, not in this country," I answered.

"That is so. There is something . . . Come you here with me and see."

I followed him to that basin where the spring bubbled. Going down on one knee, he gestured to the far side of that pool. There was enough light from the fire to show stones set there, as if at one time the basin had been broken at that point and then hurriedly built up again with rocks conveniently at hand. That they had served the purpose well was manifest in that there was no seepage from that place. But why this should so interest Godgar, I had no idea and looked to him questioningly.

"That was done, I think, for a purpose," he said.

"Why?"

In answer he beckoned me to come a little beyond the basin. Earth had drifted and tufts of grass rooted. But not enough to cover a slab of stone which was part of the small remaining fragment of pavement. Godgar dug about that stone with the point of his hunting knife, laying bare the cleavage between it and the pavement.

"I think that the water was made to pour down here."

"Why?"

"That I do not know. But it had great importance for those who did it. That basin was broken in haste. When it was patched again, it was not made to stand for all time, but so that it might be freed again."

"What meaning for us now?" I was impatient.

"Again—I do not know. Save that all things which are strange must be considered when men rest as we do this night. And—" He stopped suddenly. His hand had been resting on that block of stone and now he stared down at it wide-eyed. Then he threw himself on the ground and set his ear to the cold surface.

"Listen!" It was a command I obeyed, stretching my body on the ground so that my head might rest with his, ear on stone.

Sound or vibration, I could not say which. But it came from below. I made very sure I was not mistaken and then summoned Kyllan, and he in turn, Dahaun.

It was she who had an answer for us. "Thas, perhaps . . ." She knelt there, her fingertips resting on the slab. Her eyes were closed, as if she now called upon a different kind of sight to serve her. Then she shook her head slowly.

"What lies below the earth's surface is another world and not mine. This I say—something comes upon us from below. Fortune favors us with this much warning. I had not thought that the Thas would join the enemy. It may be that they are only curious, though why . . ." She shook her head. "To come secretly thus is not the way of a friend or a neutral."

"Your boundaries—" Kyllan broke in.

"Will hold against what walks the soil, but not under it. And look you—this stone is not of the blessed kind, but of another fashioning."

"The basin—" I got to my feet. "If it were once used to answer an attack from below as Godgar believes, why not again?"

"If they are only curious, then such a use would make enemies needlessly. But it is a thought to keep in mind. Let us inspect this water trap." Dahaun said.

She brought a brand from the fire and held it close so we could look upon the stones which had put a stopper in the broken basin. I believed that Godgar was right in his reconstruction of what had happened here long ago. It was plain that the basin wall had been shattered so that its contents could flow out at this point, and that the rebuilding of that break had been done with no idea of permanence.

"Strike it here and here," Godgar pointed out, "and it will give way again."

We went back to the stone. But this time we could hear no movement beneath it. Only, that unease which had been over me since we had come from the mountains increased a hundred-fold.

"Can the stone be sealed?" Kyllan looked to Dahaun.

"I do not know. To each his own power. The Thas can do much with earth, as the Krogan with water, and we with growing things." She picked up her torch and glanced at the place where the women and children were asleep. "I think we must be prepared. Get away from any standing stone which might be overthrown."

Godgar still squatted on his heels, his hands resting on the stone. Even as Dahaun went toward those who slept, he cried out. I think I must have echoed his cry, as did Kyllan, for the ground under us moved, slipping under our feet, carrying us with it. I caught at a stone, one of the blue ones, and held to it, as soil poured about my boots. I heard crashes and shouts from the camp, saw stones slide and bound downslope.

Something fell into the fire sending sparks and flaming pieces of wood scattering. I heard screaming. For a moment I could only hold to my rock, for under my kicking feet, as I tried to find some stable spot, the earth moved as the waters of the Krogan lake might have splashed and eddied.

Then I saw Kyllan using the point of his sword, dug into the shifting earth, to pull himself along. I followed his example, trying to reach the confusion marking our campsite.

"Ha—to me!" called Godgar. About him whirled other things, small flitting figures ringing him in, in a frenzy of attack. I cut and slashed, felt steel meet flesh and was not sure of what flesh. Then I saw Godgar stumble and go down, and things scurried to leap upon him as he fought to regain his feet. At those things I aimed strokes which sent them flying. Points of angry red sparked about us and I knew them for eyes. But in what faces those eyes were set, I could not see.

Godgar clawed at me and I used my maimed hand to draw him up.

"The pool—break the pool—drown them out—" He lurched from my hold toward the basin, fell there again, fumbling at the stones set in the break. Then I heard a sharp hammering even above the squealing of the things through which I waded to join him. There were sharp pains in my legs and thighs. I shook off a small body which leaped to plaster itself against my back and tried to over-topple me. But I reached Godgar and bent to pry at the stones.

Though we worked in the dark, fighting off the foul smelling rabble which poured out of the earth, yet by some stroke of fortune one of us loosed the main stone of that barrier. There boiled out a flood which surprised me, since I had thought that not so much force would come from a pool fed by such a quiet and sluggish stream.

The squealing of our half-seen enemies rose to screams, as if they looked upon water as a danger even greater than that steel and fire we used against them. They fled, uttering their piercing cries, while the water dashed around us with the force of a strong river current. Surely more poured from there than had ever been pent in the basin.

Godgar cried out and tried to drag me to one isde. I looked over my shoulder. Visible, glowing with some of the blue light of the stones, a tall pillar of water rose even higher, its plume crest dashing down in the flood faster and faster. This fountaining had no relation now to the gurgling, puffing bubble which earlier fed the basin.

I saw small shaggy things caught in that overflow, whirled back and down, rammed by the water into the hole from which they must have emerged. For the flood sought the stone Godgar had earlier marked, or rather the dark pit that stone had capped, and now it poured hungrily into that cavity with the activity of a falls feeding a river.

We stumbled yet further back. The torrent of rushing water was now between us and the fire. The noise of its passing drowned all other sound. Something whirled along in it clutched at my leg, nearly toppling me. In instinctive reaction I struck down to free myself from that hold, but not before swift, sharp pain struck into my thigh and brought a cry out of me.

I could not rest my weight upon that wounded leg, but fell back against one of the blue stones, trying to feel in the dark the extent of the damage. But so tender was my flesh, that I could not bear the touch of my own fumbling examination. I could only hold to the rock, Godgar gasping and choking beside me, while the water continued to run from what seemed an inexhaustible source.

There were no more of the squealing things on our side of the stream. Now across the flood the fire flared again so we had a better measure of light. I could see men there and the gleam of swords. On the very edge of the flood, the water licking eagerly at it, lay a body, face turned up and eyes staring sightlessly straight at me.

I heard a cry from Godgar and would have echoed that had I not needed all my strength to cling to consciousness. For the pain from my thigh had become red torment such as no other wound I had ever taken.

The thing was small and twisted, its arms and legs, if those four limbs could be dignified by such human applications, were thin, covered with coarse bristles which made them resemble roots with a matting of finer fibers. In contrast the body was thick and bloated and of a white-gray which grew rapidly paler while we looked upon it. This, too, was covered with hair in shaggy patches, not like any hair I had ever seen on man or beast, but very coarse and upstanding from the hide.

It had very little neck; its skull seemed supported directly by wide bowed shoulders. The jaw and chin, and very little chin there was, jutted forward to a sharp point; the nose was a ridge joined to that vee of jaw, with two openings just above the lips. The eyes were deep sunk on either side of that ridge. It wore no clothing, nor was there any sign it was more than animal . . . yet I knew that it was.

"What is it?" Godgar asked.

"I do not know." Except, all my instincts told me, that it was one of the servants of evil, as were the Gray Ones and the Rasti.

"Look!" Godgar pointed. "The water—"

That fountain, which had stood so tall and poured forth such a volume of water, was dropping lower and lower as it continued to play. The flood which had cut us from the fire was growing narrower by the moment. I watched the dwindling dully, knowing that if I loosed my hold upon the rock which supported me I would fall. I doubted greatly that I could then rise once again. The river became a runnel; the runnel, a trickle.

"Kemoc!" I heard a cry raised from the fireside and tried to answer. It was Godgar's shout which brought them to us. With Kyllan's arm about me I fell forward, not only into his ward, but also into darkness in which pain was lost.

I roused, only too soon, to find Dahaun and my brother in counsel over me. It would seem, I understood with a kind of dreamy unconcern, that the wounds of the Thas —for it was those underground dwellers who had sprung the attack—were poisoned and that, though Dahaun could apply certain temporary measures to alleviate my pain, the healing must take place elsewhere.

I was not the only wounded. There were broken bones from the falling rocks, and several more poisoned cuts among the defenders. But mine was the deepest hurt and the one which might slow our retreat.

Kyllan spoke quickly—saying that he would stay with me until help could be sent. But, catching the look in Dahaun's eyes, I knew our peril, and, in this dreamy state where her remedies had placed me, I did not fear riding. This much I did foresee: that although the Thas attack had failed, mainly by reason of that extraordinary flood, it would not be the last. To be trapped away from the Valley meant defeat.

"Tie me on Shil." I managed to get out the words, though those sounded faint and far away in my own hearing. "We ride—or we die—as well we all know."

Dahaun looked deep into my eyes. "This is your will, Kemoc?"

"This is my will."

So at dawn we did ride, I bound to Shil as I had said. Dahaun had given me leaves to chew. The sour juices in my mouth were bitter, but they kept that barrier between me and pain, leaving me aware of it yet not subject to its tearing.

We traveled under clouds, still heavy with the storm which did not break. I went as a man might go in a dream, seeing here a bit sharply, there a fraction with a clear mind, then sliding once more into a haze.

It was when we came to the river that I awakened out of that state. Or was awakened—by a mind thrust, so keen, so inimical, that I gasped and tried to right myself on Shil's back. The Renthan gave a great trumpeting cry, whirled, to race away from our party, down the bank. I could do nothing to control our going. Behind sounded shouts, cries, the pounding of hooves in our wake.

As if he would escape any pursuit, Shil leaped from the bank into the river. Water closed over me as I struggled against the ties which kept me on the back of the plunging Renthan who seemed utterly mad.

Something gave and I was free, gasping and choking. I had been well taught to swim by Otkell, the crippled Sulcar warrior our father had sent to lesson us. But my wound had made of my left leg a part which would not answer the orders of my mind. Still gasping, choking, I came against a boulder and held to it despairingly. All mist had gone from my mind, and the fierce pain of my wound left me too weak to keep that grasp against the pull of the current.

A clutch on me from behind. Kyllan! I tried to say his name. But I could not shape it. I used mind touch. . . . To meeting nothing!

The grip was very strong, pulling me away from the rock anchorage, out into the current. I cried out, thrashed about with my arms, trying vainly to turn my head far enough to see who or what held me. But I continued to be borne along, my head a little above water, away from the bank and the shelter of the rocks.

I saw Kyllan, mounted on Shabrina, look out to where I was there plain to see. Then fear closed upon me as I straight at me, but there was no sign that he really saw me. I tried again to call . . . but there was no sound from my lips. With mind touch it was as if I beat against a high wall in which there was no opening.

Kyllan rode along the bank, still visibly searching. Yet I was there plain to see. Then fear closed upon me as I was drawn farther and farther away, leaving Kyllan and those who came after him. I saw Shil climb from the water and stand with hanging head. Then the bank curved and all of them were hidden from me, so I lost my last hope.

V

I was no longer carried along helplessly in a swift flowing flood, rather did I rest upon something stable and dry. Yet I did not at once open my eyes, moved by some primitive need for learning all that I could by my other senses before betraying the fact that I was conscious. The pain in my thigh gnawed and I was more and more aware of its torment. I fought against giving way to that, to hold my mind on other things.

Wind blew chill, making me shiver and shake. I pressed one hand against the surface on which I lay and felt gravel and sand. I listened; there was a gurgle not too far off which might be water, and a sighing which could be born of the passing of wind through vegetation. But that was the limit of the knowledge I gained.

I opened my eyes. Above, far above, still hung those thick clouds, turning day into twilight. But, cutting between those and me, was a branch, gray-white, bare of any foliage, standing as a stark and dreary monument to some long dead tree.

Now I pulled up my hands, struggled to brace myself higher. The world reeled back and forth sickeningly. I retched, turning my head weakly to let a water flood pour out of my mouth, my body wracked by the force of revulsion.

Once I had finished, I struggled up again, trying with fierce determination so that I might see where I lay. My resting place, I learned as I turned my head with great caution, moving only by force of will against the waves of nausea which continued to strike, was a scrap of beach, wet only a few inches away by the lapping of the river. To my right were boulders among which were caught bleached drift, marking the rise of old flooding.

My helm and sword were gone. The bandages Dahaun had set upon my wound were loosened and new stains grew there. But as far as I could see I was now alone. What or who had brought me along the current and away from my brother and friends, had not drowned me, but left me to what might be a far crueler fate, abandonment in this place where I was pinned by my wound from any try at escape.

But we are a stubborn race, we of Estcarp; my father was never known to accept without struggle any ill which fortune visited upon him. So, in spite of the pain it cost me, I managed to drag myself to a rock which might give me support. There I sweated and groaned as I pulled up to my feet, leaning heavily on the stone, to examine farther my situation. It was not one to encourage any man.

I was not on the river's bank, but rather on a small islet in the midst of its current. An islet which, by evidence about me, was at times completely overrun by water. Nothing grew here. There was only rock and pieces of drift wedged among the stones. It reminded me of that isle where we had taken refuge on the night when Kaththea had given birth to her familiar and sent it to range the past for our enlightenment. But then I had been whole, not only of body, but also in that we three had been closeknit to one purpose.

The shores on either side were high banked, and the current was swift. Had I been whole I would have thrown off my mail and dared to swim. Crippled as I now was, I had no chance.

Bracing myself closer to the rock, I twisted around to finger my bandage, trying to draw it tighter. The slightest touch made me flinch and grit my teeth, but I did what I could. The chill air still cut at me. It was as if the prolonged summer which abode in Escore was now changing into autumn. I longed for a fire and looked at the drift. There was a light-striker in my belt pouch. But such a fire might also be a beacon for the enemy.

Slowly I surveyed the banks. Ahead of my islet was another, larger, covered in places with green. A place which had a small promise of hospitality, better than this perch. I longed to reach it, but knew I could not fight the current.

Unless . . . Again I studied the piles of caught drift. Suppose I might put together a raft? Or perhaps, nothing as ambitious as a raft—a support to keep my head above water while the current took me somewhere downstream where I could swim to one shore or the other?

Then what? Weaponless, unable to do more than crawl, perhaps—easy meat for the Rasti, the Gray Ones or any other trouble roaming this land.

Yet, because it is born in our breed not to surrender without one last effort, I leaned over, as well as I could without losing my precarious balance, to pull to me those pieces of drift within my reach. My haul was disappointing; most were light sticks, so water-worn and dried they broke easily. There was one longer piece I essayed to use as a staff, hopping along by its aid. The pain and strain of such progress was so great, I had to rest, sweating and sick, between each step. The tiny beach was so small I could not go far. The rest of my water-washed perch was rock covered and I could not venture to climb over it.

Still I pulled and threw those pieces of drift I could reach into a pile on the beach and then eased myself down there. To tie this all together was a problem I could not solve at the moment. If I still had a knife with me I might have been able to slit tie strips from my clothing. But the knife, too, was gone, and the rocks afforded no vines to be put to such usage.

Perhaps, if I took off the leather under-jerkin which kept my mail from chaffing breast and shoulders, I could make a kind of bag of that. Stuffed with the very dry drift, would it make a support? Would it float at all?

Things were a little hazy about me; my thinking no longer was connected. I held foggily to an idea, not certain it had any value. I was thirsty. Slowly I edged to where the river lapped the gravel and dipped my hand into the flood, bringing what I could cup in my palm's hollow up to my lips. It took many such handfuls to satisfy my longing. Then I splashed the liquid over my face. To my fingers my flesh felt hot and tight, and I thought I must have a fever.

I went back to fumbling with the buckles of my mail shirt, having to pause weakly many times in the business of getting it off. Now I was no longer cold, but hot . . . so hot I longed to lunge forward into the blessed coolness of that river.

Why had I taken off my mail . . . what was it I must do? I sat staring down at the folds of metal rings on my knees, trying to remember why it had been so important that I struggle so against my own weakness.

Jerkin . . . I plucked the latches of my leather undershirt. *Must take off jerkin.* But the smallest movement was now too hard, requiring such effort that I sat panting heavily between my attempts to free myself from that other garment.

Thirsty . . . water . . . I needed water. . . . Once more I hunched along, the gravel bruising and cutting my hands as I crawled, and came to the river. My hands went into the flood.

Out of the water arose a nightmare to front me!

It was fanged; a great gaping mouth stretched wide and ready to snap me in. For that moment I saw only the mouth and the teeth within it. I threw myself back and away, wrenching my wound so that I lost consciousness.

"—awake!"

"Kyllan?"

"Awake! Dussa, let him wake!"

Cool wetness on my face. But that frantic cry did not ring in my ear; it was in my mind.

"Kyllan?"

"Wake you! If you would live, wake!"

Not Kyllan, not Kaththea. This was not the known mind touch. It was a thin, keening voice which hurt my brain as some sounds hurt the ears. I tried to flee it, but it held me fast.

"Wake!"

I opened my eyes, expecting somehow to see that monster from the river. But instead it was an oval face of pale, fair coloring, and around it tendrils of spun-silver hair dried, to spring into a floss cloud.

"Wake!" Hands on me, pulling me up.

"What—who—?"

She kept looking over her shoulder, as if she also

feared what might emerge from the river. Her anxiety was plain. But to me it had little meaning, and when she looked back to me she frowned. Her thoughts were as sharp pointed knives to prick my swimming brain into action.

"We have little time. They make a bargain—with you for payment! Do you wish to be given to *those?*"

I blinked. But the urgency of her mind touch stirred within me the instinct for self-preservation that will keep a man going even when his conscious mind has retreated into non-thought. Clumsily I tried to answer to her tugging, somehow crawling to the river as she pulled and pushed me in that direction.

Then I remembered and tried to jerk out of her hold. "Thing—thing in there—"

Her grip tightened and she thought at me fiercely. "No longer. It will obey me. You must get away before *they* send for you."

So determined was her will that it overrode my small spark of rebellion and I lurched on. Then I was floundering in the water.

"On your back—over on your back." she ordered.

Somehow I did find myself on my back, and once more I was drawn along, my head held above the surface. We were headed downstream. My companion swam, but also used the current to aid our flight. For flight it was. My immersion cleared my thinking enough to let me know that we were in danger.

Then it began to rain; huge drops struck the surface about us. The clouds were at last loosing the burden with which they had so long threatened us. I closed my eyes against the beating, and I thought my companion's apprehension heightened.

"Must—must get ashore—before the floods came. . . ."

I caught her hurried thought. Then she called a call so high in pitch it faded from my mental grasp. Shortly after, there was a burst of relief from her mind. Then followed her orders.

"We must go under water here. Take a deep breath and hold it when I say so."

My protest did not register with her. So when her order reached my mind I filled my lungs as best I might. There was abrupt darkness about us. We were not only submerged beneath the water, but must also come under some other roofing. There is a fear in this for my species, and perhaps I felt it the more since I was helpless. Did she realize I must breathe—breathe—*now!*

Then my face broke water, my nose and mouth open to the air. I gulped that in, and with it a strong animal scent, as if we transversed a burrow, yet water still lapped about us. It was dark, yet my companion advanced with confidence.

"Where are we?"

"In a runway to an aspt house. Ah, now we must crawl. Hold to my belt and come—"

Turning from my back was a task which left me sweating again, but turn I did in those cramped quarters. Her hands aided and guided me, setting my groping fingers in a belt with many sharp shells set along its surface. We crawled and came into a wide circular place which had ghostly light shifting from the upper portion of its dome.

The flooring under us was piled with dried rushes and bunches of leaves, while the walls of the dome were of dried mud mixed with more reeds, plastered into some smoothness. At the apex of that ceiling were small holes to give air, though that was heavily tainted with the strong animal odor. Light also came from another source: bits of vegetable matter had been wedged haphazardly into the walls and emitted a weird grayish radiance.

We were not alone in that domed room. Squatting across from us was a furred creature. It was large. If it had stood on its powerful hindfeet it might have just topped my shoulder. Its head was round, with no discernible ears, a wide mouth with noticeable, jutting teeth, and feet provided with long heavy claws. Had I fronted it in other company I might have watched it warily. But now it smoothed its fur with its paws, combing through that thickness with its claws. It did this almost absently, for its eyes were fixed upon the girl who had brought me. Though I could not catch their thought speech, I was sure they were communicating.

She was Orsya, but why she had brought me from the islet, and from what danger we fled, I had no idea. The furred owner of the house waddled to a hole and, ducking into it, was gone. Orsya turned her attention to me.

"Let me look upon your wound." It was an order rather than a request, but one I obeyed. For the raging pain Dahaun's treatment had reduced was fast returning, and I wondered how much more I could stand.

The Krogan girl brought out a knife and cut more of my breeches and the bandage I had knotted tighter. Though the light of our refuge seemed twilight to me, it apparently served her adequately. She examined my wound intently.

"It is better than I had hoped. The woodswoman knows her herbs," was Orsya's comment. "While her roots and leaves would not heal it, yet the poison has eaten no deeper. Now let us see what can be done."

I had raised myself on my elbows to watch her. Now, with a palm flat against my chest, she pushed me flat again.

"Rest—do not move! I shall speedily return."

As the animal, she crawled through that mud arch and I was left alone. The light-headedness which had come and gone upon the islet plagued me, and with it the pain in my thigh was a fire charring to the bone.

It seemed a very long time before she came back, and I needed all my small remaining stock of fortitude to endure it. I knew that I had a fever and it was increasingly hard to keep in touch with the world about me.

Orsya bent over my wound again; her touch was at first sheer agony as she coated torn flesh with a soft, wet substance she took from a shell box. Then a coolness spread from that coating, soothing, turning the torn flesh numb. Three times she spread the coating, each time waiting for a short interval before she applied the next layer. Then she put over it some wide leaves.

When she had finished she raised my heavy head and urged into my mouth some globules that burst as I bit down on them, filling my mouth with a salty, bitter fluid.

"Swallow!" she commanded.

In spite of my distaste, I did, though it was faintly nauseating and left my throat feeling raw. Water from a shell cup followed, before she settled me back on an improvised pillow of reeds scraped up from the floor.

I slept then, my last waking memory that of seeing Orsya curl up at the other side of the house. She held something between her hands; whatever that object was, it gave off flickers of light which ran hither and thither across the walls, for what purpose I could not guess.

When I awoke again I was alone. But my head was clear and the pain in my wound was only a suggestion of ache. Suddenly I wanted out—into the clear, clean air which did not carry the animal smell, wanted out enough so that, if I still had my sword, I might have been hacking at the walls which pent me there.

Only, when I tried to sit up, I discovered that the plaster Orsya had put on my thigh was now a great weight, its surface under my exploring hands, seemingly as hard as stone. It tied me as efficiently where I was as if she had left me in dungeon chains. But I did not have long to fret about that, for she crawled in from the tunnel, carrying something wrapped in a net.

For a moment she eyed me appraisingly. "It is well," she commented. "The poison no longer fills you. Now, eat, and so grow strong, for danger stalks this land, with net and spear, to take you."

Her net bag she put down and opened to show small leaf-wrapped parcels in it. Hunger—yes, I *was* hungry— with the hunger that follows involuntary fasting. I glanced at the parcels and knew I would not question flavor, nor source, that only the substance interested me.

There were small slivers of white meat, moist, and I believe, raw. Over these she scattered a flower-like dust from another packet. I ate eagerly, and found it good, where I had been prepared to overcome repugnance because of my need. There were four or five things which might have been roots, peeled and scraped, which had a sharp flavor, a little biting to the tongue. When I had finished, Orsya folded away the net.

"We must talk, man from overmountain. As I have said, you are not free from danger—but very far from safety. At least, beyond these walls you are. The Valley is far from here. Also, those who rode with you believe you dead."

"How did I get to that island?"

She had brought out a comb and drew it through her cloud of hair, smoothing and parting those filmy locks with a kind of unconscious sensual pleasure.

"Oboro was sent to take you, or one of you. The People

65

—the Krogan as you earth walkers call us—are very frightened; and fear has made them angry against those they believe have brought them danger. No longer may it be in this land to answer no war horn except one's own. You and Ethutur came to Orais and asked for our aid. But other, and greater, lords had come before you. After you were gone they sent such messengers as we did not dare to deny hearing.

"We want none of your wars; do you understand? None!" Her mind touch was a ringing shout in my brain. "Leave us to our lakes and pools, our rivers and streams. Leave us in peace!"

"Yet Oboro caught me—"

For a moment she did not answer, but busied herself ridding one long strand of hair of a tangle, as if that was the weightiest act in all the world. But I guessed that she hid behind her comb and combing as one might cower for refuge under the spreading limbs of a welcoming tree.

"You called upon water to war with the Thas—loosed one of the ancient weapons the Krogan once built for a lord long since dead. Now the Thas, and those who sent them, cry out upon my people, saying that in truth we have secretly allied ourselves to you. Those sent among us to see we do not do such a thing, they will take toll—"

"But why was I captured?"

"You are one of those who began the troubling, one who helped to loose the flood. You were wounded and so easy to capture," she replied frankly.

Suddenly I discovered that I was watching the rise and fall of that comb in her hair with a serious attention which woke an uneasiness in me. Reluctantly, and that reluctance alarmed me even more, I looked away from her, fixing my eyes on the dome wall above her head.

"So Oboro thought me easy prey—"

"Orias ordered that one of you be taken, if it were possible. He might use such a prisoner as a peace-offering to *those*. And mayhap, if he drove a good bargain, free us from their notice."

"But if it meant so much to your people, why did you rescue me?"

Her comb was still now. "Because what Orais ordered would bring trouble also. Perhaps worse trouble in the end. Is it not the truth, that you *spoke* and one of the Great Ones *answered*?"

"How—how did you know that?"

"Because we are who we are, man from overmountain. Once, very long and long ago, we had ancestors who were of your breed. But those chose to walk another road, and from that walking, little by little, were we born. But powers shaped us, and once we answered to their pull and sway. So when one of the Great Ones stirs, then all like unto us in this land knows it. And if you are one who will be *answered*, then you might loose upon us worse than *those* can summon in their turn."

"But Orias did not think so?"

"Orais believes what he was told—that only by chance did you hit upon some spell which moved a long closed gate. His informer also said better give you unto those who can force you to put such a key into their hands."

"No!"

"So say I also, man from overmountain."

"My name is Kemoc."

For the first time I saw her smile. "Kemoc, then. No, if you have such a spell, I would rather have it serve those you company with in the Valley, than others. Thus did I come to take you from the island."

"And this?" I looked about me.

"This is a winter dwelling for the aspt. Since they are of the rivers, so are they bidable when we approach them properly. But time passes and powers walk. I do not think it will be much longer that you dare an overland trip to the Valley. It is whispered that the Shadow forces will soon have that under siege."

I rapped my hand against the stone-hard covering of my wound. "How long must I be tied here?"

Again she smiled and put away her comb. "For no longer than is needed to chip you free, Kemoc."

Chip she did, hammering with stone and the point of her knife. I thought that what she had plastered on me and left to dry must be the same healing mud as had brought my brother back from the edge of death. For when the last shards fell away there was no wound, but a half-healed scar seam, and I could move the limb with ease.

She took me out through the underwater tunnel and we sheltered warily in a thicket of reed growth, rooted where the water swirled. It was early morning and a mist clung to the surface of the river. Orsya sniffed, drawing deep breaths into her lungs and expelling them slowly, as if in that way she tested for some message which eluded me.

"The day will be fair," she announced. "That is good—clouds favor the Shadow; sun is the enemy to *those*."

"Which way do I go?"

She shook her head at me. "Way *we* go, Kemoc. To let you blunder helplessly in this land is to pick a possel from its shell and throw it to a vuffle. We go by water."

Go by water we did, first swimming with the current of the river, and then against the push of ripples in a smaller side stream to the south. Although the land seemed open and smiling under the sun, yet I paid close attention to all Orsya's directions. We lay in a reed bank once—she underwater, I with a hollow reed in my mouth for air—while a small pack of Gray Ones lapped water and growled to one another within arms touching of our hiding place.

It was irking to my guide that I could not take wholly to the water as she was able, but needed air for my laboring lungs. I am sure she could have made that journey in a third less time than we took. At night we sheltered again in another river dweller's abandoned burrow, one not finished with the skill of the aspt dwelling, merely a hole cut in the bank.

There she spoke of her people and their like. I learned that she was the first daughter of Orais' elder sister, so by their way of ranking kinship, thought closer to him than his own children. She was more adventurous than most of her generation, having slipped away from her home on numerous occasions to explore waterways where only a few, if any, of the males had ever ventured. She hinted of strange finds in the mountains, and then said impatiently, that with the coming of war such searching must be abandoned. Mention of the war silenced her and she curled into sleep.

It was midmorning before the stream we had followed dwindled to a size so we could no longer swim. Then she motioned to the heights ahead and said:

"Guide your way by that peak, Kemoc. If you take care and make haste, you will reach your Valley by sundown. I can abide for short periods of time in the open air, but not for long. Thus, this is our parting place."

I tried to thank her. But what are adequate thanks for one's life? She smiled again and waved. Then she splashed back into the water and was gone before I could finish what I was stumbling over to say.

Setting my attention on the peak she had pointed out I began the last stage of my journey.

VI

The winged sentries of the Valley had me in view long before I sighted them. A Flannan appeared out of nowhere to coast along over my head, then was gone with beating wings. I came up, not the road entrance I had known before, but a notch between two standing stones. Back door to the Green domain this might be, but here were also inscribed the Symbols on each wall. One of the lizard folk who helped patrol the heights peered down on me, jewel-eyed.

"Kemoc!"

Kyllan came running, throwing his arms about my shoulders, mind and eyes both meeting mine. In that moment our old closeness was as if it had never been broken.

It was like unto a high feast day as they brought me to the feather-roofed houses, asking questions all the way. But what I had to tell them of Krogan enmity made them quickly sober.

"This is ill hearing!" Dahaun had poured the guesting cup for me. Now she put the flagon back on the table as if she saw some evil picture. "With the Krogan ranged against us . . . water can be a bad weapon to face. But who can be these Great Ones of the Shadow whom Orais

70

fears so much that he tries to buy their favor with a captive? The Krogan are not a timid folk. In the past they have been friends to us. Perhaps a seeking—"

Ethutur shook his head. "Not yet; not until we can learn in no other way. Remember, those who so *seek* may also find themselves the sought, if they are detected and the power on the other side is equal to, or greater than, their own."

In the first excitement of my return I had forgotten something, but no longer. Kaththea—where was my sister? I looked to Kyllan for an answer. Surely she was not avoiding me... ?

He was quick with reassurance. "She rode east yesterday, when we believed you dead. It was her thought to go to a place, known here, where certain forces can be tapped; and where, with her witch knowledge, perhaps she could read your fate. Believe this, Kemoc; she was sure that you were not dead. For she said that she and I would know it if your life had been taken from you!"

I dropped my head into my hands. Suddenly it became so needful that I reach her, that I sent out a call, believing that here in the protected Valley, it could cause no harm. Kyllan's thought twined with mine, making it twofold as it went forth, joyfully seeking.

Into that seeking I poured more and more strength. I felt the tide of Kyllan's rise with it—out and out. . . . Yet there came no answer. It was not as if Kaththea was absorbed in some spell of her own, for still we would have touched her mind and been warned off. No, this was a total absense of all Kaththea meant to both of us—as total as if the walls of the Wise Women's Secret Place had once more closed about her.

Now my spear of thought grew swifter, shot in all directions. But there was no target, only that emptiness which in itself was ominous. I raised my head again from trembling hands and looked to Kyllan, saw the grayish shade beneath the weathering of his face and knew we were united in fear.

"Gone!" He said it first, in a whisper which still must have reached the ears of those about us, for they, too, looked startled and dismayed.

"Where?" To me that was most important. When I had called Kaththea from the island of the Krogan lake, her answer has been faint and hard to read, coming across miles of territory which the enemy held; still, I had reached her and she, me. In this protected Valley where there would be no barriers, I could not reach her at all.

I turned to Dahaun. "This place of power to which she went, where does it lie?"

"At the eastern tip of the Valley, up against the Heights."

The Heights—Dinzil! To me the answer was as plain as if written out in fiery runes across the air between us. My thought was clear to her.

"Why?"

So Dahaun did not dispute the possibility of my guess; she looked for a reason.

"Yes, why?" That was Kyllan. "Kaththea looked upon him with favor; that is true. But she would not go to him thus without speech between us, especially after saying that she wished to seek you through the power."

"Not willingly," I answered aloud, between set teeth.

Dahaun shook her head. "Not unwillingly, Kemoc. One with her powers could not be drawn unwillingly past our defenses. And those guard every gate of this Valley."

"I do not believe that she agreed—"

"How know you what arguments may have been used with her?" Kyllan asked.

I turned on him, and some of my fear became anger, to be directed at one within my reach: "Why did you not keep mind touch, to know what chanced with her?"

He flushed. But when he made answer he kept a rein on his temper. "Because she wished it so, saying she must hoard her energy to use in the seeing. She said that while she was learned in much, yet never had she taken the Witch Oath, nor received the Jewel, been admitted into full company. Thus she doubts at times and needs all her strength."

That sounded as Kaththea's own words, and I knew that he spoke the truth. Still . . . that he might have protected her, and had not, burned unfairly in me. I spoke now to Dahaun:

"Can Shil bear me to where Kaththea went?"

"I do not know. That he can go in that direction, yes. But whether you, who have little protection against the forces which gather there, can reach it, that is another question."

"Which only trial may answer! But let me try—"

Only I was not to have that chance. For, even before I finished speaking, one of the birds swooped down to perch on Dahaun's shoulder. Instead of the usual trilled greeting, its cries were a scream, plainly meant to announce some disaster. Ethutur and the rest were on their feet, crowding for the door. Dahaun looked to us from Estcarp.

"They move upon the Valley, even as the Krogan maid warned you, Kemoc."

So began our siege time and it was a bitter one. While the Symbols might bar the gates, yet there were miles of cliffs, and against those a motley crew of monsters climbed, flew, scrabbled to find a way at us. Storm clouds gathered about the rim we defended; wind and torrents

73

of rain lashed at us. The gloom hid those who strove to make the ascent. The lightning strikes of the force whips were undistinguishable at times from the true lightning of the storm.

It was a wild series of battles. There would come lulls, even as the most vicious hurricanes know lulls. Then once more the rush, so we had to be on the alert, for we never knew when the next attack would muster.

Some of the enemy I had seen before. While the Rasti could not climb the cliffs, the Gray Ones put on their quasi-human shapes to find holes. There were other things . . . drifting mists which were perhaps the more feared by us from overmountain because they had no substance to be hewed by steel, nor shattered by dart . . . and vast, armored things prowling about the base of the cliffs, unable to climb, but digging with taloned paws at our natural wall with sullen ferocity.

Flying things fought airborne over our heads where Flannan, bird, Vrang of the peaks cut and slew in turn. It was a struggle out of a nightmare; even those among our recruits who had gone up against the frightening other-world might of the Kolder long years past found this a more fearsome battle.

For how long we held that defense, I do not know, for day was nearly as darksome as night. When day came pillars of fire flamed green, high into the sky, from cressets along the cliff. In that light our adversaries seemed less inclined to press forward.

The Green People had their own magic that they called upon. Dahaun and others did not take actual part in the fighting, but summoned and marshaled forces which were not of any earth I had known.

I knew that the Lady of Green Silences feared the waters within the Valley, that some disaster might come from them since the Krogan were against us. But, though the lizard folk patrolled there, they found no sign that Orais had taken the field openly under the Shadow.

Once, when Ethutur spoke to a handful of the Old Race, he said, in a puzzled fashion, that all who had been sent against us were only the minor servants of evil and no Great One from the Shadow had given us a blow. This he thought sinister . . . unless the Great Ones had indeed withdrawn so far into their other worlds that they could not be easily summoned again.

We suffered losses in those grim hours. Godgar fell, taking with him a warrior's guard of the enemy. There were gaps in the ranks of the Green People also, and among their four-footed and winged allies. No one kept count of the casualties for there was no time to think of anything but dogged defense. Although Kyllan fought a distance from me, I knew all was still well with him. But, even through this, my thought for Kaththea was a gnawing. That she had gone out of the Valley, I was certain.

Some of the men from the Heights fought in our ranks. But among them Dinzil did not show. Nor did I expect him to, no matter what excuse his followers could offer for him.

Perhaps what Dahaun called down was what came to our succor at last. Or perhaps the enemy had just so many fangs, claws, bodies, and wills to throw against us, and those had become so thinned they were ready to retreat. But at last the clouds broke and the sun shone. Under that glory the hosts of the Shadow drew back. They took their dead with them, so we could not tell how great a toll we had exacted. However, they had been beaten this time, of that we were sure.

We took counsel then and knew that our own losses

had not been light. Nor could we withstand many more such concentrated attacks. So in the breathing space now allowed us, we must fortify and scout, strike back where we could.

But I had another task. And so I told them.

Then Kyllan arose and said that this would be his road also: for the three of us were one, and when that bond was broken, then we were all lessened.

Then I spoke to him alone, saying that once before we had been parted, and he, the warrior, had held to his duty, when I had been maimed and Kaththea rift from us. Now, here again, was a time when we must be what we were called upon to be. Warrior he was, and in this place his skill was needed. But with me was Kaththea even closer linked, and upon me the need to go to her was the heavier.

I think Dahaun and Ethurtur understood. But those from Estcarp did not. For, to them, long nurtured in the harshness of border war, the life of one woman weighed as nothing against the good of all. That she was a witch tipped the scales even more, for among those who fled from Karsten the Wise Ones were feared but not esteemed.

I expected no support. I took only a small supply of food, a sword, and a spark of hope, to travel east. Shil's strength was offered me, but I said I would ride only to the borders of the Valley; beyond that I risked no life save my own.

Kyllan parted from me reluctantly. I think—I know—that he was hurt by my frankness concerning the stronger bond between me and Kaththea, though he knew that I spoke the truth, and that his skill was needed here.

In the Valley it seemed that our bloody struggle, of the days just past, was an ugly dream. Shil went at a steady gallop along the river bottom. There were no traps here to be evaded and his going was swift and smooth. I saw the lizard sentries who still watched for any Krogan menace. I wondered about Orsya and what her people would do when they discovered, if they did, that she had freed me from the prison islet.

The wide grasslands and pleasant groves of the Valley gave way now to a landscape narrowing between slowly converging walls, wilder looking, with a predominance of rocky outcrops. I thought that the Valley must dwindle to a point ahead. In that point, according to Dahaun's directions, lay a little used, climbing way which led to the place where Kaththea had gone, to find that which even the Lady of Green Silences held in awe.

To each his or her own magic, as Dahaun had once said to me. The Valley's was of growth and life from the soil, the Thas' was of things underground, and the Krogan's of the water. I gathered from Dahaun that the place Kaththea had sought was akin to the powers of the air.

The Witches of Estcarp could control wind and rain and tempests, after a fashion. Perhaps my sister planned to draw upon such arts now. Only, if she had gone there with such intent, she had not succeeded.

Shil slowed pace, single-footed warily through a narrow slit between towering walls. No longer was the sun with me, though it was still some hours from setting. But here twilight abode.

Finally the Renthan halted.

"So far—no farther," came his thought.

A narrow path was before us, but I felt it, too . . . a distinct warn-off to the spirit. I dismounted and slung the strap of the supply bag across my shoulder.

"My thanks for your courtesy, swift-footed runner. Tell

them all was well with me when we parted."

His head was up; he was searching the walls above and beyond. In my sight they were sheer reaches of rock, no place on their surfaces to shelter any would-be ambusher. I had a strong feeling also that this place would not welcome such forces as we had beaten back from the Valley. Shil blew from his nostrils, pawed the ground.

"There is the taste, the smell, the feel, of power here."

"But not of evil," I answered him.

He lowered his head so his golden eyes met mine.

"Some powers are beyond our measurement—for good or ill. He who goes this road walks blindfolded in the senses we know."

"I have no choice."

Once again he blew and tossed his head. "Go in strength, watch well your footing, and keep always alert with eye and ear...."

He did not want to leave, but he could not pass some barrier there. Would it also stand against me? I went on with long strides, half expecting that I might find myself running into one of those force walls, such as had once been between us and the Secret Place where Kaththea was shut from the world. But there was nothing.

I looked back once and saw Shil still standing there, watching me. When I raised my hand in salute, once more he tossed his head in answer. Then I turned and kept my eyes only for the forward route, shutting out of mind what lay behind.

For a while the cut sloped gently upward and the footing was easy. Then I came to the very tip point of that cut. The way was very narrow here. I could stretch forth my arms and have the fingers of each hand brush the walls. Before me was a stair. Plainly no act of nature, but the work of intelligence. On each of those steps was deep graven symbols. Some were of the protective kind of the Valley, but others were strange to me. I did not quite like setting bootsoles upon those marks, yet that I must do if I were to climb. So I went. Seven steps, a landing place the width of three steps, three steps, another such landing, then nine. . . . I could not see any natural reason for such an arrangement, unless the grouping had an occult meaning.

Gradually the stairway grew yet narrower, tapering from one landing to the next. When I was on the last flight there was barely room on each step for two feet set together. I found I made the climb one step at a time, placing my feet together before I raised one for the next step. There were thirteen in this last very narrow way. I found myself counting them under my breath as I went.

The symbols here were all strange: I discovered that I did not like to look at any of them very long. No trace of warning clung to them—I was sensitive enough to the evil of Escore to recognize that—rather it was as if they were never meant for eyes and brains such as mine to sight and understand.

I was tired, though I had not felt any fatigue when I had ridden down the Valley. This was a heaviness which weighted my limbs, made me gasp a little at each step, a need to rest between. My wound had healed fast and clean after Orsya's treatment. It was not that which affected me now, but rather an all-over heaviness of body, a corresponding darkness of spirit.

The stairs were behind me at last, and I stood on the top of the cliff wall of the Valley. Cut into the surface of the stone was a path. As the steps had narrowed little by little, this followed the opposite pattern: beginning no wider than that exit, spreading out, wedged-shaped, beyond to a place where stood a forest of pillars.

Night had come while I climbed and, though I wanted to go on, the weariness was now so heavy upon me I could pull myself no farther than to where I could rest my length in a slot of the road, wrapped in my cloak. So I slept, with no drowsy fall into slumber, but a swift extinction of consciousness. Had I wished, I could not have fought that sleep.

I awoke as swiftly, sat up stiffly, to flex my arms and legs. Dawn light struck here. I ate sparingly from the food Dahaun had packed for me, drank a mouthful of water from my bottle. I must guard well those supplies, she had warned me. For, in troubled lands where the Shadow reached, a man might be brought under evil influences should he eat of what he found growing ripe and ready to his plucking.

Once more I walked that wedge road. The pillars did not appear to be set in any order, nor did they carry any marks of tooling. They might rather have been the boles of petrified trees from which crowns and branches had long since been chipped away. So strong did this feeling of being in a stone forest grow, that I kept glancing from side to side to see if those missing branches might still lie on the surface between the boles. But the rock was bare. As the wind arose and blew among those standing stones, I could plainly hear the sound present in a grove when a stout breeze sets leaves to rustling. I shut my eyes once and knew that I stood in a grove; yet when I opened them to look, I only gazed upon stone.

The rustling of the unseen wood grew louder, though the push of air against me was no more. There began a wailing, a keening, which were the cries of all the bereft of the world wailing their dead. That, too, died away, and then there was *sound*—words I thought—in no tongue known to me or any man of my kind. I did not *answer*, as had that Other I had provoked in the lowlands. No, these sounds were uttered in a space which might touch upon that in which I moved, but was not mine.

The very feeling of that awesome otherness was such that I did fall, or rather was crushed, to my knees, unable to even think of where that might be—or what lips uttered those *words*.

There followed silence as sharp as if a door had been shut, no wind, no wailing, only silence. I got to my feet and began to run on. So I came into an open space where the road ended, and I stood staring about me.

Stone and rock . . . Across that rock a splash of color, I went to that. It lay in a loose coil as if dropped only a moment earlier. I picked up a scarf, loose, silken, its fine threads catching on my scarred fingers' rough skin. It was green-blue, such a scarf as the women of the Valley wore about their shoulders in the evening. Kaththea had worn a like one when she had laughed with Dinzil at the feasting.

"Kaththea!" I felt it was wrong to raise my voice in that place, but I dared the mind call, as I stood running the soft length back and forth in my hands. "Kaththea! Where are you?"

Silence . . . that dead and awesome silence which had fallen in this place since the closing of the door. To my mind not the faintest answer, though I went seeking.

I coiled the scarf into a small handful and stowed it inside my jerkin to lie against my breast. It had been Kaththea's I was sure. Thus, perhaps, I could use it for a linkage, since a possession can be a draw point.

But where had she gone from here? Not back into the Valley . . . and the road to this haunted place ended here.

If she had gone on, it was among those stone trees and there I would follow.

The road had been a sure guide, but once I left it behind and threaded a way among the standing stones, I found I had entered a maze. There was no point ahead I could fix upon as a goal, and, as I twisted and turned, I found myself heading back into the open space where I had found the scarf. On the second such return, I sat down.

That there was a spell set here I no longer doubted. It was meant to confuse mind and eye. To counter it, I closed my eyes upon those bewildering ranks of trees and concentrated on the days I had spent in Lormt. It had been so accepted that no male could use witch power, that no guardian-ship had been put on the records. It was true that most were written in such allegorical style, with so many obscure references to matters unknown, that those not carefully schooled in witch training could make little or nothing of them. At the time I had been searching there, my one desire was to find a refuge for us, and so I had paid little attention to other secrets.

But some of what I had pushed aside along the way lingered in mind. I had the words which had brought the *answer*; those I had no intention of trying again. Now I must bring to my need other knowledge.

There was a chance. I forced a picture from memory. A page of parchment covered with crabbed, archaic writing. Of the handful of words I had been able to read, perhaps a few would serve. How much power did I have in me? Was I one who had inherited the ability of my father to overstep the boundaries of my sex and be more gifted than other males of the Old Race?

I brought out that scarf I had carried. Now I began to knead and roll it between my fingers, twisting it slowly and with care into a cord. So soft was the material it was like a ribbon. Then I knotted the two ends and laid it down before me, so that what I had was a circle, very vivid against the stone.

Fixing my full attention on it as it lay there, I brought my will into use. I had no training in such matters. All I possessed was a memory of some lines on parchment, a driving need for success, and a will which might or might not be equal to the demand I made upon it.

Kaththea . . . in my mind I built the picture of Kaththea, perhaps not just as she was in life, but as she was to me. I concentrated upon that picture for a long time, trying to see her standing within that green circle. Then —now would come the test of what I knew, or what I might be.

I moved my hands slowly and I said aloud three words.

Hardly daring to breathe I watched and waited. The blue-green circlet trembled . . . one side across. Now it was a hoop balanced on its edge. It began to roll slowly, away from the open, out among the topless, branchless stone trees. I followed it, holding to the hope that I had now a guide.

VII

Back and forth the hoop wove a path through the stone wood, and many times was I sure it turned upon itself to lead me in circles. Yet it was my only hope for passing through this ensorceled place. Sometimes I faced the now beaming sun, and then I would remember the old warnings: when a man's shadow lay behind him, so that he could not set eye upon it—that was the time when evil might creep upon him unawares. But, although this place was alien to me, I did not think of it as evil, rather as a barrier, set up to warn off or mislead those who had no kinship with it. We came at last to the other side of that pillared land and the hoop rolled into the open. It wobbled from side to side as if the energy which sustained it was failing. Yet still it rolled, and the path it followed was straight ahead; now there was no chiseled road, only rough rock worked by time and storms.

To the very end of this plateau the loop brought me before it collapsed, no longer anything but a silken cord. If what powers I had sought to fasten upon it had worked, then Kaththea had come this way. But why? And—how?

I picked up the scarf and once more folded it small, to put in my jerkin, as I moved along the edge of a drop, looking down. There was no visible means of descent; the break was sharp and deep.

When I was sure of that I retraced my steps to examine intently the spot where my hoop guide had fallen. The sun, though westering now, showed me scars on the rock. Something had rested there, under weight. I glanced to the opposite side of the chasm. There was a level space; there could have been a bridge across. But if so, that was gone. I rubbed my thigh where the wound was now but a memory and tried to measure by eye the distance between my stand and the other edge.

Only a desperate man would consider such a leap. But now, ridden by my fears, I was a desperate man. I drew my sword and tied it to the supply bag. By the strap I whirled this around my head twice and let it fly. I heard the clang of the blade against the rock, saw it come to rest a foot or so in from the lip of that other rim.

Next I shed my boots, to make them another bundle with my belt buckled about them, and flung them across that gulf. Under my bare feet the rock was warmed by the sun. I paced back toward the edge of the stone forest, though I did not venture in among those boles. Then I put my energy and determination to the test, racing for the edge of the cliff, arching out in a leap, not daring to let myself believe that I would do anything but land safely on the other side.

I sprawled forward, struck painfully, bruising my body with such force that I feared I might have broken bones. I lay there, the breath driven out of me, gasping, before I realized, with a leap of inner exultation, that I had indeed crossed. But I was sore, when I moved to sit up and look about me. I went limpingly when I once more drew on my boots and shouldered my pack.

The marks which had guided me on the other side were sharper to read here; there were scratches as if something had been dragged along the rock. For want of better track I followed those, to find, wedged in behind some rocks, my bridge; a thing made of three logs bound together with hide thongs. The fact that it had been hidden suggested that its makers thought to use it again and I wondered. Would they so have a secret way of reaching the Valley? And would it be in the best interests of those I had left behind to destroy the bridge here and now. But how? I did not have the strength to maneuver it back and send it rolling into the gulf. To set it afire . . . that was beyond me. Also I doubted if those we feared could move easily through that stone wood.

Those who had hidden the bridge left other traces of their going. I had had good training as a scout in the mountains of Estcarp. These men—if they were men—had not hidden their trail. Hoofprints of Renthan—those were plain in a patch of earth. A tuft of fleece flagged me from a thorn bush, for this side of the gulf was not all rock. Things grew here, though the whipping wind and lack of good soil stunted that growth.

I followed the trail, easier to read in the soil, down a steep slope and into a wood of grotesquely twisted trees, which at first grew hardly higher than my own head. But, as I descended farther into their stand, they stood taller, though nonetheless crooked, until I was in a wood where sunlight did not pierce and I moved in a grayish gloom. Then I saw a thick moss depending from the limbs and crooked branches, so that, though these trees were scanty of leaf, yet they shut out light. Some of this moss dripped in long, swaying masses, as if tattered curtains hung between tree and tree. But the party whose traces I followed had broken away, pulling down some of this wiry vegetation so that it lay in heaps on the ground, giving forth a faintly spicy odor.

As the moss curtains hung from the trees, so did the ground give root to a similar growth. This was soft and springing under foot and from it, here and there, arose slender stems on which trembled, at my passing, pallid flowers. There were other lighter glimmers here and there along that mossy undergrowth. As the forest grew darker about me, so these did glow with a phosphorescent light. They were star-shaped with six points. When I bent more closely to them, they would fade, and all left to be seen was a kind of grayish web spun across the top of moss tendrils.

Night was coming, and I could not follow the trail in the dark. Nor had I any wish to camp in this place. So far I had not seen or heard life within the wood, but that did not rule out the possibility that some very unpleasant surprises might lurk here.

Yet I must find a place in which to rest, or else try to return back the way I had come. For the farther down-slope I went, the deeper became the moss-grown forest. I found myself pausing for long moments to listen intently. The faint breezes, which did manage to penetrate to this place, moved the tree rooted vegetation so that there was always a low whispering. I thought it sounded eerily like half-heard words, broken speech, issuing from things which spied and followed as I went.

I stopped at last to look at one great tree which might, in spite of its gray-green curtains, provide a firm and safe wall for a man's back. Eat, drink and rest, I must. My bruised body was too tired to be forced along and I had no desire to blunder perhaps into a camp of the enemy.

The tree did provide a feeling of security as I sat with my back against it. Now, as the gloom deepened, the stars and the pale flowers were more noticeable. I was aware of an elusive fragrance, a pleasant scent carried by the sighing breeze.

I ate and drank with moderation. Luckily, the journey rations of the Green People had been long ago devised to give a maximum of nourishment to a minimum of bulk, so that a few mouthfuls sufficed a man for a day. Still one's stomach continued to want real food, chewed and swallowed for its filling. So I was vaguely dissatisfied, even though my mind told me I was well-fed on the crumbs I had licked from my fingers.

Just as, the night before, that climb up the stairs had wearied me past all previous acquaintance with fatigue, so now something of the same trembling weakness settled upon me as I sat there. It was rank folly to sleep . . . rank folly. . . . I remembered some inner warning trying to arouse me even as the waves of sleep rolled over me, and me, under them.

Water about me, rising higher and higher, choking me! I had lost Orsya, I was drowning in the river. . . .

Gasping, I awoke. Not water, no. But I was buried in drifts, waves of moss which rose to chin level, the end of the fronds weaving loosely about my head. Fear triggered my responses, my struggle to throw off that blanket. Yet, my legs and arms were now as tightly caught as if cords bound them. I could not even move away from the tree against which I had set my back, for now this tide of gray and green had lashed me to it! Would I indeed drown in it? I ducked, twisted and turned my head, and then I realized that the weaving fronds about my shoulders were not tightening about my head. While my movement was constricted, yet the fibers had not tightened to the point that either breathing or circulation was impaired. I was captive, but so far my life was not yet imperiled.

But that was small comfort. I rested my head against the tree trunk and gave up struggling. It was very dark now and the glow of the stars almost brilliant. Those caught my attention. I had not noted any particular pattern to their setting before, but now I saw two rows, leading from where I was imprisoned off to my left. Almost as if they had been deliberately set to mark a path! A path for who—or what?

The swish-swish of the tree-rooted moss whispered under some breeze. But I could hear no insect, no night hunter.

I turned my attention to the moss. The coarse strands about me were not of the ground growth, but that which was limb rooted. I could see by the aid of the phosphorescent stars that loops of it had loosened hold on branches to fall about the parent trunk and my body. Tales, told by the Sulcar rovers, of strange growths in far southern lands which had a taste for flesh and blood, which seized upon prey as might animal hunters, came far too easily to mind at that moment. Then, I discovered I could move a little in that cording, enough to change position slightly when I strove to favor, half-unconsciously, one of my worst bruises. It was as if what held me captive had picked the need for such easement out of my mind and responded to it.

Out of my mind? But that was wild—utterly wild! How could a plant read my thoughts? Or was it a plant? Oh, yes; leaf and fiber about me were vegetation. But could it be a tool—this prisoning mass—a tool in other hands?

"Who are you?" Deliberately I aimed that thought into the gloom. "Who are you? What would you do with me?"

I do not believe that I expected any answer. But—while I did not get an answer—I did tap *something!* Just as Orsya had slid off that beam used for contact between us when she spoke to the aspt, so did I now but touch for a second, to lose it again, some think-level. It was not like those of the Green People, or of the Krogan, being far less "human." Animal? Somehow, I did not believe so. I put all my concentration now, not into physical struggle against the moss, but into seeking.

"Who—are—you?"

Twice more that flicker of almost touch. Enough to keep me struggling. But it came and was lost again before I could even decide whether it was an upper band such as Orsya used, or a lower, in a level to which I had not delved before.

Light . . . it was much lighter . . . day coming? No—

from those star-beacons to my left the light streamed in visible shafts of pearl glow. There was an expectancy about them, a waiting.

"Who—are—you?" This time I plunged, down the scale of mind bands, taking a chance that what I sought lay below and not above.

And I caught, held, though not long enough for a complete thought to pass between us. What burst at me in return was excitement, shock, and fear.

Fear I wanted least of all, for fear may drive the one afraid to violent action.

"Who are you?" Once more I hit that low level. But this time with no reaction; I touched no mind. It was as if that other, still afraid, had closed a door firmly against me.

The candles which had sprung from the stars continued to grow stronger. They were not akin to the weird gray lights which we had seen shine for evil, for they did not chill me. While sun did not shine, it was now coolly pale as if in the light of a cloudy day.

Up the path came a figure: Small, yes, and hunched. But I did not feel about it as I had about those scuttling things of the dark, the Thas. This came very slowly, pausing now and then to eye me apprehensively. Fear—

When it came to stand between two of the nearer star candles I could see it better. It was as gray as the moss of the trees, and its long hair could hardly be told from that growth. When it put up gnarled hands to part and brush aside that hair in order to view me the better, I saw a small wrinkled face with a flattened nose and large eyes fringed in lashes which grew bushy and thick. Once more it made that sweeping motion to send cascades of hair back over its shoulders and I saw it was female. The large breasts and protruding stomach were only part covered by a kind of net woven of moss. In that were caught some of the fragrant flowers in what seemed to me a pitiful attempt at adornment.

Then memory awoke in me and I remembered more childhood tales. This was a Mosswife, who, according to legend, crept despairingly about the haunts of man, trying ever to win some attention from the other race. A Mosswife, reported the stories of old, yearned to have her children nursed and fostered by human-kind. And if one would strike such a bargain, the Mosswife thereafter served him richly, giving secrets of hidden treasure and the like.

Legend reported them good, a shy people, meaning no ill, distressed when their uncouth appearance frightened or disgusted those they wanted to befriend or favor. How true was legend? It seemed I was to test that now.

The Mosswife advanced another hesitant step or two. She gave the appearance of age, but if that were so I could not tell. The memories I had of the tales always described them so. Also—that no Moss man had ever been sighted.

She stood and stared. I tried again to use mind touch, with no result. If it were she whom I had contacted earlier, she held her barrier against me now. But there flowed from her a kind of good will, a timid good will, as if she meant me no harm, but feared that I did not feel the same toward her.

I gave up trying to reach her by mind touch. Instead I spoke aloud, and into the tones of my voice I never tried harder to put that which would lead her to believe that I meant her no harm, that on the contrary I now looked to her for aid. Elsewhere in Escore we had discovered that the language of this land, though using different pronunciations and some archaic turns of speech, was still that of the Old Race, and we could be understood.

"Friend—" I schooled my voice to softness. "I am friend—friend to the Moss Folk."

She searched me with her eyes, holding mine in a steady gaze.

How did the old saying go: "Whole friend, half-friend, unfriend."

Though I did not repeat that aloud, I was willing to accept from her name of half-friend—if she did not think me unfriend.

I saw her puckered lips work as if she chewed upon the word before she spoke it aloud in turn.

"Friend—" Her voice was a whisper, not much louder than the wind whisper through the moss curtains.

Her stare still held me. Then, as a door opening, thought flowed into my mind.

"Who are you who follow a trail through the moss-land?"

"I am Kemoc Tregarth from overmountain." But the designation which might mean something to others of Escore, meant nothing to her. "From the Valley of Green Silences," I added, and this did carry weight.

She mouthed a word again, and this time a flood of reassurance warmed me. For the word she said, though it was distorted by the sibilance of her whisper, was the badge of rightness in what might be a land of nameless evil—the ancient word of power:

"Euthayan."

I answered it quickly, by lip, not mind, so that she could be sure that I was one who could say such and not be blasted in the saying.

Her hands moved from the hold they had kept upon the mantle of her moss hair. They waved gently, as the breeze stirred banners on the trees. Following the bidding of those gestures, the moss strands binding me to the tree stirred, fell apart, loosing me, until I sat in a nest of fibers.

"Come!"

She beckoned and I got to my feet. Then she drew back a step as if the fact I towered over her was daunting. But, drawing her hair about her as one might draw a cloak, she turned and went down that path of the star candles.

Shouldering my pack, I followed. The candles continued to light our way, though outside the borders of their dim light the night pressed in and I thought we must still be a ways from dawn. Now those woods lamps were farther and farther apart, and paler. I hastened so as not to lose my guide. For all her stumpy frame and withered looking legs, she threaded this way very swiftly.

Heavier and heavier hung the moss curtains. Sometimes they appeared almost solid between the trees, too thick to be stirred by any wind. I realized these took the form of walls, that I might be passing among dwellings. My guide put out her hands and parted the substance of one such wall, again beckoned me to pass her in that entrance.

I came into a space under a very large tree. Its scaled bole was the center support of the house. The moss curtains formed the walls, and a moss carpet grew underfoot. There were stars of light set flat against the tree trunk, wreathed around it from the ground up to the branching of the first limbs. The light they gave was near to that of a fire.

On the moss sat my—hostesses? judges? captors? I knew not what they were, save they were Mosswives, so resembling she who had brought me that I could believe them all of one sisterhood. She who was closest to the star studded tree gestured for me to sit. I put aside my pack and dropped, cross-legged.

Again there was a period of silent appraisal, just as there had been with my guide. Then she, whom I guessed was chief of that company, named first herself and then the others, in the formal manner followed by those country dwellers living far from the main life of Estcarp.

"Fuusu, Foruw, Frono, Fyngri, Fubbi—" Fubbi being she who had led me here.

"Kemoc Tregarth," I answered, as was proper. Then I added, which was of the custom of Estcarp, but not might be so here:

"No threat from me to the House of Fuusu and her sister, clan, or rooftree, harvest, flocks—"

If they did not understand my good-wish, they did the will behind it. For Fuusu made another sign, and Foruw, who sat upon her right, produced a cup of wood and poured into it a darkish liquid from a stone bottle. She touched her lips briefly to one side of the cup and then held it out.

Though I remembered Dahaun's injunction against drinking or eating in the wilds, I dared not refuse a sip from the guesting cup. I swallowed it a little fearfully. The stuff was sour and a little bitter. I was glad that I need not drink more of it. But I formally tipped the cup right and left, dribbled a few drops over its brim to the moss carpet, wishing thus luck on both house and land.

I put the cup down between us and waited politely for Fuusu to continue. I did not have to wait long.

"Where go you through the moss land, Kemoc Tregarth." She stumbled a little over my name. "And why?"

"I seek one who has been taken from me, and the trail leads hither."

"There have been those who came and went."

"Went where?" I could not restrain my eagerness.

The Mosswife shook her head slowly. "Into hidden ways; they have set a blind spell on their going. None may follow."

Blind spell? I did not know what she meant. But perhaps she could tell me more. . . .

"There was a maiden with them?" I asked.

Fuusu nodded to Fubbi. "Let her answer; she saw their passing."

"There was a maiden, and others. A Great Dark One—"

A Great Dark One; the words repeated in my mind. Had I guessed wrong? Not Dinzil, but one of the enemy . . . ?

"She was of the light, but she rode among dark ones. Hurry, hurry, hurry, they went. Then they took a hidden way and the blind spell was cast," Fubbi said.

"Can you show me this way?" I broke in with scant courtesy. Danger from Dinzil was one thing, but if Kaththea had been taken by one of the enemy . . . ? Time— time was also now an enemy.

"I can show, but you will not be able to take that way."

I did not believe her. Perhaps I was over confident because I had already won so far with success. Her talk of a blind spell meant little.

"Show him," Fuusu ordered. "He will not believe until he sees."

I remembered to pay the proper farewells to Fuusu and her court, but once outside her tree house I was impatient to be gone. There was no longer a candle-lighted way, but Fubbi put out her hand to clasp mine. Against my flesh hers felt dry and hard, as might a harsh strand of moss, but her fingers gripped mine tightly and drew me on.

Without that guiding I could not have made my way through the moss grown forest. At last it thinned somewhat and there was dawn light about us. It began to rain, the drops soaking into the moss tangles. I saw in patches of earth and torn moss the markings of Renthan hooves and knew I was again on the trail.

As the trees dwindled to bushes and the light grew stronger I saw a tall cliff of very dark rock. It veined with a wide banding of red and was unlike any rock I had seen elsewhere. The trail led directly to it—into it. Yet there was no doorway there, not the faintest sign of any archway. Nothing save the trail led into the stone, over which my questing fingers slid in vain.

I could not believe it. Yet the stone would not yield to my pushing and the prints, now crumbling in the rain's beat, led to that spot.

Fubbi had drawn her hair about her cloakwise, and the moisture dripped from it, so she was protected from the downpour. She watched me and I thought there was a spark of amusement within her eyes.

"They went through," I said aloud; perhaps I wanted her to deny it. Instead she repeated my words with assured finality. "They went through."

"To where?"

"Who knows? A spell to blind, to bind. Ask of Loskeetha and mayhap she will show you her futures."

"Loskeetha? Who is Loskeetha?"

Fubbi pivoted, one of her thin arms protruded from her cloak of hair to point yet farther east. "Loskeetha of the Garden of Stones, the Reader of Sands. If she will read, then mayhap you shall know."

Having given me so faint a clue, she drew all of herself back into the mass of hair, and padded away at a brisk trot, into the brush—to be at one with that before I could halt her.

VIII

The rain was fast washing away the tracks of those who had ridden into the wall. I hunched my shoulders under its drive and looked back at the moss forest. But all within me rebelled against retreat. To the east then. Where was this Loskeetha and her Garden of Rocks? Legend did not identify her for me.

I took the edge of the black and red wall for my guide and tramped on, already well wet by the rain. If any road led this way it was not discernible to my eyes. What grew here were no longer trees, or even grass and brush, such as I had seen elsewhere: but, instead, low plants with thick, fleshy cushions of leaves and stems in one. These were sharply thorned, as I found to my discomfort, when I skidded on some rain-slicked mud and stumbled against one. They were yellow in color and a few had centermost stalks upstanding, on which clustered small flowers, now tight closed. Pallid insects sheltered under those leaves and I disliked what I saw of them.

To avoid contact with this foliage, I wove an in and out track, for they grew thicker and thicker—taller, too—until those center flower stalks overtopped my head. A winged thing with a serpentine neck and reptilian appearance, though it was clothed in drab brown feathers, dropped from the sky and hung upside down on one of those stalks, feasting on the insects it plucked with tapping darts of its narrow head. It paused for only an instant as I passed, showing no fear of me, but staring with small, black beads of eyes in curiosity.

I liked its looks no better than I did of the territory in which it hunted. There was something alien here—another warn-off territory such as the stone forest had been. Yet I did not sense that this was an ensorceled place, rather one unkindly to my species.

The rain dripped and ran, puddling about some of the fleshy plants. I saw tendrils like blades of grass reach out to lie in those puddles, swell, carrying back a burden of water they sucked up. It seemed to me the thick leaves swelled in turn, storing up that moisture.

I was hungry, but I was in no mind to stop and eat in that place. So I quickened pace, hoping to get beyond the growths. Then I came to an abrupt end of planting. It was as if I faced an invisible wall: here, were the plants; beyond, smooth sand. So vivid was that impression that I put out my hand to feel before me. But it met only empty air. The rain about me cut small rivulets in the ground. But—over that sand no rain fell; the sand was unmarked.

I turned my head from left to right. On one side was the cliff wall of black and red. South lay a stretch of the cushion plants. Ahead, to my right, was a line of rocks fitted together into a wall, and between that and the cliff was the smooth sand and no rain.

I hesitated about venturing out on that unmarked surface. There are treacherous stretches about the Fens of Tor which look to the eye as firm as any sea strand. But let a body rest upon them and it is swallowed.

Looking about me, I found a stone as large as my

hand. That, I tossed out, to lie upon the sand some lengths ahead. The stone did not sink. But—more weight? My sword, together with its scabbard, was heavier. I hurled it ahead.

The sword lay where it had fallen. Then I noted the other peculiarity of this ground. Ordinary sand would have been soft enough to let that weight of leather and metal sink in a little. But not this. It was as if the surface, which looked to be fine sand, was indeed a hard one. I knelt and put a fingertip cautiously upon it. It felt as soft as it looked, close to powdery, in fact. But, for all the pressure I could put into that fingertip, I could not push it below the surface.

So, at least it could be walked upon. Yet the wall which guarded it to the south had been set there with purpose. Whether this was the domain of Loskeetha, I did not know. But it looked promising.

I had ventured onto the sand, and stepped out of the storm into an unnatural complete dryness, with but a single stride.

I belted on my sword. There was a sharp turn to the north just ahead; both the cliff and the wall which paralleled it angled so I could not see what lay beyond. The wall was rough rocks. They varied in size from large boulders at the base, to quite small stones atop. They had been fitted together cunningly and with such care that I do not believe I could have put the point of my knife into any of the cracks.

At that angle I turned, to find myself looking down into a basin. The wall did not descend, but ran on to enclose three sides of that hollow, while the cliff formed the fourth. Not too far ahead was a sharp drop from the level on which I stood to the bottom. What lay therein drew my eyes. It was floored with sand: this was of a blue shade. Out of it arose rocks, solitary and rough shaped. They were set in no pattern I could follow, but the sand about them had been marked with long curving lines in and around the rocks.

As I continued to look at it, I had an odd sensation. I no longer surveyed rocks set in sand. No, I hung high above an ocean which assaulted islands, and yet never conquered those outposts of land. Or—yes, now I looked down, as might a spirit in the clouds, upon mountains which towered high above a plain; but the plain which supported their roots was a misty nothing. . . .

This was a world, but I was mightier than it. I could stride from island to island, giant tall and strong, to cross a sea in steps. I was one who would use a mountain for a stepping stone . . . I was greater—taller, stronger—than a whole world. . . .

"Are you, man? Look and tell me—are you?"

Did it ring in my ears or my head, that question?

I looked upon the islands in the sea, the mountains on the plain. Yes, I was! I was! I could set my boots there and there. I could stoop and pluck land from out of the sea and hurl it elsewhere. I could crumble a mountain with my heel.

"You could destroy then, man. But tell me; could you build again?"

My hands moved and I looked from the mountains and the islands to them. My left one moved easily, fingers curling and uncurling. But the right with its scar ridge, its stiffened bones . . .

I was no godling to remake a world at my fancy. I was a man, one Kemoc Tregarth. And the madness passed from me. Then I looked at the rocks and the sand and this time I held to sanity and forced upon my mind the knowledge of what they were and what I was.

"You are no giant, no godling then?" The voice out of nowhere was amused.

"I am not!" That amusement stung.

"Remember that, man. Now, why come you to disturb my days?"

I searched that valley of rocks and sand, to see no one. Yet I knew I was not alone.

"You—you are Loskeetha?" I asked of the emptiness.

"That is one of my names. Through the years one picks up many names from friends and unfriends. Since you call me that, the Mosswives must have said it to you. But I repeat; man, why come you here?

"The Mosswife Fubbi—she said you might aid me."

"Aid you? Why, man? What tie have you with me—kinship? Well, and who were your father and mother?"

I found myself answering the invisible one literally. "My father is Simon Tregarth, Warden of the Marches of Estcarp, my mother the Lady Jaelithe, once of the Wise Ones."

"Warrior-witch, then. But neither kin to me! So you cannot claim favor because of kinship. Now, do you claim it by treaty? What treaty have you made with me, man out of Estcarp?"

"None." Still I searched for the speaker and irritation grew in me that I must stand here being questioned by a voice.

"No kin, no treaty. What then, man? Are you a trader, perhaps? What treasure have you brought me that I may give you something in return?"

Only stubbornness kept me there as a voice hammered each point sharply home.

"I am no trader," I answered.

"No, just one who sees himself as a giant fit to rule worlds," came back in scornful amusement. "Welladay, since it had been long since any have sought me for advice, that is what you really want; is it not, man? Then perhaps I should give it free of any ties, to one who is not kin, nor ally, nor is ready to pay for it. Come down, man. But do not venture out on that sea, lest you find it more than it seems, and you, less than you imagine yourself to be."

I advanced along the edge of the drop and now saw that there were holds for hands and feet which would take me to the floor of the basin. In addition, below was a path of lighter-hued sand, hugging the wall, which could be followed without stepping onto the blue.

So I descended and went along that path. Its end was a cave which might have been a freak of nature, but she who had her being there had made use of it for her own purposes. Its entrance was a crack in the cliff wall.

I called it cave, though it was not truly that, for it was open far above to a sliver of sky. Then I faced the source of the voice.

Perhaps Loskeetha and the Mosswives had shared a common ancestor long ago. She was as small and with-ered looking as they, but she did not go cloaked in a growth of hair. Instead what scanty locks she had, and they were indeed thin and few, were pulled into a stand-ing knot on top of her head. Held by a ring of smoothly polished green stone. Bracelets of the same were about her bony wrists and ankles. For her clothing she had a sleeveless robe of some stuff which resembled the blue sand, as if the sand indeed had been plastered on a pli-able surface and belted about her.

Very old and very frail she looked, until you met her eyes. Those showed neither age nor weakness, but were alive with that fierce gleam one sees in the eyes of a hill hawk. They were as green as her stone ornaments and, I will always believe, saw farther and deeper than any human eyes.

"Greeting, man." She was seated on a rock and before her was a depression in the sand, as if it cupped a pool of water, that held blue sand like unto that about the rocks in the outer basin.

"I am Kemoc Tregarth," I said, for her calling me "man" seemed to make me, even in my own eyes, less than I was.

She laughed then, silently, her whole small, wizened body quivering with amusement.

"Kemoc Tregarth," she repeated, and to my surprise her hand rose to her head in a gesture copying a scout's salute. "Kemoc Tregarth who rides—or now walks—into danger as a proper hero should. Yet I fear, Kemoc Tregarth, that you shall now find you have gone well along a path which will prove to be your undoing."

"Why?" I demanded of her bluntly.

"Why? Well, because you must decide this and that. And if you make the wrong decision, then all you wish, all you have been, all you might have been, will come to naught."

"You prophesy darkly, lady—" I had begun when she drew herself more erect, and sent one of those disconcertingly piercing glances flashing out at me.

"Lady," she mimicked. "I am Loskeetha, since that is the name you have hailed me by. I need no titles of courtesy or honor. Mind your tongue, Kemoc Tregarth; you speak to such as you have not fronted before, witch-warrior son that you be."

"I meant no disrespect."

"One can excuse ignorance," she returned with an arrogance to match the arrogance of the Wise Ones when dealing with males. "Yes, I can prophesy, after a fashion.

What would you of me, a telling of your future? That is a small thing for which to come such a wild way, for there is but one end for any man—"

"I want to find my sister." I cut through her word play. "I traced her to a rock wall and Fubbi said she passed within, or through that, and a blind spell was laid there."

Loskeetha blinked and put her hands together, the fingers of each reaching to touch the bracelet about the opposite wrist, turning those stone rings around and around.

"A blind spell? Now which of the Great Ones, or would be Great Ones has been meddling on the boundaries of Loskeetha's land? Well, that much will be easy to discover."

Loosing her clasp on her bracelets, she spread her hands out over the hollow filled with blue sand. She moved them quickly, once up and then down, as if to fan the grains below. They puffed up in a fountain, cascading back into the cup. No longer did it lie smooth. There were raised ridges on the surface and they made a picture—that of a tower. It was not unlike those we built for watchpoints along the Estcarpian border, save it had no windows.

"So—" Loskeetha considered the picture. "The Dark Tower it is. Well, time moves when a small man tries to walk in boots too large for him." She leaned forward again as if some thought had suddenly struck her and in that thought there was some faint alarm.

Once more she spread her hands wide and the fountain of sand rose and fell. This time the grains did not form a tower, but rather a complicated symbol, like unto one of the coats of arms those of the Old Race used. But that it was no heraldic device I was also sure, for it carried a hint of the Mysteries.

Loskeetha stared at it, one of her fingers raised a little as if with its tip she traced the intricate weaving of line upon line.

She did not look at me, and she spoke sharply with none of the embroidery of speech she had used before: "This sister of yours, is she a Witch?"

"She was Witch-trained in Estcarp, but she did not take the final vow nor put on the Jewel. She has some powers—"

"Perhaps more than she has shown. Listen well, Kemoc Tregarth. There have long been those in this land who have tried for power and pulled to them rulership over forces which do not answer lightly. This desire is born into some men and eats upon them as a fever, so that they will throw to it, as one throws wood upon a fire, everything they deem will bring them what they wish. Some rose high in their knowledge in the old days; they rent this land, even carrying their struggles into places you cannot dream of, for the Great Ones have gone, still the wish to be as them comes to men—men who know a little, scraps of old learning, a fragment here and there. They strive to patch these together, to make a whole to center about them.

"There is a man in these hills who has gone far along such a seeking road—"

"Dinzil!" I interrupted her.

"If you know, why, then, do you ask?"

"Because I did not know. I only felt that he was—"

"Removed from mankind?" she interrupted in turn. "So, you were able to sense what lies in him. But you are no witch, Kemoc Tregarth. Whatever you are, or what you may be in time, you are not your sister. However, Dinzil saw in her a tool to open farther his long sought road. She was trained but not sworn, thus she was vulnerable to what influence he could lay about her. Through her he will seek—"

"But she would not willingly—" I protested, refusing to accept an alliance between Kaththea and one who played with unleashed power.

"Will can be swallowed up. If he cannot enlist her willingly, still he believes he can use her for his key. And she is in the Dark Tower, which is the heart of his secret world."

"Where I shall follow . . ."

"You have seen the working of one blind spell. How think you to follow?" she asked.

"Fubbi said—"

"Fubbi!" She threw up her hands. "I am Loskeetha and my magic is of only one kind. I can read the future—or futures."

"The futures . . . ?"

"Yes. There are many 'ifs' in any life. Walk this road and meet a beggar, throw him a coin, and he will steal behind you and use a knife between your ribs for what else you carry. But go another road and your life will run for some years more. Yes, we have a choice of futures, but we make such choices blindly—and know not sometimes the reason for or the worth of the choice we have made."

"So you can see the future. In that seeing could you also show me the Dark Tower and the way thereto?" I only half believed her then, though I was sure she entirely believed herself.

"You wish to see your futures? How may I say without looking whether the Dark Tower lies within them? But this warning I will give you, though it is not laid upon me to do so. To read the futures may weaken your resolve."

Now that I did *not* believe. I shook my head. "I go

106

after Kaththea, to that end I do not weaken."

"Be it on your own head, then, warrior who is no witch."

She reached out swiftly and caught both my hands, pulling them toward her with a sharp jerk which also brought me to my knees across the basin of blue sand. Then, keeping a tight grasp with her fingers about my wrists, she moved those hands in certain gestures and the sand fountained to make a picture. This was not a flat, two-dimensional showing such as had lain there before. Now it was as if I looked down into a living landscape, far below and small, as it had been in the Garden of Stones.

I myself was therein and before me a tall dark tower without windows. As I went toward it the wall reached out and engulfed me, but still I could see what happened. Kaththea was there. I caught her up to take her with me, but as I turned I fronted—not Dinzil—but a menacing shadow. Kaththea twisted and broke my hold and I saw a stricken look upon my face. Then—then I saw myself cut down Kaththea before she could join with that shadow!

My sharp cry of horror and denial still rang in my ears when the sand fountained again. This time I was in the Valley, riding with men I knew, to my right was Kyllan. We faced not the strange rabble we had beaten back from the walls but a shadow host. In the midst of them rode Kaththea, her eyes a-glitter, her hands upheld. From those burst sullen flashes of red which brought death to members of our company.

Then I saw myself ride forward and swing my sword, to throw it as a lance. It spun through the air and its heavy hilt struck my sister's skull. She fell, to be trampled by those she rode among.

Once more the sand fountained and cleared. I stood before the Dark Tower and from it ran Kaththea and this time I knew that she was not one of the enemy, but fleeing from them. But I saw the darkness wreathe about me. Blinded, I thrust out as if I fought with what I could not see. Kaththea, running to me for protection, was again cut down. Then the mist went and I was left alone to face my deed.

Loskeetha released my hands. "Three futures—yet the same ending. You see that, but—listen well to this—not the decisions upon which it is based. For each of those comes from other happenings."

I awoke from my daze. "You mean it is not the last act, not my strokes, that really kill Kaththea, but other things done or undone, which lead to that point? If those are not done, or undone, then Kaththea will not—will not—"

"Die at your hands? Yes."

It was my turn to catch at her wrists. But under my fingers those smooth stone bracelets turned seemingly of their own accord to break my grip.

"Tell me! Tell me what to do?"

"That is not my magic. What I can see, that I have shown you."

"Three futures, and they all end so. Can there be a fourth—one in which all goes well?"

"You have choices; make the right ones. If fortune favors you—who knows? I have read sands for men in the past and one or two—but only one or two—defeated the fates shown them."

"And . . . suppose I do nothing at all?" I asked slowly.

"You can slay yourself with that blade you seem so ready to use upon your sister. But I do not think you have so reached the end to all hope as to do that, not yet.

108

But, save for that, you will still have choices to make in each moment's breath, and you cannot help the making of them. Now will you know which are wrong and which are right."

"I can do this much. I can stay away from the Valley and the Dark Tower. I can find a place in this wilderness and stay—"

"Decision—there is a decision," Loskeetha said promptly. "Every decision has a future. Who can guess how it will be twisted to lead you to the end you fear. But, I am wearied, Kemoc Tregarth. No more can I show you, so . . ."

She clapped her hands together and that sharp sound echoed and reechoed in my ears. I blinked and shivered in a sudden blast of cold. I was on a mountainside. Below me was the cliff of red and black. It was raining and the wind was rising, and it was close to night. Shaken, hungry, cold and wet, I wavered along. Then there was a dark pit to my right and I half stumbled, half fell into a shadow cave. I crouched there, dazed.

Had there been a Loskeetha at all? And what of the three futures she had shown me? Decisions, each putting thread into a pattern. If she had really shown me the truth, how could I defeat fortune to build a fourth future?

I fumbled in my supply bag and brought forth some crumbling journey cake, ate it bit by bit to fill the aching void in my middle. I had chosen to eat. I had chosen to take refuge in this cave; had either choice led me a single step closer to one of the three futures?

Two had come at the Dark Tower, one in the Valley. Could I believe that if I stayed away from both those sites I could stave off or change the future? But, I did not even know where lay the Dark Tower. Suppose I blun-

dered along among these hills and came across it unawares? The one decision I thought I could be sure of
was not to return to the Valley.

Yet Loskeetha said small things could alter all.

I folded my arms across my knees and buried my face
upon them. Was Loskeetha right? Could Kaththea's only
safety lie in my turning my sword against myself?

In two of those futures Kaththea had been one of the
forces of evil. In the Valley she killed her friends. In the
Dark Tower it was my life she threatened. In the third,
she fled, while I was the one bewitched. In two out of
three Kaththea was no longer my sister, but a dark one.
Was I betraying all I loved best in Kaththea by trying to
save her body?

Decisions! Loskeetha had said one man, two, had defeated the possible futures. But if one did not know
which decision—

I rolled my head back and forth across my arms. My
thoughts beat in my brain. What if Loskeetha was not
what she seemed, but another of the defenses Dinzil set
up to protect his back trail? I had seen hallucinations
wrought by the Witches of Estcarp; I had been duped by
them. Loskeetha could be such an illusion, or the scenes
she showed me illusion. How could I be sure?

My head ached as I leaned back against the wall of the
cave. Night and rain made a dismal curtain. Sleep . . . if I
could sleep. Another decision—leading where? But sleep
I must.

IX

It was an ill sleep, haunted by fell dreams, so that I
roused sweating. Yet, in spite of my efforts, I would sleep

again, only to face more monstrous terrors. Whether those were born of my own imagination or the pall which lay over the cave land, I did not know. But when I awoke with an aching head, which spun when I moved, in the gray morn, I still had not made my big decision. Stay here, imprisoned by my own will, until life left me. Dare to go ahead, with belief in the rightness of my cause to arm me with courage against the futures Loskeetha had shown me. Which?

If there was evil abroad in Escore, then there was also good. I thought on that dully. But to what force could I appeal now to my arming?

There were Names from petitions made in Estcarp. But such appeals were very old and had lost their meaning for most men. We had come to look to our own strength and the backing of the Wise Women for our salvation.

I still wore a sword; I had skill in its use. I had my Borderer's knowledge of war. But to me at that moment these seemed as nothing at all. For what I would go up against now was not to be vanquished by steel. So, what had I left? Scraps of ancient wisdom culled at Lormt, but so tattered by the passing of ages as to be no shield.

And always in my mind were the three pictures Loskeetha had shown me.

There was no rain now. Neither were there any sun banners painting the highlands of the east, rather a sullen lowering of clouds. Under that gloom the stretch of land I could see from the cave was stark and lifeless. What vegetation grew there was twisted, misshapen, faded of color. There were many outcroppings of rock. These, if one looked at them carefully, had an unpleasant aspect. It was easy to picture here a leering face, there a menacing taloned paw, a mouth with gaping, fanged jaws.

These appeared to slide about just under the surface of the stone. One moment they were there, the next they were gone again—to reappear a short distance away. I wrenched my eyes from that, closed them to the gray day and tried to think. The thoughts which raced through my mind were not clear. It was as if I were in a cage and darted here and there, only to always face restraining bars.

I heard a thin wailing, such as I had heard in the stone forest where I had found Kaththea's scarf. Kaththea's scarf—my hand went to the front of my jerkin; its silken softness was between my fingers.

Kaththea—Kaththea thrice dead, and always by my hand. Was Loskeetha's magic the true sight? Or, as a small, nibbling suspicion told me, was she one of the safeguards used to befog the enemy trail?

I ate more of my rations, sipped from my flask. There was very little water left in it now. A man may endure hunger longer than he can thirst. I did not know if I would have the fortitude to stay here until death sought me out.

Nor would my nature allow me to take that do-nothing path, though it might be the highest wisdom. There was in me too much of my father, and perhaps my mother, both of whom marched to meet danger, not await its coming.

At last I crawled stiffly from that hole and looked about. I remembered, or thought I did, the look of the land about the Dark Tower in those two scenes Loskeetha's sand had painted for me. Around me now I saw no resemblance to that land. Not too far away, I could hear running water.

Danger in food, in drink, that was Dahaun's warning. But perhaps if I were to mix this water with that still remaining in my flask the danger would be lessened. Decision. . . .

I kept my head turned from the walls; the menaces which grew and dissolved there were sharper. Being sure they were illusion, I wanted none of them, lest rational thinking be disrupted.

The wailing wind in the heights tormented my ears with a keening which I would take sword-oath on were the cries of those pushed to some great extremity of terror, calling upon me for aid. Some of them seemed to be voices I knew. But, I told myself, wind around rocks can produce strange sounds.

I drew to mind odd bits of old lore. Some were of the Sulcar. It was their belief that a man would not fall in any fight unless he heard his name called aloud while the battle clamor still rang. So I found myself listening for the wind to sound some long wailing "Keeemooc."

There had been those, such as Aidan from the outback of Estcarp (where men followed the old ways more closely), who carried talismen. He had once shown me a stone with a perfect round hole in it, saying such given to one, by a woman who cared deeply, was great protection against an ill. Aidan—I had not thought of him for years. Where was Aidan now? Had he survived the border raiding, returned to the maid who had put that stone in his hand that it would keep him safe for her?

The cut I followed turned downward, leading into a wider valley. Here was more vegetation, and the shallow waters of a river I had heard before the wind raised such a doleful lament. I looked at the water. Then, with the reflexes taught me by the border years, I dropped instantly into cover among the boulders.

Not even the wind could drown out the new cries, nor the clash of metal. There was a fierce battle going on near the water's edge, even into the stream itself where the water was splashed high by the fighters. The Krogan had been trapped in a stream too shallow for them to swim. There were three of them, two men and a woman. Around and about them, apparently fighting on their side, were several furred creatures. Their opponents were a mixed force. I saw men, mailed and dark cloaked, striking out with steel, at the cornered Krogan. Farther upstream a squad of Thas rolled stones, and hurled earth into the water, trying to cut off more of the flow which might aid the aquatic race.

I saw one of the Krogan, his spear sheared off, collapse under a flashing blade. Then they had no hope at all, for, from the brush on the other bank, a second contingent of the enemy came. They held not swords but wands or staves, from which came flashes, not unlike the energy whips of the Green People. Animal and Krogan alike, they went down before those.

One of the swordsmen waded out into the water, kicked here and there at the bodies which were awash. Then he caught the floating hair of the woman, jerked up her head so that her face was fully exposed.

Orsya!

Still keeping that painful hold upon her hair, the man pulled her limp body ashore, dragged her out upon the sand and gravel. Those who held the wands made no move to join their allies. I saw a gesture or two pass between the parties and the wand people melted back into the brush.

The Thas came stumping down stream, uttering gutteral cries, to fall upon the bodies still in the water. I have seen much brutality in war. But this was of no human knowing, yet I dared not look aside for Orsya still lay there and . . .

I do not know if the Krogan were dead when they fell. But the Thas made sure that they and their furred companions would not rise again. Having fed their fury, and yet remaining unappeased, they came to where Orsya lay, the swordsmen standing about her. He who must be the Thas leader stretched out filthy claws to hook in her garment to draw her out to be ravaged by his pack.

But one of the swordsmen swung a blade warningly and those paws were jerked back, though the Thas chief set up a yammering which out-noised the wind, his ire plain to read.

Again that blade swung, in a wider circle, and the Thas retreated. He mouthed louder cries, spit and gnashed his teeth, spittle flying from his wide mouth to fleck the hair on his flailing arms, his protruding barrel of chest and paunch.

At some order from the leader of the swordsmen, two of his fellows advanced on the Thas. They were confident, arrogant, contemptuous, and the earth burrowers stood their ground only for a moment or two. Then, scurrying, they snatched at what lay staining the stream red, and, carrying burdens no one would wish to look upon, they retreated upstream. Still their leader walked backward, thumping his chest to add a hollow roll to his chittering cries.

I found my hand on sword hilt as I watched one of the swordsmen pick up the light body of the Krogan girl and drape her over his shoulder. Surely she was not dead.

My other hand was on the boulder, drawing me up. There were five of them. Let the Thas get well away . . . then follow downstream . . . watch for my chance and . . .

I could not move!

Oh, I could stand upon my feet, finger my sword hilt, turn my head to stare after those who had taken Orsya with them. Watch them go openly and without any searching of the ground around them, as men who walk their own safe territory. That I could do. But follow—no!

It was the curse Loskeetha had laid upon me, or the curse I had laid upon myself which held me there. For this was a major decision, not such a one as seeking water to drink, walking among haunted rocks, venturing forth from the cave slit. This meant throwing luck stones against fate. If I did take that trail, skulk along behind the swordsmen, try to free Orsya, then I could well be setting my feet on a road which would lead inevitably to Kaththea's blood on my sword.

I owed my life to Orsya. What I owed to Kaththea I cannot find words to say. I was torn; ah, what a tearing that was. But it kept me from following the party which had the Krogan girl. I leaned, weak as one who had taken a death blow, against the rock behind which I had taken shelter, and watched them go. I continued to stare thereafter at the empty river valley when they had passed from sight.

Then something of those bonds broke and I came down to the place of slaying. One of the animals still lay, torn and frightfully mangled, in the wash at the stream's edge, and there were other gruesome reminders of what had been done there. Without knowing why I stooped and picked up one of the broken Krogan spears. Water ran down its shaft and over my scarred hand and stiffened fingers. I watched it drip so, dully.

Loskeetha had said, no man knew what small decision would lead to a greater and more fatal one. How very right! I had made the decision to come forth from the cave, another to seek water, now I faced a third and larger. The one I had tried to avoid was one I would have named days earlier must be taken or remain a foresworn coward. A curse laid upon me—and a cursed man moved under a shadow.

The Krogan spear slipped through fingers which could not grip its smooth shaft tightly enough, and clattered on the stones.

They had taken Orsya with them and she was not dead, of that I was sure. They had not left her to the Thas, yet they meant her no mercy, I was also sure. I walked here, breathed, could touch that broken weapon, feel—because Orsya had willed to make a decision. It must not have been an easy one, for she had gone against the will of her people.

"But, Kaththea;" I said aloud. I think I meant it as an appeal, though to whom, I did not know.

Somewhere before me lay the Dark Tower; I must accept that. I had a part to be played there.

One man—two—had broken the alternate futures.

I watched the water glide by, muddied from the half dam the Thas had thrown up, stained still from what it washed here from sand and stone. Then, as one might break through a wall and see freedom, even with danger to come, I broke the spell—if spell it had been which had fallen on me in Loskeetha's Garden. To breathe, walk, live, were decisions of sorts. I could never escape them. But I could make the ones my heart, mind and training demanded of me. Those I must do with the wisdom granted me. Therefore, I must set aside this fear and do as I would have done before Loskeetha set her sand to making pictures.

I owed a deep debt to Orsya and what I would repay. If the Dark Tower lay ahead, that I would also face when the time came, with what courage I could summon.

I came away from that river point more nearly a whole

man and not one who looked ever over his shoulder for the hunter sniffing at his tracks.

Putting my scout craft to work I went again to the ridge on this side of the valley. It was very rough ground, and could not have been better designed for my purposes. I was surefooted enough to make speed from one place of concealment to another, hurrying to catch up with the party who had Orsya. My growing fear now was that they might have had mounts and those I could not overtake.

So spurred, I might have taken reckless chances, but one warning kept tugging at my thoughts. Though the Thas had seemed to withdraw, they had done so in anger. It might be that they, too, would dog the victors in that clash of wills and so be going in my direction. Thus, I not only watched downslope and ahead for those I tracked, but paused now and again, chaffing at the need, to scout behind. If the Thas did skulk there I did not sight them.

Eventually I did find those I followed. There were now four of them and in the van walked the one who carried Orsya. She was still a limp and apparently lifeless burden. Only the fact that they did see fit to take her, was an indication that she was alive.

The party which had used the flashing wands made me wary. Against such weapons my sword was no defense. I longed for one of the dart guns. Might as well long for a squad so armed, as well!

At least there were no signs of any mounts awaiting the party. Perhaps the fifth man had gone ahead to get them.

I used a convenient ridge and ran at the best speed I could dare to use over rough ground. That burst, when I peered down again, had brought me almost level with the party and their prisoner. They had come to a halt. The leader allowed Orsya to fall to the ground with callous disregard. She sprawled on a patch of grass just as she landed. But the men went a step or two beyond and dropped down, to sit at their ease, apparently to wait.

It was still a dark and cloudy day. The brush and trees along the river could afford a number of lurking places. But to reach those I would have to retreat and cross higher up. I hesitated, fearing to lose sight of the quarry lest mounts would be brought and they would go.

Four men . . . But with only a sword and the resulting need for hand to hand combat, I could not hope to win against such odds. Small use would I be then to either Orsya or Kaththea.

Yet the river drew me. Looking at the currents I thought that it ran deeper here. If Orsya could be aroused, escape into it, she might have a chance. For she would have the advantage of being in an element more at home to her than to the enemy.

Sitting here answered no problems. I was driven by the need for action. One of the swordsmen had opened a bag, and passed rations to his comrades.

I slipped off my small shoulder pack. The cloak blanket which made its cover caught my eyes. Against this barren, gray-brown land, the soft green of the Valley's favorite coloring was very noticeable. I shook it free. Then I looked to the rocks above me. Could a man seem to be in two places?

With the cloak rolled again in a wad against my chest, I climbed up between two rocks. The wind . . . in so much was the wind favoring me.

I hacked at shrubs and broke off a mass of thick twigged branches, pushing these into the cloak and fastening it about the bundle as best I could with its throat

119

buckle and the latches from my jerkin. At close sight it could not possibly deceive any one . . . but, perhaps, just at a distance with the further embellishment I could give it. Pushing and pulling I set that unwieldy package up between the rocks. I dared not wedge it too tightly lest it not give way when I wanted. My cord, a length hastily knotted of grass, would it hold at all?

Now I crawled downhill, gentling that grass thread behind me, fearing any moment to have it break apart in my hand. By some smile of fortune it did not. I measured with my eye the space of open between me and my goal. Given a stouter cord, a few other things I did *not* have, my chances would have doubled to perhaps fifty out of a hundred. But I had to be content with far less.

I opened my mouth. It had been years since I had tried this, in the days before I had taken my maiming wound. I had had no chance to practice.

Then I screamed. The sound came not from where I crouched, but from the spot where my stuffed cloak perched. So—I had not lost my skill at voice throwing! Once more I screeched, and the results were even better than I had dared to hope, since some echoing trick multipled and reinforced that cry until it appeared to come from more than one throat. I jerked my grass cord. It broke and the loose end came flying at me.

Only the strength of that jerk had been enough. The blob of green leaned, went toppling, to fall out of sight. I watched those below.

They were on their feet, weapons out, staring. Then the leader and another started for that spot where the cloak bundle had disappeared. The two remaining behind stepped closer together, their attention fixed on the heights, peering at the rocks there.

Now I snaked from one piece of cover to the next,

using every bit of skill I possessed. Once more I measured by eye. If I could continue to escape their notice for only a moment, to catch up Orsya. We would have a chance, thin, but still a chance, to get into the underbrush. This was the moment for my final move—

Once more I readied my lips. No scream this time, rather a sound like some unintelligible command, and it came from uphill beyond the two guards.

I was out and running. On sod my boots made no sound. But they turned and saw me. One shouted; both came on with bared weapons. I whirled my supply bag around my head and let it fly at the one farther away, then parried the leaping attack of the other, expecting at any moment to face two points at once. When the second did not come I concentrated upon the first.

He was good enough as a fighter, and he had the advantage of wearing mail. But he had not been schooled by the equal of Otkell, a Sulcar Marine, to whom there are no equals in tricky swordplay, since they learn to fight on board a heaving deck where skill is in high need.

Thus he took my point between his chin and the rise of his mail coat, for his helm had no evil of linked steel such as we wore in Estcarp. The fact that I fought left-handed had, I think, disconcerted him more than a little.

I looked for his fellow and saw that he lay prone a little farther off, not stirring. That my hastily thrown supply bag had done that, I could hardly believe. But I was in no mind to investigate. I caught up Orsya and crashed back into the bush, heading for the river. Behind me I heard cries; those who had gone upslope must be fast coming down again.

When I reached the bank I saw that my guess about the deeper water here had been right. There were no stones standing half dry in the sun, and the water was murky so I could not see the bottom. I took a deep breath and dived, bearing Orsya with me, hoping her gills would work automatically as we entered.

We were below surface in one great splash and I pulled her along to where a drift log plowed its butt into the bank. Under the bole of that we had a momentary hiding place. My hand was on her breast and I could feel the beating of her heart. I tucked her back with one hand and had to surface again, gasp for air. Then I saw a crevice between two water logged roots.

Moving about, I got into position, that crevice affording me a scrap of breathing room. My arms were locked about Orsya to keep her from drifting away with the pull of the water, the tree protecting us both above.

I could not see the bank, nor if they had tracked us here. For all I knew they might be waiting up there, ready to take us when those shallow gulps of air, all I could get, would not be enough.

Blind in a way, deaf also, I dared then to use the sense which in this land could be an invitation to disaster. I aimed mind touch at the Krogan girl.

"Orsya!"

There was no answer.

I strengthened that cry, though I was well aware that those who hunted us might well have the ability to track us so.

"Orsya!"

A flicker! Such a weak, trembling, flicker. But enough to make me try for the third time.

"Orsya!"

Fear—fear and hate! Blasting out along the touch with which I had reached her. My arm had just time to tighten about her firmly or she would have fought out of my hold.

"Orsya!" Not a summons now but a demand for her recognition.

It came quicker than I dared hope for. Her convulsive struggles stopped.

"What—what—?"

"Be still!" I put into that all the authority I could summon.

"We are hiding in the river. They search for us above."

I felt her thought groping, weakly, slowly, as if whatever had rendered her helpless for capture had slowed and deadened her mental processes.

"You are Kemoc. . . ."

"Yes."

"They trailed me, to take me back." She still thought in that slow, weakened fashion. "They found out—"

"That you freed me? What were they taking you back for—judgment?"

"No, I had already been judged, even though I was not there to answer. I think they meant to give me in place of you."

"Your own people!"

She was communicating more strongly now, with some of her old, firm flow. "Fear is a great governor of minds, Kemoc. I do not know what arguments the enemy may have used. There are very bad things which can be done by them."

"If the Krogan meant to give you up, then why—"

"Why were Orfons and Obbo attacked? I do not know. Mayhap the Sarn Riders are not of the same mind as those with whom Orias treated. This has always been so, Kemoc; such alliances do not hold long among those of the Shadow. An ally one day is a rival the next."

"These Sarn Riders, who are they?"

"A force which holds these hills. It is said they follow

123

one of the Great Ones who has not altogether withdrawn from this world, and that their captains take orders from a strange mouth. Wait...."

Now it was she who ordered, and I who lay silent. I could breathe through my tiny root niche, but I was still blind. I could feel her body against mine and it was rigid with sudden tension.

X

To wait blind the coming of danger is to await the full of a war ax when one stands a captive with bound hands. Orsya's mind touch was shut off. I thought she used that skill elsewhere, questing for danger, but of that I was not sure. It was all I could do to lie there.

Water splashed, washing me dangerously back and forth in my shallow hiding place. I gasped and choked as it filled my nose unexpectedly. This was no normal rippling of the river. How soon would their steel stab to spit us?

Orsya's hands fastened on my forearm. Her nails bit into my flesh. I read it as a warning. But still she did not use mind touch. Minutes drew hour long; those threatening waves subsided.

Tentatively my companion made contact: "They are gone, for now. But they will not give up the search."

"Dare we move?" I did not know how she could be so sure, but that she was, I accepted.

"You cannot take to the river deeps."

"But you can! Go, then. I am a scout and can easily throw off these bush-beaters." I tried to make my answer as certain as hers.

"The deeps lie downriver, they know that, and will be waiting.

"The Thas have left a half-dam above. There are no deeps to hide in there," I counterwarned. "Will you not have a better chance down than up?"

"You forget—my people also hunt me. Safety only lies where they do not go, where I was heading when they caught me."

"Where?"

"The river is shallow for a space, where the Thas and the Sarn forced us to a stand, but higher still it narrows and deepens again. Then it takes to underground ways. Wherever waters run the Krogan may go. I do not think the Sarn will follow that way, and while Thas lurk in burrows, still there are places they do not like." She hesitated. "I have found an old, old way, one made by those before us. There is a spell-laying there, but thin and tattered by the years, so if one is of strong will, one may penetrate it. But to sniff such will send a Thas squealing in flight, for it is a man spell, not one laid in their earth magic, but sealed with fire and air. Nor will the Sarn come, even if they find the gate, because it is guarded by one of the words of power. Of all that lies within I have no knowledge, save that such as we are not forbidden entrance. It will shelter us for a space."

"Yet upstream and past shallows," I reminded her. Though she offered me this shelter freely, yet I had Kaththea to think about now.

"It lies in the direction of the Dark Tower." Her simple answer to my thoughts at first did not make sense. Then I flinched.

"Why do you fear that?" Orsya's curiosity was as plain to me as my flare of fear must have been to her.

I told her, then, of Loskeetha and her sand reading, and of the three fates she had seen for the ending of my quest.

"Yet I believe that you cannot take any other path," Orsya replied. "The Dark Tower draws you as if it is a pull-spell. For it is not in you to turn your back upon her whom you seek, not even if you believe such a desertion may save you both. You are too close-knit, one to the other. You shall see the Dark Tower, but thereafter the fate may not lie in Loskeetha's reading at all. I have heard of her Garden of Stone and whispers concerning her sorcery. But in this land nothing is fixed and certain. For long ago all balances were set swinging this way and that. We can live but one day from dawn to sunset, one night from twilight to first dawn, and what lies ahead can change many times before we reach it."

"But Loskeetha said—decisions—the smallest decisions—"

"One has to make choices and abide by them. I know this much; any road to the Dark Tower is guarded, not only by things seen, but those unseen. I can offer you one path I believe that Dinzil and his men do not know."

There was logic in her saying. If that were the heart of Dinzil's holding, he would treat it to every defense. I could do much worse than accept her offer and go with the river. There would be trouble enough along that watery road to make a man keep his wits sharp, his eyes ever on watch.

We pulled out from under the drift refuge and, for as long as we could, we swam. If the enemy hunted, it was downstream. Orsya took the lead, using each promising overhang of bank, each large boulder or half submerged piece of drift for concealment from which to spy out clear passage beyond. We saw pronghorns come to the water to drink, and that was heartening. For those timid grazers would not seek the open if any men were about.

Finally the water grew too shallow and we must wade instead of swim. It was then that we came to the blood-stained place where Orsya's people had been attacked. Now it was twilight, gloom thickening into night. I was glad that she could not see, or did not seem to see, those stains and the carcass of the animal.

Night brought no halt as far as my companion was concerned. I was amazed at her energy, for I had thought that her hard usage at the hands of her captors would have left her weakened and not able to keep to such a steady pace.

We were well past the half dam that the Thas had made, and thereafter I tried to make my ears serve me, since my eyes could not penetrate the shadows. Now we went hand in hand to keep in touch. I heard sounds in plenty and some of them made me tense, since I could not believe they were of the normal night. But they drew no closer to where we crouched listening, and then we would venture on.

Orsya's prediction was right; the stream began to narrow and the waters arose to our middles. Here and there trails of phosphorescence in the form of bubbles spun in lines.

My companion might be tireless, but I was not. Though I did not like to admit my weakness, I began to believe there was a limit to the number of steps I could continue to take. Perhaps she read my mind; perhaps she was willing to admit that she was also not a thing forged from metal, such as the machines the Kolder used to do their bidding in the old days, but knew the fatigues and aches of flesh and bone.

Her grasp upon my hand brought us into a burrow, such as the one in which we had sheltered on our way back to the Valley. It had not been recently used, for there was no animal taint in it. It was barely large enough for both of us to crowd in very close together.

"Rest now," she told me. "There is still a long way upstream and I cannot mark my guide points in the night."

I had not thought I could sleep, but I did. Unlike the night before, my dreams were not haunted, nor could I remember dreaming at all. But I awoke hungry and thirsty. The last of my supplies had gone with the bag I had used as a weapon, and since that happening, now a day away, we had been so constantly on the move, I had forgotten food. Dahaun's warning would have to be disregarded now.

So close together had we slept that I could not alter position now without waking my burrow mate. She murmured sleepily as I slipped away, my gnawing hunger demanding that I do something about filling that far too empty middle.

I caught Orsya's thought. "What comes?"

"Nothing that I know. But we must have food."

"Surely." With far more ease she joined me in the river. The cliffs held away the direct rays of the rising sun, but the sky was light enough to let me believe the day would be a fair one.

"Ah." My companion waded along the shore. Then, as suddenly as if she had been seized by the ankles and pulled under, she was gone! I splashed after her, not knowing what I might find. Though I ducked where she had disappeared and tried to grope about with my hands

I could not locate her. But I heard a soft laugh.

Orsya stood upright again, her hands busy stripping long brown stalks from a root. Those gone, she rubbed the root vigorously between her palms, and its covering came away, so what she finally held was an ovule of ivory white.

"Eat!" She held it out with no invitation but an order.

"Dahaun said——" I held that root, looking at it hesitatingly, but hungry.

"Well enough." Orsya nodded. "Yes, there is that to be found in these lands where the Shadow has long hovered, which will kill, or will-bind, or take away memory, even the mind. But this is no be-spelled trap but a clean offering of the earth and water. You may eat of it as freely as of anything in the Valley."

So encouraged, I bit into the root. It broke crisply under my teeth and it had a clean, slightly sweet taste. Orsya dived again but was back before I had chewed and swallowed the last of my root, having found it not only pleasant to taste, but that it had juice which quenched my thirst.

She peeled another and gave it to me, before she prepared two more for herself. The banks here were steeper and higher, the water steadily rising. We finished the last of our breakfast and then began to swim.

In this I was no match for Orsya, nor did I try to keep level with her, but conserved my strength, content to hold her in sight. Luckily she paused to tread water now and then, looking about her for those guide marks she had mentioned the night before.

Once she motioned me toward the bank with a sharp gesture and on reaching me, gave a sharp jerk to my shoulder, ordering me to hold my breath. We went below surface.

"A Rus watcher on the heights," her thought explained. "They are keen-eyed, but water distorts all which lies within it. If the Rus drops no lower, I do not think we need fear."

A moment later her hold on me relaxed and I was able to break surface. But we kept close to the right hand bank. This seemed to me as wild and desolate country as that which held Loskeetha's domain, even if it lacked the growth of strange fleshy leaved plants, and our road was a waterway instead of rock.

Down the walls of the river banks looped vines, some thread-fine, others as thick as my wrist. Orsya's warning to me to avoid them was not needed, for they were so loathsome looking that no one could believe any virtue existed in them at all. They were a very pallid green with a sickly oversheen, as if they were wrought of some living rot. From them came such a stench of decay as to make one choke, dare he draw a heavy breath near them. I noticed that, though they tendriled down from above, as if seeking water, yet those strands which had touched the river surface were withered into thin skeletons. The more wholesome water must have killed them.

Things lived among those vines, though none of them did I ever see clearly. They moved in fluttering runs under the leaves, the shaking of the foliage marking their progress, but did not come into the light and air. Nor had I any desire that they do so.

"Ah, not far now." Orsya's thought carried a feeling of relief.

She treaded water where the river bank made an outward curve. The vines were less thick here and out of their noxious wreathing protruded a weather-worn lump. But was it a lump of rock? I reached Orsya and peered up in a more detailed examination.

Not a rock—some hand had worked there for a purpose. It had been, I thought, meant to be a head. But whether of man or animal, monster or spirit, no one now could say. There were two deep pits for eyes, and to see them from below as I did (the head being inclined so it looked down while we stared up) gave one a disturbing sensation that, from those holes, something still did measure all below.

"A watcher, not of our time, and one we need not fear, whatever once may have been its purpose. Now—" She swam but a short space on before she turned to me again.

"For a Krogan this would be no task, Kemoc. But for you . . ." She was plainly doubtful. "We must enter here under water, and for a space beyond remain so. I do not know how well equipped you may be for such a venture."

I flushed; it was plain she considered me the weaker party, one she must tend. Though logic told me that in the waterways she had the right of it, still my emotions could not be altogether governed by logic.

"Let us go!" I breathed deeply several times, expelling all I could from my lungs and refilling them. Orsya bobbed below, to search out that hidden entrance and see if it was still open. Now she reappeared just before me.

"Are you ready?"

"As I ever shall be."

I took the last breath and dived. Orsya's hand on my shoulder pointed me forward into darkness. I swam with what speed I could muster, my lungs bursting, the need for reaching the upper air so great it filled my world. Then I could stand it no longer and headed up. My shoulder, the back of my head, struck against solid rock. I kicked, sending my body on, felt my arm scrape painfully, and then—my head broke water, and I could breathe again!

But I was in utter darkness. And, as soon as my first gasps of relief were ended, I felt a rising unease. There was nothing but water about me, and the dark, pressing in thick and stifling in spite of the chill cold.

"Kemoc!"

"Here!" By so much had that terrible feeling of isolation and loss been broken.

Fingers scraped my upper arm and I knew she was close beside me. Her words pushed aside the dark and made this all a part of a real—if different—world again.

"This is a passage. Find a wall and use it for your guide," Orsya told me. "There are no more underground waterways—at least now as far as I was, when I first came here."

I splashed about until my outstretched fingertips touched rock.

"How did you come here—and why?"

"As you know, we communicate with other water dwellers. A Merfay told me of this and showed me the opening below. He came hither to hunt quasfi; there is a great colony who have taken shell rooting in here. A stream washes down and brings with it such food as the quasfi relish and these have grown to an unusual size. Since I have a liking for strange places I came to see, and found that I was not the first who was not Merfay or quasfi who traveled herein."

"What did you find, then?

"I leave that for you to see for yourself."

"You can see it? This dark is not everywhere?"

Again I heard her soft laughter. "There is more than one kind of candle, Kemoc from overmountain. There are even those suited to a place such as this."

But still a dark passage held us as we swam on. Then I became aware that the dark was not quite so thick beyond and that the graying gradually increased. It was not as bright as any torch or lamp, but compared to what we had come from, it was as passing from midnight to dawn.

Then we were out of the tunnel into a space so large, and yet so dim, that I could only guess at its size. A hollow mountain might have held it. The light was not diffused throughout, but spread in patches of radiance from underwater, approaching a short stretch of pebbled beach not too far away.

I swam for the beach. It presented to me such a promise of safety as I had not thought to find. As I waded out on it I saw that the light came from partly open shells which were in great clusters, rooted to the rocks under the surface.

"Quasfi," Orsya identified them. "To be relished not only by Merfays; but the deeper dwellers are more tasty."

She left in a dive which took her out of my sight. I stood dripping on that small patch of dry land and tried to learn more of this cavern. I could detect no sign of any intelligent remains here. Whatever Orsya promised to show me did not lie within my present range of vision.

The Krogan girl came out of the water, her hair plastered tight to her skull, her clothing as another skin on her body. She had a net bag in one hand—I was reminded of how she had carried one during our flight to the mountains—and from the bag glowed the light of the shellfish. But as she left the water it faded and by the time she joined me was almost gone.

In a very practical way she opened the shells with a knife she borrowed from me. A quick jab dispatched the creatures, and she offered one to me, its own outer covering serving as a plate.

Long ago I had learned that it was not good to be squeamish in such matters. When one was hungry, one ate, whatever one was lucky enough to find. The life of a Border scout did not provide dainty food, any more than it provides warm, soft beds, and uninterrupted sleep.

I ate. The meat was tough and one needed to chew it vigorously. The flavor was strange, not as satisfying as the taste of the roots. But neither was it too unpleasant, and looking at the wealth of quasfi beds about us, one could see starvation was no menace.

Orsya did not throw away the shells we emptied, but put them once more into her net, setting them therein with care, their inner surfaces pointing outward, small stones in the middle to keep them so. Having twisted, turned and repacked, she stood up.

"Are you ready?"

"Where do we go now?"

"Over there." She pointed, but now I could not say whether our direction led north or south, east or west.

Orsya waded into the water, having carefully made fast the net bag to her belt. As I followed more slowly I saw that once the bag dipped below the surface, it began to give out ghostly light as if the water had ignited the shells.

We headed away from the beach. There were fewer of the quasfi beds now, more dark patches. But under us the bottom was shelving and shortly thereafter we waded, water waist-high. I judged, since I saw cavern walls looming out into the half gloom, that we were now in a rift, leading back into the cliffs.

As the water fell to our knees, Orsya unhooked the bag from her belt and dragged it along at the end of one of its tie cords, being careful to let it go under the surface so its light continued.

The rift widened out again. Once more I saw the glimmer of living quasfi beds. But— I stopped short, straining.

Here were no rocky beaches providing the shellfish with housing space. Instead, they rooted on platforms on which towered, above the waterline, carved figures. These were set in two lines leading from where we stood to a bulk I could only half discern in the limited light.

Water lapped around their feet and lines of dead quasfi, their shells still cemented fast, strung about them, thigh-high, suggesting that in another time the statues had been even further submerged.

They were human of body, although some of the figures were so muffled in cloaks or long robes that their forms could only be guessed at.

Yes, human of body—but they had no faces! The heads set on those shoulders were blank of any carving, being only oval balls, though in each oval were deep eyepits, such eyepits as had marked the carving on the cliff outside.

"Come!" Still trailing her shell bag, Orsya moved forward down the avenue between those standing figures. She did not glance at them as she passed, but headed straight for the dark mass ahead.

But I had an odd feeling as I followed her that through each set of those eyepits, we were watched, remotely, detachedly, but still watched.

I stumbled, caught my balance and knew my feet were on underwater steps, which led up out of the flood. Before us was a wide platform and on it a building. So poor was the light that I could not be sure of its size. Darker gaps in its walls suggested windows and doors, but to explore it without proper lighting was folly. I said as much to Orysa. It was well out of the water and her quasfi shell lamp would not serve us here.

"No," she agreed, "but wait and see."

We stepped together from the top of that stair onto the platform. Once more I halted with a gasp of amazement.

Because, as our feet touched pavement, there came a glow from it, thin, hardly better than the radiance from the shells, but enough to make us sure of our footing.

"It is some magic of this place," Orsya told me. "Stoop —place your hands upon the stone."

I did as she bade, as she herself was doing. From the point where my flesh touched that stone (or was it stone? —the surface texture did not feel like it) light gleamed forth even brighter.

"Take off your boots!" She was hopping on one foot, pulling off her own tight foot covering. "It seems to kindle greater from the touch of skin upon it."

I was reluctant to follow her example, but when she went on confidently and then looked back in some surprise, I pulled off my light boots to carry them in one hand. She was right; as our bare feet crossed that smooth surface, the glow heightened, until we could really see something of the dark structure before us.

There were no panes in those windows; the doorway was a wide open portal. I wished that I had the sword I had dropped back by the river. Orsya had returned my knife to me and there was a good eight inches of well-tried blade, but in such a place imagination is quick to paint perils which could not be faced by so small a weapon.

I saw no carvings, no embellishments about the doorpost, nothing to break the severe look of the walls, save the stark openings of the windows. But, as we ventured inside, the light which followed the pacing of our feet, flared up to twice the brilliance. The room in which we stood was bare. Fronting us was a long wall, and set into that were ten openings. They had doors shut tight, nor could I see any latch, any way of opening them. Orsya crossed to the one directly facing us and put her hand against it, to find it immovable.

"I did not come so far before," she said. "There was an old warn-spell then—today it was gone."

"A warn-spell!" I was angered at the danger into which she had brought us. "And we come here without weapons—"

"A warn-spell very old," she returned. "It was one which answered to our protective words, not to *theirs*."

I must accept her explanation. But there was one way to test it. From left to right I looked along that row of closed doors. Then I spoke two *words* I had learned in Lormt.

XI

They were not Great Words, such as I had used when the power had *answered* me, but they would test and protect the tester.

As they echoed along that narrow room where we stood, the light under our feet blazed so high my eyes were dazzled for a moment and I heard Orsya cry out softly. Then followed on the roll of those *words* a crackling, a splintering, low and far off thunder. And in that new light I saw the door to which my companion had set her hands was now riven, falling apart in flakes. Orsya leaped back as they struck and crumbled into powdery debris.

Only that one door had been so affected. It was as if Orsya's touch had channeled whatever power the words had into striking there. I thought, though I could not be sure, for it all happened so quickly, that the breakage had come from the very point where her fingers rested.

Now came an *answer*—not such a one as had before, but a kind of chanting. It was quickly ended, and of it I understood not a word.

"What . . . ?"

Orsya shook her head. "I do not know, though it is very old. Some of the sounds—" She shook her head again. "No, I do not know. It was a guard set, I believe, to answer such a coming as ours. What was opened to us, we need not now fear."

I did not share her certainty about that. I would have held her back as she went confidently through that door, but I was too far from her and she eluded my grasp easily. There was nothing left to do but follow.

The light enveloped us with a cloud of radiance, and was reflected by a blaze of glitter.

This was a square room, in its center a two step dais on which stood a high-backed, wide-armed chair: the chair had an occupant. Memory stirred in me. That tale of how my father and Koris and the other survivors of shipwreck had found, high in a Karsten cliff, the hollowed tomb of the legended Volt, who had been seated so in a chair, his great ax across his knees. Koris had dared to claim that ax. After his taking of it, the remains of Volt had vanished into dust, as if he had waited only for the coming of some warrior bold enough, strong enough to wield a weapon which was forged not for human hands but for one deemed a half-god.

But this was no time-dried body which faced us. What it was I could not say, for I could not see it. A blue light veiled what rested in that chair so one was aware only of a form somewhere within. But it was not alive. This I knew was a tomb, even as Volt's rock hole had been.

One could have no fear, no feeling of morbidity about that mist in the chair. Rather there was a kind of welcome . . . I was startled when my thoughts read my feelings so.

"Who . . . ?" Orsya took another step forward, a second, a third; now she was very close to the foot of the dais, staring up at that column of mist.

"Someone," the words came out of nowhere into my mind, surely Orsya had not sent them, "who means us no harm."

About the dais were piled small chests. Some of these had rotted and burst. From them trickled such treasures as I had never seen gathered in one place before. But my eyes came quickly to the first step where there lay by itself, very plain in that light, a sword.

My hand went out of itself, fingers flexing, reaching for the hilt. The blade did not have the blue cast of fine steel, but rather a golden glow—or perhaps that was only the reflection of the light in the room. Its hilt appeared to be cut from a single piece of yellow quartz in which small sparks of red, gold, and blue like unto the mist flashed, died, and flashed again. It was slightly longer, I thought, than the weapons I knew. But it showed no signs of any eating by time.

I wanted it more than anything I had ever wanted in my life before. That desire was as sharp in me as physical hunger, as the need for drink in a desert.

Had Koris felt this when he looked upon Volt's ax? If he had I did not wonder that he set hand to it. But Volt had not denied him in that taking. Would I—did I dare —to do the same here?

To rob the dead—that is a dire thing. Yet Koris had asked of Volt his ax and taken it, and thereafter wrought great things for his chosen people, using that weapon.

To take up a dead man's sword, that was to take to one a measure of him who had first carried it. The Sulcar believed that in the heat of battle a man using a dead man's sword can be possessed by the ghost, inspired either to such deeds as he would not dare alone, or driven to his fate if the ghost proved vengeful and jealous. Yet still Sulcarmen have been known to plunder tombs for none other than swords of story and fame: Not in Estcarp, but in the northlands where once they had their home ports before they made their alliance with the Wise Women. They sang sagas of the deeds of such men and such swords.

I tried to fight that eating desire to take into my hand that hilt of gold. But there are some hungers which are greater than any reason, even for such as I who have tried all my life to put thought before action. And this time temptation won.

So I brushed past Orsya and went down on one knee. But the hand I put out to clasp that hilt was not the left, rather the maimed right: It went so naturally. Those fingers which could still move closed about the half. Yet, even as they did, for the last time prudence warned. I broke that queer eyelock which riveted my attention to the sword, looked up into the blue mist.

Within it was a core, a dim seen figure; that it did exist there was all of which I was sure. Koris had taken Volt's ax, but boldly, as a gift, not as one who plundered. Could I do less here and now?

I drew back my hand, though it was hard to break that hold, as if my fingers, against my will, decided to keep what they had grasped. Though I did not rise to my feet,

I spoke aloud to what the mist cloaked.

"I am Kemoc Tregarth out of Estcarp, overmountain. I seek that which has been unlawfully taken; I have lost my sword in honorable battle. Do I go forth from here empty-handed, then already is my cause part lost. I claim no hero's name nor fame. But I can say these words and not be blasted—"

Those *words* from Lormt, which had opened to us this doorway, once again I spoke. But this time in no challenge or as a war cry, but rather as identification, so that this throne and its occupant, would know that I was not of the Shadow, but of those who raised shield against the Dark.

I do not know what I expected to follow my speaking. Anything might happen. That which sat within the blue might rise and welcome me, or strike me down. But there was nothing, no blaze of heightened radiance, not even an echo.

So I felt a little foolish. But not so much so that I did not hesitate to raise the hand, which had been curved about the hilt, to he or she who sat above, in the same salute I would have given a war leader.

Then I picked up the sword. It was not time marked. No rust pits marred its surface. Its point and edge were as sharp and clean as a man might wish. Again my scarred and stiffened hand closed about the hilt with an ease I had not known since the healing of that old wound.

I got to my feet and fumbled in my jerkin to bring out the scarf, now wet and like a string. This I looped to make an improvised baldric, since it would not fit into the empty scabbard at my belt.

"You have done what must be done." For the first time in long minutes Orsya's thoughts reached me. "We do not

141

see the patterns woven by the Great Ones, only a thread now and then which belongs to us. You have taken on you more than a sword; may the bearing of both be not too heavy a burden."

I wondered if her people shared the Sulcar beliefs concerning dead men's weapons. But the blade did not seem heavy. Instead, handling it was fired with a sense of impatience new to me, a desire to push on, to hurry about my self-appointed task.

Already I had turned to the door. But Orsya did not follow me. Surprised, I glanced back. She was slowly circling the throne and the misty figure, surveying the moldering treasure boxes. Had she been emboldened by my appropriation of the sword to go hunting on her own? I would have protested but had a second thought. Orsya must do as she believed best, with no right of mine to question.

She was behind the throne now, and she lingered there. When she came forth she carried in her hand a short rod. It was cone shaped, rising to a sharp point at the tip she held upright, and it was not smooth, but ridged with corrugations which spiraled along its full length. In color it was ivory-white, and, when she moved her hand, I thought I saw a spark of white light or fire dance for a second on its point.

It was not long enough, nor shaped to suggest a weapon. Nor was it bejeweled, set into any precious base. What it was, or its purpose, I could not guess. But Orsya held it carefully as if it were to her as meaningful as the sword to me. Now she faced the misty figure. She did not kneel as I had to take the sword and make my half plea. She spoke—not by mind touch—in that curiously toneless audible speech of her people.

"I am Orsya of the Krogan, though they no longer own

142

me as daughter or friend. I am one fit to hold what I have taken from its casket. Powers I have, if not great ones, and weapons I have, if they are not forged by fire out of molten metal. This I take because I know it for what it is, and what it may do, and because I am what I am, and I go where I go."

She lifted the cone-rod, holding it out between her and the shrouded one. This time it was no spark which showed at the tip, but a darting streak of white fire. Then she turned and came quickly to join me.

We did not speak as we went back to the platform outside, to look back along the road we had come, past those faceless statues with their holes for eyes. I was about to retrace our path, when Orsya stopped me with uplifted hand. Her head was forward a little, turning slowly from side to side, her nostrils expanded as if she were testing for some scent. But all I could sniff was that odd smell which hung about all these water-logged caverns. It was plain she was alerted by something I could not detect.

"What...?" I asked in a half-whisper.

"Thas," she replied in a sound as muted, "and something else."

I unslung the sword I had taken. Underground was the Thas' home. I and perhaps Orsya, would be at as great a disadvantage as I was underwater. I tried to pick up any scent in the air, but my sense was not as acute as hers.

"They come—that way." She pointed along the way of the statues with her cone-rod. "Let us go this—" Her choice ran to our right along the front of the building. I did not see how that could favor us, but Orsya had been here before, and there was a chance she knew more than she had shown me.

I put on my boots, even as she latched her scaled foot

coverings. To dim the light of our going was a prudent move. Then we hurried past those blank oblongs of windows to the end.

The tomb had been constructed to the fore of the platform which ran on back for quite a distance more, to a shadow which might denote the wall of the cavern. Again Orsya held her head high, sniffing.

"Do you feel that air?" she asked aloud.

Even as she spoke, I did. There was a distinct inward flow of air current coming from the rear of the platform.

"Water—fresher water." She began to run while I lengthened stride to keep up with her.

As we retreated from the tomb, so did the light recede. Orsya's shell lamp was useless out of the water, and we headed into a dark which increased near to the thick black of that first passageway through which we had come. I listened, as we went, for any sound behind us. How about ahead? The Thas must burrow; what if they waited for us wherever Orsya led?

"No Thas." She picked up my thought. "I do not think that this is a place they have ever visited before. They leave their stench wherever they push their foul runways. But—I wish I knew what they brought with them, or what ranges before them now, for its like I have never scented."

We reached the end of the platform. Orsya moved beside me and there was a glow of light: enough to show that she had shed one foot covering and planted her flesh against the floor to give us that gleam.

The wall of the cavern was there, arching up and back over our heads. Between it and the platform was a channel in which ran water. This came from an archway to our right and gurgled on, to be lost in the dark. Orsya replaced her boot and that momentary glimpse was gone.

"That scarf—the one you use to sling the sword—hold one end; give me the other. Now get down into the water."

I did as she bade, feeling the sharp twitch as she gripped Kaththea's scarf, lowering myself gingerly into the water which I hoped was not deep enough to close over my head. But it was only waist-high. Once more immersed, Orsya's shell lamp came to life.

She headed for the archway. I discovered that this water had a current, and we were walking against that force. After a few moments I was aware of something else; the shell lamp was radiating a dimmer illumination and I feared that it was actually dying away. At my questioning Orsya confirmed that alarming fact. The quasfi shells did not hold their natural illumination for long after they were emptied of their indwellers. Soon the light would be completely exhausted.

"Do you know this way?" I asked, for reassurance.

She held the cone-rod tight against her breast with the scarf end, while with her free hand she scooped up a little of the water and touched her tongue tip to it. "No; but this is water which has run in the open air, under sun, and not too long ago. It will lead us out."

With that I had to be content.

The increasing dark was hard for me to take. Never have I favored underground ways, having to fight a feeling that around me walls were moving in to crush. Perhaps because we walked in water Orsya did not appear to be affected in the same way and I hid my feelings from her.

There was an urgent jerk on the scarf. I stopped, listened. She did not try to reach me by mind tough, rather did her hand slide down the scarf to close upon mine, and I did not need the cramping of her fingers to know this was a warning.

My senses in this deep hole might not be as acute as hers, but now I could hear it too; a splashing ahead. The last glimmer of our shell lamp was quenched and we were in the dark. I swung out my sword in a short arc ahead and to the right. Its point scraped wall and with that as my guide, I drew to it, bringing my companion with me, feeling somehow the safer with a solid surface to my side. In spite of my wishes to deny it, that splashing sounded nearer. What kind of monsters patrolled these darksome ways?

For the first time Orsya spoke. She was very close to me, so that her breath was against my cheek as she whispered:

"This is none of my knowing. I cannot reach it with a hail call. I do not know if it is of the water world at all."

"Thas?"

"No! Thas I know." There was loathing in that.

We listened. To retreat before it was still possible, but we might reach the cavern of the tomb, only to find Thas waiting for us. In that moment I longed for Kyllan's gift, for it was in him to touch and act upon the minds of beasts, bringing them under his will. He could have turned that splasher, sent it off from us—always supposing it *was* an animal and not some unknown abomination loosed by the Shadow in this place.

Suddenly Orsya's grip tightened. Though we now stood in utter dark, yet ahead were lights—two grayish disks just above water level. From them came a little diffused glimmering. Those disks were set in a line—

Eyes! But eyes which glowed, which were equal in size to the palm of my hand: eyes far enough apart to suggest a head of proportions beyond any beast I had ever seen!

I pushed Orsya against the wall behind me. The sword was in my maimed hand; now I tried to transfer it to my left. But found, to my dismay, that I could not clasp it as well, that even with my stiff fingers it was better in my right hand.

The eyes, which had been close to the surface of the water, now suddenly jerked aloft to a level above my own head. We heard a sibilant hissing as the thing came to a full stop. I had no doubt that it had sighted us, though the beams of light those eyes cast ahead did not reach to where we now stood.

Since the only target I had were those gray disks, those must be my point of attack. The hissing grew stronger. A fetid puff of air struck me full face, as if the creature had exhaled. I brought up the sword and, though I have used a blade since childhood, it seemed to me that never had I held one before which felt like an extension of my own body.

The eyes swung downward, and now, though still at water level, they were much closer. Again a puff of stinking breath.

"Kemoc!" Orsya's mind thrust was harsh. "The eyes—do not look into them— Ahh! Keep me . . . keep me with you . . ."

I felt her move stiffly, trying to break the pressure of my body, to slip from between me and the wall.

"It wills me to it! Keep me—" Now she cried aloud as if terror had filled her.

I dared not wait any longer. With a push from my shoulder I sent her stumbling back and heard a splash as she must have fallen into the water. But whatever compulsion those eyes exerted on her, they did not hold for me.

One could not rush nor leap through the current of this stream. It was rather like wading through slipping sand and I dared not lose my footing. Those eyes, at the level of my own waist . . . if the thing had a skull shaped in proportion to their size, its jaws must now be submerged.

"Sytryl"

That was no word of mine, but it had come out of me in a cry like unto a war shout. Then it was as if I were no longer Kemoc Tregarth, but another, one who knew such fighting and was not dismayed by either the dark or the nature of the unseen enemy. In my mind I seemed to stand aside and watch with a kind of awe the action of my body. Just as my maimed hand was put to use it had not known since that wound years ago, so did I thrust and spring in waves in which I had never been trained.

The golden sword went home in one of those gray disks. A bulk arose high, with a terrible scream to tear through one's head. But my hand held to hilt, and, though I was hurled away with a punishing stroke from what must be a great paw, yet I kept my weapon and struggled up to my feet again, back to the wall, facing straightly that bobbing single disk.

It struck at me and I flung out my arm, the sword straight pointed, in what I deemed a very short chance at any victory. My blade struck something hard, skidded down, to slash open that other disk. Then I was crushed back against the rock wall as a vast, scaled weight fell upon me. Had I been pinned below the surface of the stream I would have died, for that blow had enough force to drive both wits and breath out of me. When I struggled back to full consciousness I felt a weight across me waist-high, but it did not move.

Cautiously I used my left hand to explore: Scaled skin, and under that the general shape of a limb, now inert.

Revulsion set me to working for freedom. I wavered finally to my feet, the sword still in my hand as if nothing but my conscious will could ever dislodge it.

"Orsya! Orsya!"

I called first with voice and then mind. Had she been caught in the struggle, lay now perhaps crushed under the body of the thing I had apparently killed?

"Orsya!"

"Coming—" Mind touch and from some distance. I leaned against the wall and tried to explore by touch any damage I had taken in the encounter. My ribs and side were sore to any pressure, but I thought they were not broken. My jerkin was rent from one shoulder.

But I had been very lucky, too lucky to believe that it had been good fortune alone which had brought me through. Were the Sulcarmen right? When I had taken that sword into my hand, had I also taken into my body some essence of the one to whom it had once belonged? What meant the strange word I had hurled into that face (if the monster had a face) when I attacked? I would not lose it now . . . I never could. . . .

"Kemoc?"

"Here!"

She was coming. I put out my hands, touched skin and instantly her fingers were about my wrist in a fierce, hurting hold.

"I fell into the water; I think I was dazed. The current carried me back. What—what happened?"

"The thing is dead."

"You killed it!"

"The sword killed it. I was merely one who held it for the kill. But it seems we have picked a dangerous road. If we have met one such surprise, there may be others ahead."

"The Thas are coming—and with them that other . .

"What other?"

"I do not know. Save that it is of the Shadow. It is not even remotely human-kind and they even fear it, though they are bound to its company for the present."

So our road must still lie ahead. We struggled over the monster bulk of the dead thing. Behind it the waters of the stream arose, partly dammed by the body. Where the current had washed only a little above our knees, now it rose rapidly. We quickened pace for I feared it might choke the passage.

"The eyes—you said that the eyes drew you." I questioned as we went.

I read her surprise. "Did you not feel it? That there was naught to do but to surrender to it—to go to it as it wished? But, no, you could not, or you would not have fought! Truly, you have your own safeguards, overmountain man!"

As far as Orsya could explain, the gaze of the creature had overpowered her will, drew her to it. I wondered if that was not the manner of its hunting in these dark passages, so that it brought its prey easily within reach. Yet my own immunization to the spell puzzled us both. It might have something to do with the sword. For, folly though it might be, I was convinced that the blade had in the past been used against just such a monster and what had come to me was a memory of that other battle.

To our relief the waters did not reach higher than our breasts; and I wondered what the Thas would make of that bulk stopped in the tunnel when they blundered into it.

The waterway opened into a pool and there was the splash of a falls. Light, daylight, though grayed and dim from the distance, danced down to show us those falls, laced with foam, which cascaded from an opening far above.

XII

The spray from the falls was a mist of rain over us. But at least we could see. I drew Orsya with me back against the wall farthest from the falls, from where I could see best those openings (there were three of them) above us.

It was clear we could not climb near the falls; the rock was too much under the blanket of spray. The second opening was no good to us either, for it was in the roof of the cavern and only a winged man could reach it. So I studied the third. It was a narrow slit, to the right of the falls, out of the direct force of the water for most of the climb.

But even if we could reach that opening to the outer world we did not know what awaited us on the far side, nor in what part of the country we would emerge. I said as much to Orsya, but she shook her head.

"We are in the highlands. You still have the Dark Tower ahead."

I could not see how she was so sure of our direction. But I did not argue about it.

"Can you climb?" Whether her webbed feet could find toeholds as easily as mine, I did not know.

"One does not know without trying," she said.

As I feared, even here the stone was slick with water.

We were beyond all but the edge of the constant dampening of the spray and the wall was rough enough to give us purchase for our hands and feet, bared to grip more firmly. However, it was not a progress to be hurried.

I went first, testing each hold before I risked setting weight upon it. Now and then I glanced back to be sure Orsya was following. She did not seem in any distress, though she moved deliberately. About two thirds of the way up I came across a fault in the rock, hidden from below, a small shelf which could hardly be termed a ledge, but which would give us a resting place, sorely needed after those hours of flight.

I lay down on the ledge and reached my hands to Orsya, helping her up and over beside me in that narrow space. But her head turned to a very narrow crevice in the wall at our backs, her nostrils expanding as she tested the air.

"Thas!"

"Here?" This shelf was no place on which to face a fight. Nor did I want to start to climb again and be attacked from below.

"Not now," she reported after a moment. "But this crack leads to one of their burrows. We had better not linger."

She was right. The entrance to a Thas run was no place in which to take our ease—especially not when a slight push could send us both over and down. I got to my feet, tried to forget the pain in my shoulders, the aching weariness of my arms. Behind lay the longest stretch. *Keep my mind only on the few inches before me—the next hand hold—and then the one after that—*

It was a slowly rising agony, that last part of the climb. My maimed hand was numb. I could watch it move and hold, but I could not feel the stone beneath the awkward fingers. Always with me was the fear that that grasp could slip.

But that was the hand which I at last pushed through the opening into the outer world. The light was not that of the sun and I wondered if we were coming out into a storm. But, as I struggled through, I discovered we were still at the bottom of a rift. The stream which made the falls in the cavern poured along there. The rest was only rock walls and sand. I turned to draw Orsya up beside me.

We were a wild looking pair, our clothing tattered, with raw red scraps of skin on our arms and legs, along with dark bruises, the grime of mud and other signs of our journey. But the sheer relief of getting out of those ways made me feel light of head and heart—though some of that might have been due to lack of food.

Orsya went to the edge of the stream, fell on her knees by it, staring into the water intently, as Loskeetha might have consulted her bowl of sand. Then she made a quick dart with one hand and brought it up clasped about a wriggling, fighting creature which was so long and slim of body it seemed more snake than fish. She knocked this against a rock and left it there, then made another grab. Hungry as I was, I could not find any appetite for her catch. But she gathered them together carefully and put them in the bag from which she dumped the quasfi shells.

We started along the cut, I on the narrow bank, Orsya in the stream. Twice more she made a raid into the flood swirling about her feet and added to her bag.

Twilight was dim about us as the ravine widened out and vegetation and grass began to show in ragged clumps. We drew away from the water a little and I found a place where a boulder and part of an ancient slide from the heights, together with the cliff wall, gave us a corner of protection. Orsya borrowed my knife to work upon the fish, while I piled stones to add to our shelter.

I did not relish the thought of raw fish, but when she handed me some, I accepted it and tried not to think what I was eating. It was not as unpleasant as I had expected and, while I would not choose to live upon such foodstuffs, I could chew and swallow my share.

It was already dark, but Orsya brought out the cone-rod, unwrapping Kaththea's scarf. This she sat on the ground before us with much care.

When it stood point up to her satisfaction, she bent her head and breathed upon it. Then, with her hands she made certain signs, one or two of which I recognized, for I had seen Kaththea sketch their like. I knew better than to disturb her concentration at such a time. But I wondered what Orsya was, and if she were indeed the Krogan equivalent of a Wise Woman.

She sat back at last, rubbing her hands together as if they were either cold, or she would free them of something clinging to her skin.

"You may sleep without fear of surprise," came her thought. "We have such a guardian as had not been known since my mother's mother's mother's time."

I longed to ask her what manner of magic she had wrought. But the first law of power is that explanations must not be asked for—if they are volunteered, well and good. And, since she did not tell me, I could only wonder. Yet I believed in her promise of safety. This was good, for I do not think I could have stood any watch that night, my fatigue of mind and body was as a burden heavy enough to push me to earth.

When I awoke Orsya was not curled in sleep, but rather sat, her hands arched over the cone-rod, not quite touching it, her position being that of one who warms herself at a fire. She must have heard me stir, for she gave a start as one awakened out of deep thought and turned her head to look at me.

Her hair, well dried now, was a silvery cloud about her head and shoulders. Somehow at this moment she looked more unhuman, more alien, than she had since our first meeting by the guest isle.

"I have been screeing. . . . Eat." She nodded at what rested just beyond my hand. "And listen!"

There was about her such an air of command as I had seen in the Witches of Estcarp, and automatically I obeyed. Screeing? The term was new to me, but I thought she meant foreseeing, after Loskeetha's pattern, and I wanted no more of that.

Orsya read my thoughts and shook her head. "I deal not with futures, possible or impossible, but with dangers which walk this land. There is much abroad here—"

I glanced from her to the wider stretch of valley. There was nothing I could see except scanty growths of brush and the stream.

"The eyes of the head cannot be trusted here," she answered my thought once more. "Whatever you see, look twice, and thrice, and with the mind also."

"Illusions?" I guessed.

Orsya nodded. "Illusions. They are deft at weaving such, these who deal in the powers of the Shadow. Look now." She placed her right hand so that the point of the cone must touch the palm, then she leaned forward to touch my forehead.

I blinked, startled.

A rock not too far away was no longer a thing of rugged stone, but rather of warty gray hide, of large, questing eyes, of claws to tear.

"Look now upon your sword," Orsya's thought commanded.

I must have unconsciously reached for its hilt when I sighted the rock-monster. Along its blade red runes glowed; they might have been written in freshly shed blood. But they were in no language I knew.

"Illusion? Or is it really there? And, if it is, why does it not attack?"

"Because we have also a protection of illusion about us."

She raised her hand from the cone and I saw only a rock. "How long we can maintain our cover and—" She hesitated and then continued, "there is also this. We can go together only while we travel by water. I can not take wholly to land. Thus the last part of the journey will be yours."

"None of it need be yours," I told her swiftly. "You have the means to make yourself safe. Stay here—" I could not say "stay here until I return," for I was sure that returning was not one of the things I could read into any future. This quest was mine alone and Orsya need not bear any of its burdens.

It was as if she neither heard my words, nor read them in my mind. Instead she had gone back to studying the cone-rod.

"The sword will warn you. It is not in my power to read its history, for it is of war and warriors. My gifts lie with the waters and, a little, of the earth across which they run. But there are tales which travel from one people to another across this riven land of ours. A blood runs on that blade when evil is nearby, as you have seen. Therefore, when we must part, you must use it as a touchstone to try the truth of what you see: the fair, the safe, those may seem foul or dangerous. The seeming foul may be harmless. Do not trust your unaided sight. Now, it is day—let us go."

"That thing out there—" I stood up, sword in hand, half expecting to see the rock turn into a monster ready to charge.

"It is a guardian, I think." Orsya was rewinding the cone in Kaththea's scarf. "Give me your hand, and walk softly with me in the stream. It may be able to sense that we pass, but it will not see us."

I kept my eyes upon that rock—fearing that the illusion might hold so that I could still be seeing it while what it covered was stalking us.

"Think not of it," she ordered. "And no more mind touch—such creatures cannot read it, but they are alerted by its use."

Hand in hand we hurried down to the stream and stepped into the water. As we had in the tunnels, we waded in a current which flowed with some power, and which reached our knees. I held the sword before me, watching the bared blade. The runes blazed as we passed the rock, and then they began to fade.

The second time that warning showed we were well out in the canyon valley. But this time the danger was visible: small, scuttling things moving around the open end of a cut in the cliff—Thas!

They were bringing forth baskets of earth and rocks, dumping it in piles, running back again in a fury of work. I felt Orsya's hand tighten about mine, read the wave of disgust which filled her.

We rounded a curve in the canyon and saw another portion of Thas labor. They were building a road with earth and rocks, angling it up along the side of the cliff. Among them were man-like figures wearing saffron yellow cloaks, and those carried staffs, but wore no swords.

They were plainly in charge of the operation, ordering the Thas here and there, consulting maps or rolls of instructions. The reason for the labor was a mystery to me, but that it had great importance to the enemy was clear.

Orsya raised her fingers to her lips in warning, having dropped my hand for an instant. Then she snatched my fingers up again as if even so small a break between us might be disastrous. Silence, she had cautioned, and I gathered that stood for mind touch also.

Some distance away, more Thas worked along the river, some piling rock out in the stream bed, though they entered water with very visible reluctance and had to be constantly urged to it by two of the saffron robes who kept constant watch over their activities. How we were going to pass them if we kept to the water I did not see.

With my sword blade I motioned left. Orsya studied the ground there and then nodded. It seemed to me that our splashing progress out of the stream would surely alert the workers. But we gained the far bank unobserved.

I guessed that Orsya had by some means rendered us invisible to those workers. The illusion had protected us —so far. But I breathed more freely when we were in cover in broken country. The footing was less smooth, but this type of lurking was familiar to me. Threading in and out among the rocks and brush, we worked our way safely past the activity by the river. I wished I could learn the reason for it. That it meant no good to us I could guess.

"Listen; I will climb . . . see what lies ahead."

"Take care. When we are apart, the illusion does not cloak you."

"This is a game not unknown to me," I returned with confidence.

Orsya pushed back between two rocks, crouching

158

down. I fastened the sword to my belt and began to climb behind a chimney, which was weather sculptured almost free of the cliff wall I had nearly reached the perch I had selected when there was a whistling screech behind. Had that attacker not so made clear its intentions, I would have been easy prey. But at that cry I pushed away. My spine and shoulders were now firm against the parent cliff, so narrow was this portion of the break through which I crawled, though my feet were still in place on the chimney. I freed the sword as death on wings hurtled down at me.

It made one pass over the top of the chimney, screeching, and the wind of its wing flapping nearly upset my precarious balance. Then it circled and came back, landing on top of the chimney, striking down at me with a murderous beak. It had a long neck which was very supple. The head was small, and seemed mostly to be that beak, with eyes to guide its attack.

The runes on the sword blazed high as I brought the blade point up at the darting head. With my shoulders so wedged I could not strike freely. It seemed I was cornered, unable to either defend myself or retreat.

Again the beak reached for me. I tried to move the sword and the red runes on it dazzled my eyes. The blade touched something by pure fortune, for I could move it only a few inches either way. There was a screech broken off in mid-cry and that snake neck tossed. I saw that the beak had been slashed off close to its roots. The thing took to the air; cries came from it as it flew wildly back and forth, as if bereft of whatever wits it ever had. One of those swoops brought it crashing into the cliff wall and it hurtled, end over end, broken and writhing down to the ground below. I stared at the sword in unbelief. As it had when I had faced the monster in the tunnel, it answered some life or purpose of its own. I had certainly not aimed that blow, had tried feebly to use it in defense. What power-things had I brought out of that long sealed tomb?

Then my mind turned sharply to the present. Surely the cries of the winged thing would draw the attention of those working at the river. The sooner we were away from here the better. I pulled up to the perch and gave a hurried survey to what lay ahead.

The canyon opened on hilly country, less high than the heights behind us, but very broken and rough. I could see movement here and there, but a haze hid much of it. Farther to the left was the streak of what might be a road. But I did not sight any buildings. And the broken land promised lurking places in plenty.

I dared remain no longer to spy out the best route. However we went we would have to cross that road. Thinking about that I dropped from hold to hold, to find Orsya waiting for me at the foot of the chimney.

"Come!" She held out her hand. "They will come to see why the Rus cried. If they find it they will know strangers are abroad. I do not know if I can hold an illusion against searching."

"Do you know where the Dark Tower stands?" To venture just blindly on was utter folly.

"Only that it stands somewhere near. But you have a better guide than my scant knowledge."

"What?" I did not understand her.

"She whom you seek. If the tie is strong between you, open your mind and heart, and it will draw you."

"Perhaps they can detect us so." I remembered how Kaththea had once warned me against such seeking.

"If you use magic, perhaps. But use your heart hunger

rather, Kemoc. You have said that you three are a part of a whole in a way which is to no other born. Therefore, think upon her, using no lore you have learned, but only your own longing."

"I do not know how." I could think of Kaththea, fear for her, long to see her—but was that what Orsya meant?

"Set aside your fears, for this land holds much which feeds happily on fears and will in turn use that to weaken you. Think rather of when you were all together and happy in that joining. Set her in your mind as she was in those days. Now this also will I tell you, Kemoc; beware of illusions. Fair may be foul, foul fair. . . ."

"You have said that before."

"And never can I say it enough. For danger from beast and weapon may walk this land, but greater danger than that we carry in our own minds."

We had been making our way along, shoulder to shoulder. Though Orsya spoke as one certain, yet still I shrank from trying as she had suggested, to find Kaththea in that fashion. Mind touch I knew, but this other kind of seeking was something new—unless it was like unto that which I had used to guide me through the bewildering stone forest. That magic in the scarf had worn away, but it had served its purpose. Could such be tried again?

Swiftly I told Orsya what I had in mind. She listened, and then looked, with narrowed, speculative eyes upon the scarf now wrapped about her cone-rod.

"To use magic within this land is perhaps the same as lighting a fire in a beacon basket to draw the attention of half the countryside. But there is this—the scarf has shrouded this for long now, and that will give it virtue. You might not be able to command that virtue. . . ." Now she turned that speculative look upon me. The question she asked next was one which I would never have expected to hear in that time and place, for it seemed to have no relation to what was to be done.

"Tell me, Kemoc; have you been with a woman and known her after the fashion of male and female?"

Startled, I answered, "Yes." That was long ago during border leaves and it might have happened to one who was no longer me.

"Then it would not work for you. But for me . . . What were the words you used to send the scarf seeking before?"

I repeated them slowly, in the softest of whispers. Her lips moved soundlessly as if she shaped those words. Then she nodded again.

"I cannot go far from the stream-side. Once we are in those broken lands we must find a place where I can shelter while you go ahead, if your path leads from the water. Then I shall lay a spell upon this. You must hold the picture of Kaththea in your mind. For her I have not seen, nor does there stretch any tie between us. Once that is done, the scarf may once more lead you—only, remember; it must be your heart and not your mind which sets it on its way. This"—she held the cone tighter to her breast—"cannot work for any save a virgin. Even if it is taken into another's hand some of its virtue will depart. For it is the horn of a unicorn, and it carries great power for those who can use it."

Only the top protruded from the wrapping of scarf, but I looked at that, startled. The forces which could be channeled through such rare objects were more than just legends. We still named our years for beasts of old— Firedrake, Griffin, and there was a Year of the Unicorn.

We made our way from one bit of cover to the next

until we came to the road. Orsya put up her hand in warning, though I did not need that gesture, for the runes on the sword ran red. There was no way of passing over it, and we trailed impatiently along beside it until we came to where a stream cut across the land. There was no bridge to carry the road as one might suppose— rather the pavement ended abruptly on one bank to begin on the other, and Orsya smiled.

"So . . . as yet they have not mastered water."

"What is it?"

"Running water." She pointed to the stream. "Evil cannot cross it without some powerful, nature-twisting spell. They can build on one side and the other, but they cannot yet successfully span it. This is our road."

She splashed joyfully into the stream and perforce I followed. We kept well away from either bank, but as we passed the two ends of the road, my sword appeared to drip crimson drops, so shimmering were the runes.

Once beyond the road I wished to go ashore again, lest in the open river we be too visible, but Orsya insisted that our covering illusion held. We were still arguing the matter when she gave a little cry and pointed downstream, the way we had come. I turned my head.

There was something swimming there against the current, a vee of ripples, but nothing making them. I looked to the sword which I swung into readiness. The surface was cool and gray, no bloody runes along it. Yet something moved toward us at good speed and it was invisible.

XIII

Orsya took one step and then another toward that rippling in the water. I had the testimony of my blade that it was no danger, yet the unseen and unknown will always be feared, for that is inherent in us.

"Kofi!"

At my companion's hail, the vee of ripples veered, pointed to Orsya. Then there were splashings and movements in the water as if whatever swam there was now treading water.

"What is it?" I demanded.

"Merfay," she answered before her lips shaped soft twitterings, not akin to any speech I have ever heard. Nor did "Merfay" mean anything to me.

The invisible one swam forward again, splashing us with waves made in his passing. Orsya caught my hand once more.

"Come! Oh, this day we are favored! Kofi will lead us to a safe place."

"Can you see him—her—it?" I asked.

Her eyes went wide in surprise. "You do not?"

"Nothing but water rippling as if something swims there."

"But he is there—plain—"

Not to me. Nor have I ever heard of a Merfay.

Orsya shook her head. "They are like unto us in some instances, save smaller, and closer akin to the furred and finned ones than we. Mostly they dwell apart, not needing others. But Kofi—he is of like mind with me, one who

164

explores beyond the haunts of his people. We have shared ventures in the past. He is not subject to the illusions, since his mind is so unique he cannot be so entrapped. He has roamed the water lands here for a space, watching to see what the enemies do. They are preparing for a great march of men, to the west—"

"The Valley!"

"Perhaps so. Yet, the hour has not yet come when they muster. They await some order or sending."

I thought of Dinzil and what Loskeetha said he might do, now that Kaththea was within his hands. The need to seek the Dark Tower, even though that seeking might lead to disaster, boiled within me. So that I quickened pace, pulling Orsya after me by our hand clasp. While ahead of us that guide I could only trace by ripples swam steadily onward.

More and more vegetation grew about. Orsya plundered here and there, finding more of those edible roots, cleaning them and storing them in her net bag. We munched some and they were better to me than the fish. Always the Merfay served as our scout. Once he (though it seemed odd to grant any identity to a wedge of ripples) made a wide detour about a block of stone which had fallen into the river. Orsya followed his lead, beckoning me well away from any contact with it.

As we passed, I saw that the stone had been dressed, and that once it might have been a pillar. There were others like it lying in confusion on the shore, as if they had been tumbled this way or that by some titanic blow of nature or man. They were not blue, as those in the havens experience had taught me to watch for, but rather a yellowish-gray, unpleasant to the eye.

"An ancient place of power," Orsya explained. "But no power we would wish to raise."

As we passed that place, I felt a clammy chill, or perhaps my imagination furnished that.

The brush became trees, weirdly leafed, resembling the blasted forests we had found on the Escore side of the churned mountains, where the witch power had set the ancient barrier between Estcarp, the refuge, and this country, the threat. Those leaves might have been living, still they had a skeleton look which made one think of ashes, of something long since dead and dry. The grass was a tall, sword-edged, spiky growth which could cut skin if one were unwary, and there were other nasty looking things which one certainly did not want to touch at all.

But among all this rank and poisoned vegetation, there were islets and ways which had normal looking foliage growing. The unseen Kofi turned into a side stream, banked by such growth, leading to our left.

I was still hazy about directions. This territory beyond the Heights made one unsure of any north or south. But I thought now we might be heading once more east, so further and further into the unknown.

Splashing began ahead as the stream grew more shallow. It would seem Kofi now walked as we did. My boots were almost rotted on my feet, and I wondered at how I would replace them to go overland. Perhaps bindings cut from my jerkin would serve.

The trees here were of a species which grew thickly along waterways. They arched over our heads, meeting in a canopy which, while it did not shut out all light, kept away the sun. Within that tenting floated wisps of the haze I had seen from the survey point back in the hills.

"Good!" Orsya broke the quiet for the first time since we had left the main river. "Our thanks must be to Kofi."

Her ejaculation appeared to be caused by the rise of a humpbacked hillock in the midst of the stream. It was, in spite of the brush growth rooted on it, too symmetrical to be a product of nature. My companion identified it.

"Aspt house, and very large. We shall find an entrance along the bank. The stream must have shrunk much since this was built and abandoned."

A branch waved vigorously at the bank, not pulled by any wind. Orsya laughed.

"We see, Kofi. Thanks to you again," and then she twittered.

There was a hole there. I pulled out a tangle of roots and some stones before we could crawl within, to find ourselves in a very darkish chamber like the one where Orsya had tended my wound. Luckily there were holes in the roof, where portions of the covering had fallen away, so that I was not moving blind. Our guide had led us well; we could not have found a more snug or safe place in which to spend the fast approaching night.

A small pattering noise drew my attention to the opposite side of the chamber. Nothing—or did Kofi now share our quarters?

"Right!" Orsya answered my thoughts. "I wonder . . . yes, let us try."

She edged around behind me and leaned forward to place her two hands on my forehead just above my eyes. "Watch," she ordered, "and tell me if you now see aught."

I blinked and then blinked again. A wisp of mist against the dusk? No, it was not the floating mist which had found its way inside, rather it was a shape taking form. So, I saw Kofi.

He was small, about as tall as my mid-thigh. Unlike the aspts, he was humanoid in form. That is, he had four limbs, of which the upper two appeared to function as arms. He was like, yet unlike, the lizard folk of the Valley. Though his skin was scaled, his feet and hands were webbed as Orsya's, the webs extending close to the tips of the digits. His head was round, and seemed to have very little neck. Front and back his body was covered by a shell which was shaped in a wedge, wide at the top, narrowing to a point between his legs. When I turned my attention on him, his head snapped down into the shoulder part of that shield, so that only the snout and two eyes could be seen.

"Kofi." Orsya took away her hand and there was nothing to be seen.

I put out my right hand in the universal peace sign, holding it palm up and empty. For want of better reassurance to this strange water person I gave the formal greeting of the overmountain men.

"To Kofi of the river, greeting and peace from Kemoc Tregarth."

There was another faint sound. Then, for an instant, on the thick scar of my wound ridge I felt a delicate touch, as if one of those webbed hands had rested there in acknowledgment of understanding that I meant well and was no unfriend.

Orsya opened her net and divided the roots she had harvested along the river, setting aside a half dozen of them. We ate, but Kofi did not share; I asked why.

"He has gone hunting. He will hunt for more than that to fill his middle, for he will bring us news of aught which comes near this clean place."

She gathered up the roots she had put aside and said: "Put these in your belt pouch, Kemoc. They will furnish food when you may need it. This is truly a land where you must heed Dahaun's warning, and eat not, even when it might seem that you look upon food you know well. Now, let us rest. With the morning may come great demands upon us."

Whether Kofi came back to share our shelter, I do not know. But this night I did not sleep sound. There was an abiding sense of something lurking just beyond the borders of what I could see. Whether it was aware of me and waiting to attack, of that I was not sure. In fact, perhaps I would have been less uneasy has I been certain *that* was so.

Orsya appeared no better at resting than I. I heard her stirring about. Then I saw a faint white spark and guessed that she had once more set up the cone-rod and with it wrought such protective magic as she knew.

We were both up and eager to go when the first gray of dawn lit up the deserted house. She had once more wound Kaththea's scarf about the horn, and she tried to impart to that tie with my sister some virtue of her talisman.

"Kofi?" I looked to her for enlightenment.

"Waits us outside."

"We came into a thick mist curtain. There was a splash in the reeds and Orsya turned her head to twitter. She listened and then looked to me.

"The Tower lies ahead. But you must leave the waterways to reach it and Kofi says it is spell-guarded. Most of the garrison who were once there have been sent away, and it is no longer warrior held, but protected in other ways. We can go with you to the beginning of the climb, but beyond that . . ." She shook her head. "Land for the Merfays is less hospitable even that it is for me. Without water I am only a burden. But what I can give you, I shall."

Once more the unseen Merfay splashed ahead of us. The mist was so thick that we were only shadows to one another as we moved. But the stream made a road we could not wander from. However, if this fog continued to hold elsewhere I did not see how I could find the Tower.

"Did I not say that this, and your heart"—Orsya held up an end of the scarf—"would be your guide? Wait and see before you despair."

Loskeetha's prophecies of death and disaster at the Tower . . . Perhaps I had escaped the third fate of the Valley meeting, but there remained the other two.

"No!" Orsya's thought struck sharply, to clash with those in my head. "Believe that you have no foreseen future, that you can control fate. Listen; if all else fails, and it seems that you have indeed to face what Loskeetha read in her sand, then—use the *words* which brought that *answer*. You can do no worse ill than Loskeetha showed you, and you may break fate by matching one power against another. It is a fearsome thing, but in times of great peril men will call upon any weapon."

The mist-filled world through which we moved held no sense of time. It was day because of the light, but how long since we had left our night's lodging, I could not tell. I was aware that the stream grew shallow, and that more and more reefs of rock broke it.

Orsya halted on one of these. "This is our parting place, Kemoc. Now—"

Slowly she unwound the scarf from the horn. Her mind was abruptly closed to me, but I think she was rapt for those moments in her own use of power, pouring into the scarf what she could to strengthen the tie between it and she who had once worn it. For a very long time it lay across her knees, with her hands—still holding the horn, as one might cup a lighted candle—resting on the bedraggled green stuff. Orsya's lips moved; she might have been chanting, without voicing aloud the words.

Then she made a scooping motion with the horn, caught its tip under the fabric and so flipped it over to me.

"What I can do, I have done. Think on your Kaththea, and see what comes of it. Remember, it must be the Kaththea with whom you were the most closely tied, even if she lives now only in the past."

I took up the length which was no longer whole, nor as bright in color as it had been when I had found it in the stone forest. I gathered it tightly in my closed fists while I did as she bade, or tried to.

How far back was the Kaththea with whom Kyllan and I had been truly one? Not in the Valley, nor during our journey into Escore, nor in those years when she had been in the Secret Place of the Wise Women, while Kyllan and I had plied our sword trade on the borders. So year by year I slipped back in time until I came to those days when we had been at Etsford, children still, when my mother had come riding with a stricken heart because Simon Tregarth, her lord, had vanished, no man knowing where, save that the sea had taken him.

Then we had been indeed one. I dragged from that well of memory the Kaththea I had known in those days before the discipline of the Wise Women had tried to mold her into their accepted image.

How true was my remembering I did not know, but that it was the way she seemed to me then, of that I was sure. I built her picture in my mind as vividly as I could. That was Kaththea who was the third part of something greater than any one of us. Kaththea to whom I was tied past any breaking of bonds.

Then the silken stuff I prisoned in my hand seemed to fight against the pressure of my fingers. I released it and a green rope coiled upward, swung down to the ground.

This time it did not form a loop, but writhed as might a snake across the rock.

So intent was I upon following it that it was not until later I realized I had said no farewell to Orsya, nor was I even sure I could find again that reef-ridge in the stream where I had left her. But I knew without being told that if I allowed other thoughts to distract me from the re-membered image of Kaththea I would lose this guide.

I climbed the bank, giving my green ribbon full atten-tion. Above the cut of the stream the mist thinned. For a space there was good and wholesome foliage about me, as there had been all along the waterway. But that began to grow sparser. Then came herbage of another kind of which had the noxious look of evil growth. I had taken time by the stream to reinforce my boots with strips cut from my jerkin, and now my upper body was bare to the chill which lingered over the land.

On wriggled the scarf and I followed. The ground rose steadily, but as yet the slope was not difficult to breast. I kept the sword in my hand, looking now and then to it for the glowing of the danger runes.

Orsya had masked us in illusion. That would not hold for me alone. But as yet the land seemed deserted; that in itself struck me as strange and sinister, as if I walked now into a trap, my way made easy until the lock of the cage clicked behind me.

Up and up, and colder the air I shivered in. Kaththea ... I sought Kaththea. She was to me as a missing arm, a part lopped off to leave me crippled.

Then the sword blazed scarlet. Someone came running lightly through the last tatters of the mist. She whom I sought! But the sword was red—

"Brother!" Her hands reached for mine.

There had been another Kaththea who was illusion,

who had almost tricked me once, in the garden of the Secret Place.

Or was this such a future as Loskeetha had seen. If I turned steel against this smiling girl, would my sister's blood flow over it?

Trust to the sword, Orsya had said. *Fair is foul . . .* if it says so.

"Kemoc!" Hands out . . . then that green ribbon flowed across the rock. She gave a croaking cry which could never rightfully burst from any human throat, as if that silken thing was a poisonous reptile. And I struck.

Blood fountained up to bathe the blade, showered in crimson drops over my hand. Where those drops touched my skin, fire ate. What lay writhing on the ground was a thing out of deep nightmare. It died still trying to reach me with great grasping claws.

Did he who ruled the Dark Tower know that I came? Or was the form this guard had used to mask its evil lifted just now from my mind? For the Kaththea who had run to meet me was the youthful Kaththea I thought on. I thrust the sword into the sand, whipping it back and forth to cleanse it of the smoking blood. The drops I smeared from my hand left blisters rising on the skin. Then I hurried to catch up with the green ribbon which had not paused.

It dropped over a bank into a road, rutted by use, and that not too long ago. To my unease the ribbon wriggled now in one of those ruts. But there was naught I could do, save follow, even though such a path must lead me directly to whatever guards Dinzil would have placed here.

Towering rocks walled in this way and, as it had been in the road away from Loskeetha, it seemed that things slid to peer, leer, threaten under the surface of the stone, to be sighted from the corners of one's eyes, to vanish when one looked directly.

I heard weeping as a low wail such as the wind might make, but it grew louder as I went. From the top of a rise I looked down into a cup, from which the road went up again on the far side. In that hollow was a woman of the Green People, her clothing rent from her, her bruised body lashed across a rock so that her spine was arched at a painful angle. She wailed and then babbled as might one who had passed too far the threshold of pain and terror.

The sword flamed—

Too good a touchstone was that for Dinzil's traps, or those I had met so far. It would be easy to pass this counterfeit of his devising, yet to leave a live enemy at my back—that was folly. So persuasive was the illusion that I had to force my hand to the use of the warning sword.

The woman vanished as blood ran. There was a man in her place, choking in death. Man? He had a human body, and human features, but what I saw in the hate-filled eyes he turned upon me, what he screamed as he died—those were not of mankind.

A dead monster, a dead seeming-man. Did Dinzil know when they died? Did I so alert him against my coming?

I pulled up to the top of the rise beyond the cup and saw it.

This was the Dark Tower of Loskeetha's pictures. I hesitated; two visions she had shown me. In one I would meet with some bewilderment before I reached the Tower and, during that, cut down Kaththea. Therefore, beware; watch for any troubling. . . .

The green ribbon flowed on to where that black finger

pointed as if in defiance to the sky.

It was in truth, a dark tower. The stone of its walls was black; it had about it that suggestion of terrible age which was in Es City, in some of the places where the Wise Women carried out their sorceries. As if not only the years men knew had passed over it, but another withering and aging which was not of our reckoning.

There were no breaks in its surface, no sign of door or window. It stood on a mound covered with a thick growth of short grass, a gray grass. The road I followed ran only to the foot of that mound. There had been traffic on that road, yet those who used it might well have leaped forth from the ground at that spot; there were no signs they had ever passed over the grass.

I went forward slowly, alert always to any hint that Loskeetha's prophecy was about to be fulfilled. When I reached the mound I breathed easier. Two of her pictures had I now defeated, that of the Valley, and the fight before the Tower.

The scarf had paused before the mound side. One end of it arose to wave in the air, back and forth, as if it would climb that rise but dared not rest upon the grass. I saw that the runes were red when I pointed the sword at that slope.

I touched the scarf with the sword and was amazed as straightway the silk wreathed itself about the length of golden metal, writhed up over it to my arm, and there wrapped itself around and around flesh and muscle. There was a warmth to it which spread over my shoulder into the rest of my body.

But I was no nearer my goal, the interior of the Tower. Now I put the thought of Kaththea to the back of my mind while I considered the problem immediately before me. There was a spell here to which I had no key.

Or did I? There was one mentioned in old legends, but it was danger above danger to use it in such a place. For, while it opened the doors of the Shadow, or was said to do so, it also threw away some of the defenses of him who used it, rendering him easy prey.

How much can one trust legends? Since we had come into the fields of Esocre, we had come to believe that there was more truth than fantasy in the tales of Estcarp. I could take this road, knowing I had thrown away some shields, and prove whether or not this particular story was also true.

To linger here, hoping for blind chance to perhaps throw me a favor, was folly. I had no other key, so let me turn this one.

I set off to walk around that mound and Tower widdershuns, against the light of the sun, open-eyed into the ways of those who served the Shadow. If I did it with my teeth set, my hand locked upon sword hilt, that was only return for the danger I was sure I faced.

Three, seven, nine, those are the numbers which have power in them. One of those three I was sure I must use now. Three times I walked that ringing, from the road's end to the road's end. Nothing happened.

Four times more I made that journey. The warmth from the scarf was in me; the sword showed the only danger was on the mound.

Three and seven had not availed me; now I must try nine. When I came to the road's end for the ninth time, there was at last an answer. The grass vanished in a shifting the eye could not follow. My door was open and it led, not to the tower above, but into the mound on which that sat. An open door in which no guardian stood —who knew what waited inside?

Holding the sword before me, fully expecting to see it burst into fiery runes, I advanced step by cautious step. But the warning I thought to see did not come. Before me was a passage with unbroken walls having a cold gray glimmer. That passage ran on and on.

I walked, my eyes going from wall to sword, to wall again, seeking a door, a stair, some way into the tower above. While there was none of that shifting movement under the surface here, as there had been on the rocks without, still there was an odd, distracting distortion when one looked too long at those walls, a queer sickening feeling.

How long did that passage run? It seemed to me that I had traveled leagues and that I ached with weariness, yet dared not vary my pace nor sit to rest in such a place. At last there was an archway and through it I came into a round room which might indeed have marked the foundation of the tower. There were other doors here, set about the walls, so that if similar passages to that I had followed ran from them, they would be spoked as a wheel. But there were no stairs, no way aloft.

I moved about that round chamber, trying each door. They had neither handles nor latches; not one gave, even when I put my shoulder to them in full strength. There was only the road I had come from.

Then I went to the middle of the room. I could retreat without accomplishing anything. So far Loskeetha's third future had not materialized. There was no sign of Kaththea, nor of any shadow form to which she could betray me.

Kaththea! I laid my left hand over the binding of the scarf about my upper arm. Into my mind I resummoned the memory of Kaththea. Under my touch the tie stirred, began to unwind. I withdrew my fingers but continued to remember. The ribbon length crept down, wreathing about the sword to reach the pavement.

XIV

I had expected my silken guide to seek out one of those barred doors. Instead it drew in tight coils to the mid-point of the chamber, almost at my feet, and one end pointed up, to the roof. I leaned back, but to my eyes there was no hint of any opening there.

Illusion? This was a place in which illusion was a weapon. What was the answer to illusion? Suddenly I thought of those scraps netted in Lormt. To use counter-magic here was to open my defenses further, yet there was nothing else I could do. The sword was an emblem of power; how much power, I could not guess. But it would provide, or I hoped it would, the spark I needed. I closed my eyes and held the sword high, pressing its blade to my face, so that I felt the metal touch my eye-lids.

I did not say those ancieent words aloud in this place, rather I thought them slowly, picturing them in my mind as I had seen them on that crumpled, time worn parchment.

Three there were, and then three more. Then after them the mind picture of a certain symbol. I put down the sword and opened my eyes, to see how well I had wrought.

There was a stair before me, a ladder of stone blocks.

Up it went the scarf. So . . . by this much had my learning worked; I had my door into the Dark Tower. I began to climb, watching the sword for warning of ill to come. But, as in the passage and the room below, there was no sign of glowing runes.

Up and up went that steep stair. Though I had seen a ceiling over my head when I stood below, yet now it seemed that that was also an illusion: that there were no floors above, only this stair leading up and up.

Though I could see the stone steps immediately before me, farther ahead they were concealed by a shifting. Fearing giddiness on such a steep perch, I dared not watch them.

The scarf continued to rise confidently ahead. Around the stair there was a sense of open space in which that core of stone ladder was the only secure thing. Thus I could look neither to left nor right, lest light-headedness assault me.

Under my breath I muttered some of those words of power. The sensation that I might lose my balance at every step and go spinning off one side or the other, into that nothingness, grew stronger, until it was close to torment.

But there did come at last an end to the stair. I emerged through a well opening, to stand in a circular chamber, not unlike the one in which the stair was rooted, save that it was smaller. The scarf coiled there, one end aloft like the head of a reptile, weaving back and forth.

There were doorways here, also, but these portals were open, with no locked barriers. Only, each of them opened upon nothingness! Not fog, nor mist, but upon open space. When I had glanced at them I sat down on the floor, my sword across my knees, unable to move because of the panic which comes to all of us with a dream of falling. For those doorways drew, beckoned, and I was afraid as I had never been before.

What kind of a place that was I did not know. But that it was an entrance way into areas where my kind was not meant to venture, of that I was convinced. Yet the scarf brought me here.

Kaththea! I closed my eyes, fastened my will upon a mind picture, put my desire into it. Then I opened my eyes again. The scarf—it was no longer coiled—moved toward one of those portals open upon nothingness.

I thought this was another illusion, that the scarf had at last betrayed me, and once more I applied the ritual which had freed my sight below. I raised the sword to my eyes and repeated the potent charm.

When I looked again, there was no change. The scarf was coiled before the doorway directly before me; it fluttered one end up and down as it had when it had come to the mound and dared not touch the evil grass there.

I could not get to my feet, so little did I now trust my sense of balance. I crawled on hands and knees, pushing the sword before me. Then I was behind that questing scarf facing nothingness. In that moment I almost broke, being sure that it was not in me to go through that door into whatever lay beyond.

My hand went out and fell upon the scarf and once more that wreathed about my hand and wrist, moved up my arm. In my despair I voiced a call:

"Kaththea!"

As I had set my will on the scarf, so did I now bend it. I had used mind touch all my life, but this time I put into it all my energy. The effort left me weak and gasping, as if I had run clad in full mail to the top of a hill and then plunged at once into fierce swordplay.

I lay flat upon the floor of that chamber, my forehead

on the blade of the sword. Perhaps it was the virtue in that which helped me now. For faint, very faint, and from far off, came an answer:

"*Kemoc?*" No louder than a sigh. Yet it was an answer, and there could be no illusion in it.

So . . . she still lived, even though she might be pent in this place. To reach her I must—*must*—go through that door. In that moment I was not sure I could force myself to do so.

What had I to serve me? The scarf which Orsya had bespelled for me, the sword which had not been forged by my race, some words which might summon help, or call down doom. . . . I was a blind man, wandering unguided.

I began to crawl; it was beyond my strength to stand erect and march as a man should. As I crawled part of me, deep inside, shrieked and struggled against such folly, such willed self-destruction. For it hammered in my brain that to go into such a place without mighty protection was advancing to certain death, and not only that of the body.

Now that I was on the very threshold of that doorway, I had to shut my eyes. To look upon that nothingness churned all the thoughts in a man's brain and made him mad.

My will gave me the last thrust through—over—

This was the old nightmare—falling, falling, falling . . .

Not only my thoughts were twisted—pain—such agony as a man cannot bear, I felt. Yet I did not escape into unconsciousness—I fell—and felt.

I was no man now, only a thing which cried, screamed, whimpered, suffered.

Color, burst of wild color— What was color?

Crawling . . . across a flat surface. Great sweeps of that

raw, eye-hurting color bursting in explosive action from surface to over head. A dull drone of noise . . . crawl . . .

My eyes were full of tears; they were also full of fire which burnt back into my head.

MY? Who was *my*? What was my?

Crawl on . . . keep moving. Shut eyes against another violent blast of flaming color. Do not cease to crawl— Why?

It is hard to put into words what possessed that "my" in that time. I cannot tell how long it took for a small sense of identity to seep back to that thing which crawled, wept, flinched from every burst of the earth-sky flames. But come it did—first as dim questions, then as fragmentary answers.

There came a time when I stopped crawling, looking with my watering eyes at what had become my body. I was not—a man!

Green-gray, warty hide with straggling patches of hair-fine tendrils of flesh growing out of it. My hands were paws, webbed, thickened; my feet like them. I tried to straighten my back, found that my head was set forward between high, hunched shoulders. But around my right arm was wound a strip of green flame—flame? Slowly I raised one of those misshapen paws and touched it. It had no substance, being a mist, into which my paw sank.

But that movement, the sight of the band, awoke in me a greater stirring of memory. Scarf— But there had been something else—a sword! The word slipping into my sluggish mind acted as a key to turn a lock, open a coffer from which flooded full memory.

The sword! I looked about me frantically; I dared not lose the sword!

There was no sword. But on the ground before me, that stony surface splotched with searing color, was a shaft of golden light. As did the green mist about my arm, it too soothed my irritated eyes. I reached for it. Again my paw sank into light and fear struck at me. I could no longer hold it!

But I must! I opened and closed that paw as best I could. It swept back and forth through the shaft of light, grasping nothing. I pounded my paws on the rocky floor in fear and rage. Pain came from that. A thick, greenish fluid oozed from the bruises. I folded them against the distorted barrel which was now my chest and rocked back and forth, moaning with a mouth I could guess was of no human shape.

How had that shaft come here? I had been crawling when my wits began to return to me. I had not carried the sword, yet there it lay. Therefore it had somehow come with me, though I had not borne it.

I rubbed the back of the warty paw across my face to clear away the sticky tears, shrinking from that touch of unwholesome flesh against flesh. There was one way to learn how that shaft had come with me, and that was to travel on and see what happened. But not crawling—no! This hideous form which I looked upon was not my own, though I seemed now to inhabit it. But I was a man, and as a man I would now go to meet the unknown on my feet—so much had resolution returned to me.

But to get onto those paw feet and then balance erect was a labor which seemed almost beyond my determination to accomplish. My hunched back pushed my torso so far forward that I was top-heavy. I could not screw up my head to see more than a few steps ahead. I tried to learn more of this body. The hunched back, the thick shoulders tapered to abnormally slender loins and legs. Cautiously I raised a paw to touch my face, almost afraid of what that examination would tell me. My mouth appeared to be a wide gash with little lip, in it teeth which were sharply pointed fangs.

My nose had ceased to exist; in its place was a single gash which served as a nostril. There was no hair on my head, but a ragged growth of flesh stretched from ear to ear in a quivering band. The ears were very large, though lobeless. In truth, I was such a monster as to send any but the stoutest of heart screaming from a first meeting.

Flinging out my arms to balance the top-heavy weight of flesh and bone, I took one unsteady step and then another, as one who walks a narrow and perilous bridge above a gulf. The shaft of light moved, always the same distance ahead of my tottering advance.

Heartened by that, for I thought that the sword, even in this strange new form, was the best talisman I could have, I practiced walking. I discovered that a slow shuffle would carry me along.

Along—where?

I had come into this hellish place seeking Kaththea. Kaththea! Glancing down at the loathsome body I now had, I recoiled from the thought that it if had fared so with me, then it must also have been with my sister. Where was this place? Surely far outside the boundaries laid upon any normal world known to human kind.

If the Dark Tower guarded a gate, and it would appear that was so, I did not believe that Dinzil had meant for Kaththea never to return. Loskeetha had said Dinzil looked upon Kaththea as a means of gaining mastery over new forces. He would not willingly lose such a key.

If he had not taken steps from which there was no retreat.

I paused, strained to lift my monster head the higher in order to see what might lie ahead. There was no horizon in this place, nothing but the eternal explosions of color and the hard ground over which I moved so slowly.

The colors . . . perhaps I was growing more accustomed to them. My eyes did not water so much, neither was the pain so sharp when I looked about me. I began to count and found they followed a pattern. The pattern they followed was the old one: three, seven, nine. Not only could I count that between bursts, but certain colors showed in flashes of the same grouping. Thus what abode here was in tune to a power.

But I must have a guide.

"Kaththea!"

Just as once I had seen certain *words* take shape and fly visibly before me, so now in this place I saw my sister's name do likewise. Brightly green as the scarf which was now a ring of light, it took wing, speeding to the right of my path.

I shuffled to follow it. Then it was hidden in a burst of purple fire, a fountain of angry crimson.

"Kaththea!"

Another bird-thought skimming ahead. Under my feet the gold of the sword moved with me. I put my hand-paw once more to the band of the scarf.

"Kaththea!"

Bird-thoughts flying, if they only would continue to lead me! Yet she did not answer, and I could only trust that what I followed was the truth and not bait for a trap.

I saw nothing but the springing flashes, the ground under my feet, until, when a spout of dark blue shot high, I sighted a massive bulk a little to the left of the path the winged thoughts set me.

It was a sullen crimson in color, its hue not affected by the constant play of contrasting shades. I thought it first a rocky outcrop, and then some very rudely wrought and ancient statue.

It crouched upon wide haunches, its hands upon the ground on either side just beyond the upjutting of its knees, its head turned a little to watch in the direction my thoughts flew. It was obscenely female, huge pendulous breasts flowing over its knees. But the face was unfinished—there was no mouth, no nose, only pits for eyes. From those pits flowed steadily two streams of darker red, like unto blood, which dripped and stained the rest of its body. In size it was twice, three times, that of the body I now wore. From it spread such a dampening of the spirit that I nearly wilted under that blow, which was not to the body, but the soul.

Whatever it might once have been, it was now a prisoner, and the agony of its spirit was a shadow over the land on which it crouched. I shuddered away from it, yet did I turn twice to look back. Monstrous though it was, it stirred my pity

The last time I turned, I forced up one of my paws. I tried to mouth aloud what I would say. But human words could not be shaped by the guise I wore. So I thought, the very old words which we had used many times along the border, to wish to rest those who had been shield mates and sword brothers in our company. For I knew no other comfort for the suffering spirit.

"Earth take that which is of earth. Water, accept that of water, and that which is now freed, let it *be* free, to follow the High Path—Sytry willing—"

Those last two words, they were not of my belief. But I had only a moment to think that. For once more I saw thoughts speed through the air, not green this time, but golden, the golden of the sword. They flew to that crouching red thing which wept blood. Then they were gone as if they had entered it, some in the featureless head, some in the body.

There was no sound, only a wave of feeling. But I was buffeted by it to the ground as a man may be beaten down by a storm of great force. I lay under it, fighting to hold my own identity intact. Then it was gone, and I pulled once more to my hands and knees. That what had wept was crumbling, falling apart, as unbaked clay will yield to water. Swiftly it went, until there was nothing left but a heaped pile of red dust.

Shaking, I got clumsily to my feet. Something lay there. Startled, I saw that the light which had traveled with me had taken on a more substantial form. Once again it had the outline of a sword. When I went painfully back down on one knee to grasp it, I discovered that, while I could move it a little way, I still could not pick it up.

Once more I stood as erect as I could, for the first time becoming aware of another change. There was an alteration in the feeling of this land, a kind of troubling. I began to wonder if, in my pity, I had not done something which would bring on me such notice as no traveler here would care to court.

"Kaktheal"

I sent the thought and tried to speed the pace of my shuffle, also puzzling as to why my sword had changed.

Sytry willing— The words I had used from no memory of my own. Further back, when I had fought the monster in the underground channel—what had I called on? Sytry! Was it a *name* or a *word* of power? there was a way to test that. I came to a stop, staring down at that gold shaftblade.

In the name of Sytry! I thought. *Be you again a weapon to my hand, a thing of power!*

There was no buffeting wind of emotion this time. Rather a trembling which shook my body as if some invisible thing shook me to and fro. A flash of light exploded, to dance wildly along the length of the sword, making it blaze until I shut my eyes and uttered a beastly kind of mewling sound. But when I forced them open again—

The sword—no light beam now—but seemingly a weapon as complete and concrete as that which I had carried out of the tomb. I was on my knees where that shaking fit had left me; for the third time I reached for the hilt. It was hard to flex my paw about it, yet I did so. From that grip a new kind of strength flowed up my arm into me.

Who was Sytry? Or what? In this place it had some governance. Would it also restore my own form so that I could go into battle, if need be, as one in his proper body?

In the Name of Sytry, I tried that thought, *let me be as the man I was*—

I waited for that shaking, for some sign that the spell would work again. But nothing came; I did not alter. Then I got wearily to my feet. The sword was a thing of Sytry; I was not. I should not have hoped it would be so.

"Kaththea!"

Once more I loosed the winged thought and continued on this endless journey across space, bound by no dimensions known to me. Though my shuffle was hardly more than a painful hobble, I did make progress. Some time later I saw looming in the flashes of color something else above the surface of the plain. This was no giant hunched figure but a band of light which did not leap

188

and die, but was constant. Great gems cut in facets to reflect might have looked so, for these were diamond shaped, one narrow point rooted in the ground. Again the system of numbering prevailed—three yellow, seven purple, nine red—making a wall to rise well above my bowed head.

Yet my thoughts sped over that wall; for whom I sought must be behind it. I came to it, moved right for many steps, and then went in the opposite direction. Both ways the wall continued on and on as far as I could see. There was no climbing it, for the surface was slick; there was nothing for my poorly coordinated paws to cling to.

I squatted down before one of the red stones, my weariness a great aching in my bones. It would seem I had come to the end of my journey. As I sat there, I slid the flat of my paw back and forth across the blade of the sword. No runes blazed there; it was as if they had never been. The metal was cool, somehow reassuring. I continued to finger it as I stared at the stones.

The narrow points . . . how were they based? Set immovable in the surface of this land? Now on my hands and knees I crawled to the place where I could examine the setting carefully. Yes, the wall was not an integral part of the ground; there was a thin line. To me that seemed the only part to attack.

My only tool was the sword. Almost I feared to put it to such a test. To break the blade—what would I have left? On the other hand, what would an intact sword profit me if this was indeed the end of my quest?

My clumsy movements made it a far harder business than was necessary, as I began to pick and dig with the point at that juncture between the red stone and the ground. I tried to search my memory for anything out of Lormt which might now lend me strength, either of arm or purpose. But to think of Lormt was also a struggle, and when I did so, my arm grew weary at once and I missed my aim.

Lormt, then, was no aid. What of Sytry?

For the first time the sword hit true, just where I had wished to aim it!

"By the power of Sytry, under the Name of Sytry." I paused and then experimented. Three times I repeated that name in my mind and then gave a thanks word, seven times, and again thanks, and at last nine times—

The sword was out of my awkward grasp. It stood erect at an angle, to work in sharp picks and jabs as I wanted. There was a humming along the gem wall, a buzzing—it filled my head. I raised my paws to my ears, tried to blanket out that sound. Still the sword worked on.

Now small fragments, chips of red glitter, flew splinter-like to the ground. Some of them cut my warty hide. Yet I dared not take my paws from my ears to shield myself. The sword moved faster, a blur of light. Sometimes in my teary sight it was no longer a sword but a dart of pure force.

The tall stone shivered, trembled. Now the sword rose in the air, turned to a horizontal position and launched itself straight at the side of the diamond about halfway up. The stone cracked at impact, crashed down into crimson shards. The splintering spread to its two neighbors, so they, too, fell apart in a rain of vicious fragments. Along that wall the breakage continued to spread.

I did not wait to see how far it would carry. I got to my feet and held out my right paw. Back through the air swung the sword, to fit itself there securely. Then, wincing at the cuts that carpet gave me, I crossed the broken barrier into a vastly different place.

Alien had been the world of color: This had a superficial resemblance to the lands I knew. At first I thought that perhaps I had been returned to Escore. Before me ran a road among rocks, and down this road I had gone trailing behind a green scarf which moved, a ribbon-serpent, to the Dark Tower.

As I stepped onto that rutted way I saw that any resemblance was indeed only superficial, since there was no stability to anything there. Rocks melted into ground and grew again in another place. The road flowed and I struggled through it knee-deep, as I had walked streams with Orsya. Those things I had sensed being below the surface of rocks, now showed themselves plainly, so I must keep my eyes from looking at them or be lost in madness.

There was only one stable thing in all this—the sword. When I looked upon it for a space and then to what lay before me, that too was solid, had some security, if only for a small fraction of time.

I came to a dip which had been the dell in which I slew the guard. But this brimmed with a bubbling, stinking stuff which might be poisonous mud. There was no way for me to go except down into it.

XV

Bubbles rose to the surface of that slime pit and burst, releasing fetid puffs of gas. Swim? Could I put this twisted body of mine to such effort? I tried with my teary eyes to discover footing which might lie either to the left or the right. But in both directions was only that shifting which was so confusing; I quickly looked away.

If I were to go it must be by this road. Once more I put my paw to the scarf about my warty skin. Then I gripped the sword as tightly as I could and went down into that mass of half liquid corruption. It was too thick for swimming. I sank into it slowly, though I flailed with my arms, kicked those weaker legs and feet.

I was not engulfed as I had feared. My desperate struggles brought me some progress, though it was so slow! The sickening fumes made my head light, kept the tears flowing from my eyes.

It was a little time before I noticed that where the sword rested a path opened through the stuff. Once aware of that I applied the blade with cutting strokes, carving a slit through it.

At long last there was a rock ledge facing me and I pulled out on stable land, though the mess sucked avidly at my body as if it would not let me go. I had to turn and cut with what strength I could still muster to free myself.

Then I lay full length on that rock, breathing in great gasps, even though the major part of each breath I drew was the foul gas from the bubbles. Up . . . an inner warning pricked at me . . . up and away.

Once more I was reduced to crawling, leaving smears from my caked body on the rock. Up . . . still that inner urge was a lash, growing in intensity.

I heard a sound from the morass behind, louder than the bursting of those bubbles, more akin to the sucking which had come from my own struggles. My paws gripped again and pulled feebly, bringing up the weight of my heavy body. The sword I held between my fangs, cutting my lips when I moved them incautiously, but in such safety as I could devise.

The sucking sound was closer, but I could not yet turn my head. Fear lent the last impetus to reach the top of the rise, to drag myself along the lip. Then, somehow, I hunched to my knees, swung my body around.

They were coming through the muck with a speed I could not equal. There were two of them and—

Spent with my efforts to reach this point I could not get to my feet unaided. But I wriggled to one of the stones and with its help was somehow erect again, my back against it, facing those things.

They were gray and warty of skin; they had heavy arms and thick shoulders, toad faces (though the mouths were fanged). Ridges of ragged flesh arose across their skulls from one great ear to the other. These were kinsmen of the body I inhabited!

Their gashes of mouths opened as they yammered in no understandable speech. Each carried in his hand an ax, as mighty of blade as that of Volt which I had seen often in Koris' keeping, but far shorter of haft. It was plain they were hunting me.

There was no running from this, nor would I, I believe, even if I could force my weary body to the effort. The axes resembled those used by Sulcar borderers, which could be used either as a hand weapon, or to be thrown from a distance, with fatal results if the axman was expert. Whether these toadmen were, I did not know. But in such cases it is always best to give high credit to your foe's fighting prowess rather than underrate him.

I had the sword and for that to be effective I must wait until they were closer. If they were going to throw those axes, I did not believe it was possible for them to do so while they pushed through the mud. If I retreated no farther from the rim, I could dispute their landing, giving me one small advantage.

But I was so slow of body, so worn from my push through that fetid hole, that I could not move fast. I might not even leave the support of the rock against which I had set my back. When I brought up my sword in a swing meant to suggest defense, my arm answered my will so reluctantly that I felt this was indeed a fight already decided in favor of the enemy.

"Sytry!" I tried to raise the hilt to the level of my lips, the point thrusting at whatever sky this space owned. "Steel, I hold by that Name, battle I do, in that Name. Whatever favor cometh from powers I know not, yet are of the White and not the Shadow, let it rest upon me now! For I have that to do which has not been done, and there is yet a road before me—" A jumble of thoughts, ill chosen, but in that moment the most I could muster to express a plea of which I was not sure anyone, or anything, would heed.

If I could have taken only two steps forward, thrust while they were still scrambling up out of the mud, then I would have had a small advantage. But I knew that effort was not in me. Take those two steps and I would not meet them on my feet, but groveling before them, my neck bent and ready for the fall of their axes.

They must have believed me easy prey, or else they were so slow of wit that they knew only one method of attack and that a forward run, weapons aloft, yammering out what might have been war cries. I tried to swing the sword as I would have done had I had my normal body.

Its hilt loosened in my hold, spun out of my grasp, and hurled on through the air. Once more it no longer appeared a sword, but rather a flash of golden light. So swift was its passage that my eyes could not follow it, to see what it wrought in my defense. What I afterwards witnessed were wounds gaping beneath the lower jaws of the toadmen, pumping forth purplish liquid; saw them stumble and sprawl forward, sliding across the stone, their axes, falling from paws suddenly lax, striking ringingly, while I cowered back against my support, gaping foolishly.

There was another ring, louder than the axes had made, almost bell-like in tone. The sword lay there, no longer a flashing fury of destruction. I pushed away from my support, tottered to it. But the effort of stooping to pick it up made me topple and fall in turn. For a moment or two I lay there, the steel of the blade under my body. From its touch against my noisome skin spread, first a kind of warmth and then, following that, a renewal of strength. So heartened I braced myself up on my forepaws.

Where the bodies of the toadmen had lain puffed a shimmering fog of blackish motes, as soot might rise from the disturbance of a place where many fires had burned and then been quenched. And, as soot, the particles settled again to the surface of the rock, ringing—

Not the toad bodies I had seen fall to the strokes of the sword, but two lighter frames, so close to skeletons that one could see the bones plainly through the too tightly stretched skin. These, in spite of the extreme emaciation, were those of normal human kind!

The strength which had come out of the blade was in me, so I got to my feet, shuffled through the black dust to the nearest of those skeleton-men. His features were very sharp in his skull face. Looking upon him I thought that once he must have been of the Old Race or kindred blood. Death had broken some ensorcelment and returned him to his true self. Death? I glanced down at my own paws, the warty skin on my arms. Was death the *only* way of return?

The skeleton was changing again, falling into dust, as had the weeping, female thing on the other side of the gem wall. The other followed it into nothingness.

I turned my back on them as quickly as I could, faced in the other direction, to see as I expected that I would, the rise of a tower upon a mound, waiting for me even as its twin had before.

This one loomed very black and harsh, with more of a distinct outline and clarity of bulk than anything else I had seen in this eerie other world. The mound on which it was based was also dark.

Once more I walked the road into which my paw feet sank, and which was a river, but not of water. When I came to the foot of the mound there was no need to work any spell to open a door, for there it gaped, very black, already waiting. I thought "Kaththea!" to see it wing in before me, quickly vanishing in the gloom.

With the sword hilt grasped in both paws, I lumbered unsteadily on, past the portal of the mound, to enter this Dark Tower. Would it also have a staircase and doorways into more distorted worlds?

The black-dark which had seemed so thick when looking in from outside was here enlightened by a glimmer of yellowish-gray. I realized that was shed by my own body. By it I caught glimpses of floor and walls, all of huge blocks of black stone, close set. Again the walls ran without doors, to bring me into a circular room from which a stair climbed. But this was not shrouded in any spell, nor were there any other doors about that room.

My paw feet were not made for use on stairways. Once more I had to grip the sword between my teeth, go on all fours, aware that any side slip would send me crashing down upon the hard pavement below. So I went very slowly.

Then my head emerged into a lighter place, no hint of which had reached below that opening. It was as if I came into a place of ghosts. But they were not of things which had once lived and breathed. The thin, cloudy, half pictures I saw were of furnishings. There were chairs, a table which supported many jars, flasks, and tubing I did not understand. Against the walls were chests and cabinets with closed doors. All as insubstantial as river mist, yet plain to trace against the stone.

I put one paw to the edge of the table. It touched no surface, but passed easily through in a sweep which met no resistance.

There was another stairway leading aloft. This was not in the center of the room, but curled up against the wall. However it was stone and solid, not like the ghost furnishings. I shuffled to it. Since the incline here was not so steep, I managed to take it step by step, still standing, slipping my body painfully along the wall as far from the unguarded outer edge as I could get.

No sound; the tower was wrapped in silence. I tried not to make any noise, but in that I was not too successful. Even my heavy breathing stirred the air loudly enough, I feared, to alert any who walked sentry here.

There was another room above, and once more the dim, misty furnishings ringed me around. Here was a table with two chairs drawn up to it, and it was set as if for a meal. Mist goblets and plates at each place.

I swallowed. Since I had left Orsya—centuries ago—I had not eaten. Until I saw that table I had not thought of food. But now, in an instant, hunger was a pain in me. Where would I find food? What food did this toad body need for nourishment? Unwillingly I remembered those skeleton bodies. Had they gone famishing until their deaths?

There was some pretension in the furnishing of this chamber. Cobweb tapestry cloaked the walls. So thin was it, I could not detect any pattern. There were chests with the suggestion of carving on their fronts, the kind of work one might see in a manor house.

Once more another flight of stairs urged me up and on. Laboriously I climbed. Here the way was shut against me at the top by a trapdoor. I steadied my back as best I could against the wall, put the sword between my teeth, and pushed up against it with all the strength I could summon.

It yielded, rising, to fall back against the floor above with a crash which was doubly startling in the silence. I followed as quickly as I could, sure that must rouse any who sheltered here.

"Welcome—bold hero!"

I strained my head up and back on those crooked shoulders, trying to see.

Dinzil—yes, Dinzil!

But not in any disfiguring toad man disguise. He was as tall, as strong, as fair of face, as when I saw him last in the Valley. But added to that a vitality, as if in him some fire burned high, not consuming the flesh which held it, but giving an energy and force such as human kind did not know. To look upon him dazzled my eyes, and the tears dripped fast down my distorted jaws, but still I held that gaze. For hate can be a force to strengthen one, and I knew that all the hate that I had tasted before in my life was nothing to the emotion now in me.

He stood with his hands on his hips, and he was laughing—silently, his amusement a lash of contempt and scorn.

"Kemoc of Tregarth, one of the Three—I bid you welcome. Though it would seem that you have lost something, and gained something—not for the rest of your spirit, nor to delight the eyes of those—if there now are any—who look upon you with kindliness. Would you see what those would see? Behold!"

He clicked his lips and straightway there appeared before me a burnished surface on which was painfully clear what must be my reflection. But the shock was perhaps not what he had expected, since I had already known of my changed body. Perhaps my composure startled Dinzil a little, if he were still able to be touched by human emotions.

"They say," he smiled again, "there are places where what a man sees is not his outer form, but the inner; the thing he himself has fashioned through the years by his ill desires, his hidden lusts, the evil he has thought on doing but not had the courage to act upon. Do you recognize your inner self now—when it is turned to outer— Kemoc Tregarth, renegade from overmountain?"

I was past such needling.

Kaththea! I thought that not at him, but as I had before, sending it seeking. Here, what showed as that thought was no longer a bright green flying thing, but rather a bird sore hurt, fluttering, trying to reach a goal, but hindered from it.

I saw Dinzil turn his head, follow it. There was startlement in his eyes for an instant. He swept up his hand in a forbidding gesture and the thought-bird vanished. Now he looked to me again and he was no longer amused.

"It seems that I have underrated you, my misshapen hero. I will admit, I wondered how you could come this road without misstepping somewhere along the way. So you still have the power to find Kaththea, have you?" He appeared to think for a moment and then brought his hands together in a sharp clap, laughing once more.

"Very well. I have weaknesses; one of them is for heroes. Such constancy and devotion must be rewarded. Also, it will be amusing to see if your tie is strong enough to really show you Kaththea."

He said a *word*, raised both hands over his head and plunged them down. There was a whirling about me, with nothing to cling to—

We stood in the round chamber. On the floor lay the trapdoor I had pushed back. It was as it had been, save that all which had been ghostly was now solid. The tapestries on the wall were woven in time faded colors, but jewels and metallic threads gave them sparkling life. The chairs, a chest or two, were heavily carved and plainly old. Dinzil still fronted me and now he made mock reverence.

"Welcome, welcome. I would give you the guesting cup, my poor hero, but I fear what you would quaff from it in this place would be the death of you. And that is not my wish—not yet. But we tarry too long. You have not come a-guesting—have you?—but to see another."

He turned his head a little from me and I followed his glance. There was a small table and on either side of it stood a sconce as tall as a man, in which candles burned, with a mirror between. Before that mirror, as if someone sat there, a comb with a jeweled back moved slowly up and down, in the motions of one smoothing long, loose locks of hair. But that was all, just the moving comb.

I shuffled toward the mirror and table. My thought went out in a sharp call:

"Kaththea!"

Did she in truth sit there, unseen by me? Or was that moving comb but a trick Dinzil used for my torment?

In the glass I saw something. But it was my toad self pictured there, no reflection of the beauty which was my sister's.

The comb fell to the floor. There came out of nothingness such a scream of terror as I have never heard. Dinzil threw out his arms, folded them about something invisible to me.

Yet all of this could be his trickery and no truth.

"Ka33thea!" Once more I called, mind to mind.

"Evil!" That was no answer, but a feeling of loathing strong as any physical blow, and following it, *words*, some of which I knew. She was using a spell. Dinzil did not trick me; no one but Ka33thea could do this.

"Evil indeed, my love." Dinzil spoke as one soothing a child. "This thing would have you believe it is Kemoc come seeking you. Hush; waste not your wisdom which cannot harm a thing of this place."

"Ka33thea!" To the mind call I added two *words*. If she was not entirely lost to all she had been, then those would assure her that nothing of the Shadow stood here, but one of the light.

"Evil!" Again that blast against me. Stronger this time. But not buttressed with any word of power. "Send it hence, Dinzil!" that voice which was my sister's cried out of empty air. "Send it hence! To look upon it chills my heart!"

"So be it, my love!" He loosed his hold on that invisible body and then raised his hands once more and spoke a *word*. We whirled, to come again into the room furnished in mist.

"She has chosen, has she not, my hero? Let me show you something."

Once more he brought out of nothingness that mirror. But this time it did not reflect me, or the room. There was a thing—female—akin to the monstrous weeper. That is, part of it was. But on the twisted shoulders of that foul body sat my sister's head; over those shoulders and sagging breasts flowed her hair. Her hands were not paws but white and human.

"This is Kaththea as she now is."

My hate for him was a poison rising in my throat. He must have known, for his hand moved and I was planted to the floor as if roots sealed my paws to the stone.

"You see in me one who can vanquish the dangers of this place. I am Dinzil; I remain Dinzil. Slowly Kaththea is learning. When she is wholly as I am, then will she be wholly Kaththea here as well as in your own world—outwardly. She learns well and fast. All women shrink from the monstrous. I let her see a little of her present self—not telling her, of course, that she was the one upon whose form she looked, but letting her think that that is what might happen unless she speedily puts to use the safeguards I could teach her. Since then she has been most biddable. No, you are more than I thought you, Kemoc Tregarth. I had believed that most of the power was your sister's. However, one must not lightly toss aside any potential weapon without considering carefully the possibilities for future use. So—we shall put you in safe keeping until I can make a decision."

Once more his signs and the warping. Then I was in a stone-walled cell, where only the yellowish aura given off by my body provided the light. The walls about me looked solid, with no break in them. I crouched down in the middle of that small, cold space and tried to think.

Hero—Dinzil had been derisive when he named me that, and rightly so. I had done naught to defend myself, to reach Kaththea, save what my enemy had forced upon me. The battle had been no battle at all, but a pitifully inept encounter which had gone exactly as Dinzil wished.

But to con the unhappy past was no good stepping-stone to any future. That Dinzil had powers I had known since I had begun this so far ineffective quest. On my side were only the facts that I had won to the Tower, which he had not expected, that I still had the sword. Ha—I held the sword across my knees. Had Dinzil let me keep that weapon because he scorned the use of steel, or had he seen it at all?

That speculation lingered. Suppose to Dinzil the sword had been as invisible as Kaththea had been to me! Why? Or why had I not tested it upon him when we met? It was, looking back, as if I had been in bonds of a kind, unable to raise hand against him.

The Tower was his fortress. It could have safeguards in plenty, none of which were wrought of stone, steel, or even things visible. I could have been subject to them from the time I entered the mound door.

I had not once thought of using the sword, not until this moment when Dinzil must believe me safely caged. The sword had picked away the support of the gem stone wall. Could it do as well against the stones of my present prison?

Once free—if I were still in the tower—what could I do? Kaththea had fled from me to Dinzil. She had not accepted my call of identity. And she was already under the change Dinzil had set upon her. That thing he had showed me—now I wished it was wholly monster, knowing what the changes meant.

Kaththea had knowledge out of Estcarp. But much of the lore of the Wise Women could be only used by a virgin. They had held it against my mother that she had managed to retain her power even after she had wedded my father. Dinzil could not make her wholly his without destroying her usefulness.

Dear one—the words he had used to soothe her. . . . My rage was choking; my paw closed tight upon the sword hilt. Then the other arose to touch the band of light which had been Kaththea's, on which Orsya had set magic of her own.

That had been woman's magic also. It had served me, but from the outside, not the in. What had Orsya said? *Seek with the heart*—

The heart . . . What had I used to set the scarf seeking? Not Kaththea as she was but as she had been, before any magic save that which was born in us—which we used as naturally as we breathed, slept, walked, talked—was known to us.

I could not really touch the scarf which was now only a band of light. But I put my toad paw firmly into the glow, kept the other on the sword hilt. I began to make magic—not Dinzil's, nor any of this land, nor of Escore, but of the past. I sent back my mind, far, far back, to the first memory which had been mine, and Kyllan's and Kaththea's. We were on a furry rug before a fire which sent sparks flying upward now and then.

Anghart, who had been our foster mother, spun and the thread came smoothly between her fingers, her skillful everbusy fingers. Kaththea's thought reached me—

"There is a fairy wood, and there are fairy birds in the trees—"

Looking into the fire, I saw it as she did.

Then Kyllan thought: *"Here comes our father riding with his men."*

And flames rode manwise on some mountain horses.

"Mountains beyond—" That had been my addition, little guessing then how mountains beyond would change

our lives. No, do not think of what happened later. Keep memory clean and clear!

Anghart had looked down on us; very big Anghart had seemed then.

"So quiet; so quiet. Listen; I will tell you of the hoar-frost spirit and how Samsaw tricked it—"

But we had not been quiet; we had been talking to one another in our own way. Even then we knew that that was something those about us did not do and we kept it for our secret.

Memory after memory I pulled from my mind, trying to recall each small detail to make a vivid picture. Once we rode in the spring fields. Kyllan broke a branch from the Tansen tree, and its white flowers with their pink centers gave forth the sweetest fragrance. I had caught up flowering grass and made of it a crown. We had put them, crown on head, scepter in hand, on Kaththea, and told her she was like unto the Lady Bruthe, who was so fair that even the flowers blushed that they could not equal her.

"I remember—"

It had stolen so into my thought weaving that at first I was not aware. Then I took tight rein upon my emotions. Immediately I summoned up another memory and another. She who had been so drawn now joined with me. Together we knitted a tapestry of how it had been with us. I did not venture to approach her along that line of memory, only bind her tighter to me in the sharing.

"You—you are Kemoc?"

It was she who broke the spell with a tentative, uneasy question.

"I am Kemoc." I acknowledged that, but no more.

XVI

"If you be Kemoc"—there was rising tension in her thought—"then this is no land for you! Get you forth before ill comes. You do not know what happens to those who do not have the proper safeguards. I have seen— monstrous things!"

She had seen what Dinzil had taken good care to show her. "Dinzil!" Her thoughts ran even louder. "Dinzil will protect you; use the counterspells—"

So was she caught in his net that she turned instantly to him when there was need for aid.

"I have come for you, Kaththea." I told her the simple truth. If she had not gone too far down that road on which he had set her feet, then I might reach her, even as the memories I had spun had drawn her.

"But why?" There was a simplicity in that question which was not of the sister I had known. She had never been one to lean upon another, but held to her own mind. This was a different Kaththea.

I tried to make my thoughts simple, to keep her holding that slender tie between us: "Did you believe that we would let you go, uncaring what chanced with you?"

"But you knew!" her retort was swift. "You knew that I had gone to a place of power, to learn that which would make us all safe against the Shadow. And I am learning, Kemoc, much more than the Wise Women ever dreamed of. They are really small-minded, timid. They but peer through doors which they dare not enter. I marvel that we are in any awe of them."

"There is knowledge and knowledge. You yourself said that once upon a time, Kaththea. Some can pass through man and come into flower—some men cannot hold, unless they change."

"Men, yes!" she caught me up. "But I am of the Witches of Estcarp, who are adepts. What man cannot hope to do we can! And when I have garnered what I came here to find, then I shall return and you will rejoice at what I bring with me."

Loskeetha's third picture. Suddenly that was vivid in my mind and I saw it as sharply as it had appeared in the sand bowl. There rode the hosts of the Shadow and among them Kaththea, hurling her bolts of force against us, her kin.

"No!" Kaththea's cry of denial was sharp. "That is a weaving of evil, not a true foretelling. You have been deceived; you believe that I—one of the Three—could do so? Dinzil has said—"

She hesitated and I prompted her. "Dinzel has said—what?"

But she did not answer at once, and when she did there was in her reply a coolness, such as had been in her in the Valley.

"You wish me to have no true friends, but to keep me to yourself. Kyllan, he is larger of heart; he knows we shall still be united, even though we walk apart. But you will not admit it; you would prison me in bonds of your choosing."

"This Dinzil has said, and you believe?" He had been wily, but what else might I have expected? This was an argument, my own actions to free her would bolster, past my being able to refute.

"You do not like Dinzil. He has other unfriends. He did not need to tell me this; I had already seen it in you, in others of the Valley. Yet now he strives to gather such power as will deliver all of them. Do they believe they can turn sword steel and a few mutterings of lesser learning against the Great Ones whom rebellion in Escore now rouse? It takes forces beyond most men's knowledge to face those."

"Dinzil can summon such forces, control them?"

"With my aid, yes!" There was an arrogance, a pride in that which might have had roots in the confidence of the Kaththea I had known, but which had grown to turn her stranger.

"Go back, Kemoc. I know you love me, though that love is a thing of fetters for me. Because you came in love, I wish you well. Dinzil will see that you return to the world suited to you. Tell them there that we come with such powers behind us that the Shadow, seeing what marches with us, shall be routed before the first blow is struck."

I shut my mind to her words, to this Kaththea who was the monster Dinzil had shown me. Deliberately and with all the energy I could summon, I thought again of the Kaththea I had known and loved, who had been a part of me—

"Kemoc!" The arrogance had gone out of that cry; it was one of pain. "Kemoc, what would you do? Stop, stop! You lay your fetters on me again and it takes strength, such strength to break them. That strength I must save for the tasks set me here."

I thought. Kaththea who was young of heart, clean of heart, happy, danced in a green meadow and charmed birds out of the sky to come to her singing. . . . Kaththea, laughing, put up her hand to break off a dripping icicle from the eave edge and suck it, while before her the land was frost and snow, yet gem-beautiful under a winter sun. She took the icicle from her lips to trill a call, to be answered by the snow hawk. . . . Kaththea diving cleanly into the river flood to swim with us, but forgetting all contest when she found a watercub tangled in a reed bed, freeing the captive tenderly. . . . Kaththea in the firelight, sitting between us, listening to Anghart's tales . . .

"Stop!" Weaker that plea. I pushed it from me, concentrated on the pictures, on my touch upon the two talismen I trusted in this place which Dinzil believed he ruled.

Kaththea running lightly between us to the harvest field where we worked under the sun with all the manor folk to bind the grain. Kaththea chosen to take the Feast bowl to greet passing strangers that day, to gather the Earthtithe after the old custom, bringing it back jingling and ringing, laughing at her success because a whole troop of Borderers had passed and each had tossed a coin into it.

But never Kaththea in use of her power—never that! For to be Kaththea of the power was to open the door to this Kaththea of the here and now, whom I did not know, whom I feared.

"Kemoc—Kemoc, where are you?"

For a second or two I thought that was the cry of the Kaththea of my memories; for it was young, and strangely uncertain, almost lost.

I opened my eyes and looked about me. Where *was* I? In some place Dinzil deemed safe keeping. But now my confidence rose. I might have little on which to base that confidence. But when a man reaches a point which seems to have no future at all, then he can make a firm stand. In such stands are weak causes sometimes won, simply because there is nothing left to fear.

"Kemoc, please—where are you?"

"With you, soon," I made answer. I did not know if I spoke the truth.

I struggled to my feet, held the sword. "Kaththea!" Once more I sent the winged thought. It flew to the wall immediately before me, was gone. I walked to the wall.

Stone, solid under my touch. But still my confidence held. I set the sword point to the stone, and once more made my reckless magic. For I combined the word "Sytry" which was the sword key, with the phrases out of Lormt.

The hilt in my paw burned. But in spite of the pain I held it steady. The point chewed at a line between two of those blocks. Began to chew, that is, but as I continued to recite those names the stone itself yielded to my weapon, which cut as it had cleared my path through the mud pit. I came out of the prison where Dinzil had put me, and once more I stood in the underground chamber from which raised the stair into the Dark Tower.

Once more I climbed, coming into the first chamber. But now the furnishings were more substantial, less ghosts of themselves. When I put out a paw to touch one I almost dropped the sword. Had I put forth a paw—or a man's hand? Now I could see fingers! Then once more they were hidden in monster flesh—to appear again—back and forth.

I was shaken. The creature Dinzil had shown me and said was Kaththea on this plane—woman's head and hands combined with loathsome body. She had used her hands, her head, to work forces here. He had said—when she was all human seeming again—then she would be completely sealed to his purposes. Now—I brought forth my other hand to look upon it. Yes, there, too, was a flow from hand to paw. Still the paw had greater substance; the hand was but a ghost.

Using magic here, had that linked me to the world of
the Shadow, brought about that change? Yet there was
nothing else I could have done. I crept up the next flight
of stairs to the dining room. Again firmer lines, colors I
could now see. Kaththea, would she still be invisible to
me, and I the monster who roused only fear in her?

The last stair. At its top the door was this time open to
me. If Dinzil once more waited he would have the advantage, but that was a risk I must escape. I raised the
sword before me. Never in this other world had the runes
blazed to warn me, but now so great was my dependence
upon it that I had as much confidence in it as a commander in the field has upon long tried and tested scouts.

At least I had not been blasted as I moved. Laboriously I gained the top of the stairs. There was the mir-
rored table. Almost I expected to see the comb in action.
But to my first inspection the room was empty of any life
save my own.

"Kaththea!" I summoned sharply. My winged word
sped for the darksome other side of that chamber where
tapestry hung. Then out of the gloom shuffled the thing
Dinzil had shown me—save that now the hands hung
white and distinct from the swollen wrists, and the head
was more misty, looming behind it an ovoid such as
matched the weeper of the plain.

Her gait was as shuffling as my own, and there was a
frozen horror on her face—as one who faces a nightmare
come to stalking life.

"No!" Her protest was shrill, near to a shriek.

Even if I would now lose her, I could take but one
step. "As this place shows me—I am Kemoc!"

"But Dinzil said— You are not evil; you cannot be so
loathsome. I know you—your thoughts, what lies within
you—"

I remembered Dinzil's spiteful suggestion that this plane turned a man inside out, showing his spirit. But that I did not accept. If he had said the same words to her, I must break that belief and speedily, lest we both be lost.

"Think for yourself. Do not take Dinzil's thoughts for your own!"

Had I gone too far, so that, under his spell, she would turn again to believe I spoke out of jealousy?

Then I put out one of those paws which tried to be hands now and again. I saw her gaze fasten on it, her eyes widen. So much had I made her attend to me. I raised the paw, tried touch her. She shivered away, yet I persevered and caught firm hold on her, pulling her around to stand before that mirror. Whether she could see what I did, I did not know, but I kept my other hand upon the sword and willed that she do so.

"Not so! Not so!" She jerked loose, cowered away so she did not see the mirror. "Lost—I am lost—" She turned that head, which was now a featureless lump, now her own, to look at me. "You—your meddling has done this, as Dinzil warned. I am lost!" She wrung her hands, and never in all my years had I seen my sister so distraught and broken. "Dinzil!" She looked about and with a passion of pleading in her thought-voice: "Dinzil—save me! Forgive me—save me!"

Inside I felt the pain of seeing her so broken. The Kaththea of the past might have suffered deeply, but she would have fought to the end, asking aid only as might one shield mate from another.

"Kaththea—" I tried to put my paw on her again, but she backed farther and farther from me, her eyes wild, her hands warding me off. "Kaththea, think!" Could I reach her anymore? Though I was loath to give that which abode here any deeper rooting in me, yet that I must do, or perhaps lose her utterly.

I held the sword by the blade so that the hilt was between us. Then I said a *word*. Fire shimmered once more, to burn me, but still I held fast to that column of golden flame.

"Kaththea, are you one who harbors evil within you? Those of the Wise Ones often examine their spirits, look well upon their motives, know the pitfalls and traps which await all those who put out their hands to the powers. Long you dwelt with them, and your unwillingness to join with them came from no evil, but because you had stronger ties elsewhere. Since you left Estcarp and came into Escore, what ill have you done by design —or thought on doing?"

Was she even listening to me? she held her hands before her face, but did not try to touch it, as if she feared that the flesh there would not be human.

"You are not evil, Kaththea; that I will not believe! If you are not, then how can it be that you see your inner self? This is only an illusion; we are among those to whom illusion is a common tool. You are only monster on this plane, as I am monster."

"But Dinzil—" she thought.

"To Dinzil this is his place; he has made himself one with it. He has said so, just as he also told me that when you were one with it, not part monster, then you would be locked to him and his cause. Is that what you wish, Kaththea?"

She was shivering, great shudders shaking her squat, unlovely body. More and more her face faded and I saw the eyepits, the ovoid head of the weeper.

"I am monster—lost in a monster—"

"You dwell within a covering forced upon you in this

place. For many powers fair is foul, as well as foul is fair."

I thought she was listening now. She asked slowly: "What do you want of me? Why do you come to pull at me with memories?"

"Come with me!"

"Where?"

Where, indeed? I might recross that plain, pass through the remains of the gem barrier, back beyond the weeper's place. But then where? Could I find an exit, leading from the Tower, anchored in Escore? I was not sure, and she knew my uncertainty and fastened upon it.

"Come with you, say you! When I ask where, you have no answer for me. What would you have us do, wander in this place, brother? It holds dangers the like of which you cannot imagine. Do not doubt Dinzil will come hunting."

"Where is he now?"

"Where is he now?" she mimicked me shrilly. "Do you fear that he will come into the here and now to face you?" Then suddenly her eyes changed and the old current flowed between us.

"Kemoc?"

"Yes?"

"Kemoc, what has happened to us, to me?" She spoke simply as might a child bewildered by all she now saw and felt.

"We are in a place which is not ours, Kaththea, and it seeks to mold us into its own forms and ways. There is a way back—do you know it?"

Her blob head on which the traces of her normal face had almost disappeared, turned slowly as if she now

214

gazed about her with new eyes, to which this was much of a puzzle.

"I came here—"

"How?" I believed I dared not press here too hard, yet if she did know of Dinzil's door between the worlds, and it was not the same one through which I had entered, there was a chance for our escape.

"I think—" That hand which was still human raised uncertainly toward her head. Clumsily she turned to face the tapestry covered wall. "This way—"

She shuffled, her hands out before her. Then she picked up one edge of the tapestry, pulled it out. There, set in the wall, glowing an angry purple-red, was a symbol. I did not know it but its far-off descendant I had once seen, and I knew it for a symbol of such a power as I would not dare to summon.

I felt my sister's thoughts writhe to shape a *word*, before I could protest. The symbol in the stone coiled as if a loathsome reptile had been loosed. Round and round it ran, and I would not look upon it, for there was a siekness in me that Kaththea knew that *word*. Then the stone vanished and only those glowing lines ran, and ran, spilling down into a pool of sullen, molten color on the floor, and that began to trickle away.

I stumbled forward, pulling at Kaththea to save her from the touch of that pool. Ahead was nothingness as there had been in that other tower through which I had plunged into this place.

"The door is open," Kaththea's thought was once more chill and assured. "For the sake of what lay between us in the past, take your freedom and go, Kemoc!"

The arm which still bore Orsya's bespelled scarf was about her shoulders before she could dodge me. With the sword in my other hand I plunged on, using the weight of my body to bear her with me. I think she was too surprised to resist. It might not be Dinzil's door, but in that moment I saw it as the only hope for both of us .

Falling—falling—I had kept no grasp on Kaththea after we went over the drop. That she had come with me was the thought I carried along into nothingness.

Once more I awoke to pain and a dulling of mind. But in awhile I noted that no color flashes leapt here, rather there was dimness and chill walls about me. I thought that Dinzil, by some trick, had me again in prison. The sword—where was the sword?

I raised my head where I lay prone on hard stone and looked about. Then I saw a glimmer beyond my paw— Paw? So I was *not* free from that other place. A vast misery of disappointment fell on me as a crushing weight.

But—my head strained higher—the paw was at the end of an arm, a human arm! On that the faint tracing of a scar I knew well; I could remember the fight in which I took it.

Now I levered myself up to look down at the rest of my body. It was no longer that of a toad man; remnants of human clothing covered me from the waist down. But the paws—I hardly dared to touch my face with those misshapen things, as if some of their foulness might rub off. But I must know if I still wore a toad head on my shoulders.

Beyond me, in the gloom of that place, something else moved. On my hands and knees, dragging the sword with me, I went to see what.

A human body wearing the riding dress of the Valley people, a woman's body. At the end of her slender arms were red paws even more formless than mine. Above her shoulders was an ovoid, hairless featureless, save for two eyepits. At my coming the head swung and those pits looked at me as if organs of sight hid somewhere in their depths.

"Kaththea!" I stretched forth my paws to her, but she once more avoided me. Only raised her own paws to set beside mine, as if to emphasize their monster form. Then she cowered away and brought up her arms to hide her head.

What moved me then I do not know, but I plucked at the scarf about my arm, no longer a band of light, but once more silken fabric. I now held it out to Kaththea.

The pit eyes peered at it over the top of one of her shielding arms. Then her paw came forth and snatched it from me, winding it around and around her head, leaving but a small slit open for sight.

Meanwhile I looked around. We were either back in the Tower rooted in Escore, or its double. We sat on the floor near the staircase as steep as a ladder. The doorways through which one could pass into those other worlds were closed, but the sooner we were away the better. I turned to my sister.

"Come—"

"Where?" her thought demanded. "Where can I find a place to hide what I now am?"

Fear touched me that perhaps her terror was rooted in truth, that we had brought back from the place Dinzil knew permanent disfigurement, since we had wrought there with powers of the light, but which, perhaps, had been distorted by the Shadow.

"Come—"

Somehow I got her to her feet, and we went down that breakneck stair and stood in the corridor of the mound. Once more the runes ran red on the sword, and those I watched. But still I set paw to Kaththea and drew her with me. She went silently beside me, moving as one stricken so she cared not where she went, nor to what future.

We came out into a gray day with sullen rain falling heavily. I wondered at how I was to find our way back to where I had left Orsya. But this rutted road we could follow in part.

Kaththea's mind was closed to me, though I tried to get her interested in our escape. She walked dumbly, behind a barrier I could not pierce. I kept my eye upon the sword, though after we emerged from the mound, the runes cooled, nor did they fire again as we passed through the dell and climbed the rise on the other side.

From here I surveyed the ground, marking landmarks I had set in mind when I came this way. Surely it had been over there that I had slain that monstrous thing which was one of the guardians of the Dark Tower.

The hunger of which I had been aware in that other world was now pain and I brought out from my belt pouch the roots Orsya had supplied. I offered one to Kaththea.

"It is good—untainted—" I told her as I put another to my lips.

She struck it out of my grasp, so it rolled out of sight into a crevice between two rocks. Still her mind was closed to me. My hatred of Dinzil was such that had he stood before me I would have tried to rend him with teeth and nails, as might a woodland beast.

Kaththea began to waver back and forth, stumbling now and then, so I steadied her. Suddenly she twisted and shoved me from her, so I fell. Before I gained my feet she was staggering back toward the Tower.

I caught up with her, and, apparently, that last rebellion had drained her energy. She did not try to throw off the hold I kept on her, though I was alert to any move she made.

We went downslope and the footing was rough. But we might have walked through a deserted world. The sword runes did not light, and we saw no living thing. I thought I knew the brush ahead, though it was not mist-wreathed today. At last we came to the stream and the reef of rock where I had last seen Orsya. Somehow, I do not know why, I had expected to sight her there still, waiting, just as I had seen her last. When she was not I knew a surge of disappointment.

"Did you think you could depend upon the water wench, my foolish brother?" That hard, unknown Kath-thea's thoughts cut into my brain. "But it is as well for her."

"What do you mean?"

Laughter now, inside my head—such laughter as I had never thought to hear except from one as far along the path elsewhere as Dinzil.

"Because, Kemoc, my dear brother, I might ask a boon of you and, I think, I could make you grant me that boon, and thereafter it would not be well with your water wench."

"What do you mean?" I demanded again since she had left down the barrier. Only that dreadful laughter rang in my head. I guessed I had lost Kaththea for now, even though she walked unwillingly beside me.

Our road out was the stream and beyond the river. So plain was that I did not need Orsya's guidance. Yet I still worried about her—hoping that she had prudently with-drawn to safety, and not that she had been captured by some roving danger of this land.

We came to the deserted house of the aspt and under my urging Kaththea crawled into the chamber ahead of me. She settled herself against the far wall, as far from me as was possible in such confined quarters.

"Kaththea, in the Valley they know much, more than we. They will know what to do!

"But, Kemoc, my brother, I know what to do! I need only your water wench for the doing. If not her, there will be another. But she is an excellent choice, being what and who she is. Bring her to me, or me to her, and we shall make such magic as shall astonish you—Kemoc who thinks he knows something of mysteries and only cons tatters discarded by those far greater than he."

I almost lost my patience. "Such as Dinzil, I suppose."

She was silent for a long moment. Then once more that laughter rang in my mind. "Dinzil—ah, there is one who climbs clouds to tread the sky. He wants so very, very much, does Dinzil. But whether he will have even a handful from the full measure he thinks upon, that is another question, and Dinzil must come to face it. I think I hated you, Kemoc, for what you wrought when you brought me forth. But now, thinking on it the more, I see you have served me even better than I could have ordered for myself. There I was subject to Dinzil—you were so right to fear that for me. Dear brother, for your services there shall be a reward." The head so closely shrouded in the green scarf nodded.

I was chilled within, wondering what manner of thing had come to dwell within Kaththea, and whether it could ever be expelled. I thought of those two fates Loskeetha had foreseen, though neither had come to pass. In them Kaththea was one with the enemy. Now perhaps I could accept that she would be far better dead.

Only all men cling to hope and if I could get her back to the Valley surely there would be those who could deal with her, taking away not only the monster face, but the monster inner dweller also.

"Sleep, Kemoc; I swear to you that I shall be here when you wake. I want nothing more now than to go where you go."

She spoke the truth, I knew. But now it was not what I wanted to hear. Whether she slept, I do not know. But she lay quiet, her bandaged head upon her arm. At length I could watch no longer, for weariness overcame me.

XVII

We crept forth from that den in the morning. Again I offered Kaththea some of the roots and she refused, saying she had no hunger for such. When I pressed as to what food she needed, she shut herself off from me. Still she went with me without urging.

Once more the mist curdled the air about the stream. I welcomed it, for the water made a path plain to follow and the fog, I hoped, would shelter us. I watched in the stream for any movement which might show Kofi was here, for I held in mind the thought that Orsya might have left the Merfay to await us.

Or had the Krogan girl believed my mission to the Dark Tower so hopeless that she saw no reason to prepare for any return?

The scraps of vegetation looming through the fog were clean of that taint which streaked the land. But they were beginning to wither from nature. It was much colder and I thought winter must be now the closer. I could not control my shivering and longed for a cloak such as I had used to make my puppet along the way.

As we went I also paid attention to the sword for rune warnings. The mist deadened sound in a curious way and I thought that the blade might be our only alert against some dangers.

We could follow the waterways back to the Heights, if we were very lucky. But I would not attempt a return through the underground passages. Therefore, we must somehow win across the land.

To do so was a fool's folly. There was every reason to believe that we could be tracked down between one sunrise and sunset. Still I turned to the Heights and kept on. There was no other way.

Laughter—faintly jeering laughter. I turned my head quickly and looked to Kaththea.

"Impossible, my dear brother? You have an excellent forefuture reading, according to your gifts. But, remember, you do not walk alone, and I can show you some tricks which even your water wench or the Wise Ones of Estcarp could not truly lay name to. We shall get back to the Valley, never fear. If we will it, both together, that we shall do."

Again arrogant confidence in herself, the mocking half-note in relation to others. Yet that confidence carried conviction that she knew whereof she spoke. It was just that, within me, I shrank from any aid she would give me, whereas I had welcomed that of Orsya.

"What . . . !" Her scarf swathed head turned from me; she was staring into the water which was curiously agitated where the mist curtain touched it.

"Kofi!" I cried. "Orsya?" I sent a thought call. But there was no answer. The rippling in the water drew closer as the Merfay treaded water, waiting for us to catch up.

"What is it?" demanded Kaththea. "I cannot thought-scan it. But there is life here. What *is* it?"

"A Merfay. It guided us into this country."

"A friend to your water wench?" Kaththea stopped as if she did not want to approach it any nearer.

Suddenly her designation of Orsya rasped me. "Her name is Orsya and she, too, is a holder of power. With her only did I find you." My reply sounded sharp, even in my own ears.

"Orsya," Kaththea repeated. "Your pardon, brother—it shall be Orsya. So, she aided you to me? That I shall remember also. It is her magic which has strengthened this scarf of mine. But to return to this messenger we cannot see, nor mind-touch—he is a messenger, is he not?"

"I hope so."

I went down on one knee in the shallow wash of the stream and held out my hand—that paw hand—much as I had when Orsya lent her sense of sight to mine so that I could see Kofi. The disturbance in the water drew closer, but this time I felt no light touch of alien flesh on mine. Perhaps Kofi could not bring himself to such contact with the thing which now served me as a hand. For that I could not blame him. But I hoped my gesture of good will would be accepted as a greeting between us.

The splashing moved away, downstream. I did not know whether he wished nothing more to do with us, or was trying to be our guide once again. Since we must keep to the river for now, I was willing to hope it was the latter.

It must have been that, for he did not leave us behind, but kept to a pace which matched ours, though some strides ahead. Once the runes blazed red and I threw up my hand to stop Kaththea, listening, watching that thick curtain of mist. There was a muffled cawing, a series of cries splitting the silence. Then nothing, though we stood very still to listen. After a while, the runes faded.

"He hunts—" Kaththea's thought came to me.

For me now there was only one "he." "Dinzil—for us?"

Again her laughter. "You did not truly believe he would let me go so easily, brother? After he had gone so far to gain my aid? I think now Dinzil needs me more than I need him. Which makes a good point for any future bargains."

"Bargains?"

"I do not intend to go misshapen in this or any other world, Kemoc!" Her confidence cracked a little; behind it I thought I read deep anger.

"I thought you knew a way to help yourself." I pursued the subject even though I knew it was painful, for no other reason than I must learn all I could of what she thought Dinzil might do, or what she was prepared to do. I no longer trusted this Kaththea.

"Oh, I do. But it would be like Dinzil to make trouble afterwards. The road I must take can only be walked once. Also—" She checked her thought flow quickly and once more there was a barrier between us.

I shivered almost convulsively. The chill ate into my half bare body. Kaththea's head swung around so that the slit which gave her eye room faced me. Then she raised one of her red paws.

"Bring me some of those—" She motioned toward reeds growing nearby.

Though my paws were not shaped for such work, I pulled a goodly handful and held them out to her, at her gesture laying them across her two paws. She bent her head and breathed on them. Though her mind was now closed to me, I felt a kind of stirring which came from the use of power. The reeds lengthened, thickened, became part of one another, and she held a thick, wadded jacket, such as we wore in Estcarp in autumn. I took it from her and drew it on. Not only did it shield me from the chill of the wind, but also it appeared to radiate warmth, so I was now as comfortable as if I walked through a warm spring day.

"You see—power can be used to smooth the way in little things as well as big," Kaththea's thought came to me.

I rubbed the front of the jacket. It felt very real. I only trusted that the spell would linger.

She caught that. "As long as you have the need, it will, for it is shaped to your use."

We reached the main river, the mist disappearing. I still kept watch, but Kaththea marched along through the shallows as one who had naught to fear. Before us the vee of ripples marked the swimming Kofi. So he still accompanied us.

Far off sound again. Not the cawing this time, but rather a baying, such as the way the hunted hounds of Alizon (those bred for the harrying of men) sound when they course their prey.

"The Saran ride—"

I only realized since Kaththea went veiled how much one reads in the expression of one's comrades. Could I be sure that the emotions aroused by her thoughts were hers —or mine? I thought she was excited, but not as if the hunt had any connection with her. She might have been an onlooker. Was she so sure that Dinzil valued her to the extent that if his hunters came upon her she need have no fears?

"Dinzil know what he needs." So again she read my thoughts. "Dinzil has not climbed clouds to assault the high skies without being careful of all he must use along the way—until he is finished with it. Dinzil had fitted many tools to his task in the past, but he has never had one from Estcarp. So he now faces a surprise."

The baying grew louder. I saw the vee mark of Kofi dart to the opposite shore. There was a waving in the weeds; the Merfay must be going into hiding. I looked about me, but we were in such a place as had no natural defense spots. We could take to deep water, but when I said so, Kaththea gave a definitive negative.

"Your Orsya likes her mud holes and to slink along the bottom of water reaches. But I am not Orsya, nor do I have gills. As neither do you, dear brother. What of that sword of yours . . . ?" She put out her paw as if pointing a finger and then gave a small cry, jerking it back to nurse against her breast.

"What do you hold there?"

"A weapon and a talisman." Somehow I had no desire to share with her the story of from whence it had come and what it did for me.

The runes were taking fire, standing out upon the golden blade. Not for the first time I wished that I had the knowledge to read them, to know just how much this weapon could do for him who carried it, so that in danger I could call upon all it had to offer and not blunder in the dark.

There was a stirring along the ridge on the other side of the river. I tried to push Kaththea into deeper water, but she eluded me, stood to front what came as if she no fear of it. So, perforce, I had to stand with her, sword in hand, while the runes on it ran so bloody that one might think to see their crimson drip from the blade.

They came: three wolfmen running on all fours, and it was these who bayed. Behind them came men such as the ones who had captured Orsya. In their rear were two more, and they were as those who had used the lightning rods to kill the Krogan.

Again Kaththea's unearthly laughter rang in my head. "A paltry handful, brother, not meet to think to drag us down! Dinzil forgets himself to offer such insult."

Her paws rose to the scarf about her head of horror and deliberately she began to unwind that covering, all the time facing those who came. In my paw-hand the hilt of the sword heated.

The jaws of the Gray Ones were agape, showing their fangs, while they drooled slaver. Their eyes were red sparks of pure evil. Behind them the others slowed their mounts to a trot. I saw that the animals they rode were not Renthan, but closer in appearance to the horses of Estcarp, save they were larger and more powerful, and all were black. They rode bareback, with no use of bit nor rein. I remembered the Keplian, that horse-demon which had almost slain Kyllan.

So they came to the river bank and looked across to us, the water flowing between. The Gray Ones crouched at the edge of the stream, the others ranged behind them. The swordsmen were, as Dinzil had been, outwardly sons of the Old Race, or enough to pass unnoticed among them. But the two who bore the fire weapons were alien. They rode masked with hoods. But the hands—ah—there I saw paws like those I now was doomed to wear. I thought that, could I pull off those hoods, I might see toad heads. Dinzil must have summoned these henchmen out of that other world to which the Tower was the dread entrance way.

The folds of the scarf dropped away from Kaththea's head. In this open daylight that monstrous face which was not a true face was pitilessly revealed. For the first time I saw it completely and could not help an involuntary shrinking though I fought it instantly.

No mouth, no nose, only those eyepits in the red ovoid of head. Remembering my fair sister, I understood how such a happening could well nigh turn her brain, make her seek any remedy she knew of.

The Gray Ones did not advance into the stream, and I recalled Orsya's saying that running water was a deterrent to certain types of evil. But I had seen the fire weapons of those hooded ones spit across another river and I waited tensely now for one of those rods to point in our direction.

Kaththea raised both paws as high as her shoulders, held them outwards, the paws pointed to that assorted company. She used thoughts and her hands moved as if she waved them on at the enemy. What words they were I did not know. I wanted to run from her, for in my mind was a tearing, a burning, such as no man of human birth could stand. But I held to the sword and the warmth from the hilt traveled up my arm, into me, finally reaching my mind and there set up a barrier against the forces she summoned, so that, though her paws still waved and she continued to hurl her thoughts, it meant nothing to me.

The Gray Ones threw back their heads and broke into a wild, tormented howling, like unto the cries of those damned and doomed. They dashed back and forth, finally away from the river, retreating into the broken country behind.

After them the Keplians neighed, reared. Some threw their riders before they followed the wolfmen. Some of the men managed to keep their seats, but those who fell lay prone, unmoving, on the ground as if struck dead. Only the two hooded ones slid from their unhappy mounts, which plunged off, and stood together, watching Kaththea. But they made no move to turn their weapon tubes upon us.

My sister's arms dropped to her side. She spoke by open mind thought so I understood her.

"Say this to your overlord: The hawk does not hunt when the eagle flies. Nor does one who wears the cloak of power send to an equal less than a Herald of Banners. If he would have words with me, let him say them as we have always dealt—face to face." She laughed. "Remind him of what you see now; it will hearten him, for there can be a bargaining."

They gave no outward sign that they understood, any more than they replied; they simply turned and walked away, presenting their backs to us as if they had no fear of any attack. Now Kaththea again fastened the scarf back in shrouding folds.

"You sent a challenge to Dinzil," I said aloud.

"I sent a challenge," she agreed. "He will not again, I believe, dispatch underlings to hunt us as if some slaves of his were escaping. When he comes, it will be full in the power he thinks he has."

"But—"

"But that is what you fear, brother? You need not. Dinzil thought to make of me a tool, as one uses pinchers of iron to take a blazing coal from the heart of a fire. For a while"—she tucked the loose ends of her scarf into the front of her jacket to keep them tight—"he might have had a small part of it. Only—you see—he exposed me to much he had learned. Since I had already been well taught in another school, I could fit that learning into a new pattern which he does not know. Let him believe I have power and he will be twice eager to treat with us. Shall we go?" She turned her muffled head from one side to the other, and then pointed to our left." I dislike water walking. I do not believe we shall again be challenged by anything in this land. The Valley lies that way."

"How can you be sure?" Her arrogance was growing. She snapped her thoughts now as a hunter snaps a riding whip against a boot. Surely the Kaththea I had known all my life was further and further from me.

"The Valley is a reservoir of power, surely you cannot deny that. As such it puts forth a signal for all those who can feel. Try it yourself, brother, with that mysterious fire sword of yours."

So much was I under her command at that moment, that I did raise the sword, holding it only loosely to see if it could act as a pointer. I swear that I did not incline it, but it did point in the same direction she had indicated.

Against my will we left the river, though I knew that sooner or later we would have had to do so, since I would not have gone underground again.

We were quickly through that wholesome growth along the stream bed and into the blasted land which laced this rolling country. Kaththea marched straight ahead, as one who has no need to fear, but I held the sword as a guard against what might lie here, avoiding, making her avoid, certain bushes, stones, and the like, when the runes warned. We had not gone far before I knew that we had skulkers to our right and left, also trailing behind. Some of the shapes I sighted were ones I had seen before in the ranks of evil, others new to me. Not all were foul or monstrous seeming. If they were illusions they were proof against my desire for clear sight.

None of these moved to obstruct us in any way, save that they were ready to close in upon the command of their warlord. I kept ever alert, waiting for Dinzil to appear and accept Kaththea's challenge.

For such a battle I was ill-equipped. I had but one ultimate weapon, as Orsya had pointed out. There were those *words* from Lormt which had been *answered*. I might call again on what had so *answered*. Though to do so was a risk only to be taken by one in the depths of despair at a time of complete loss of hope.

Good spots appeared here and there in this seared land, mostly, I noted, about springs, pools, or small runlets, as if water was a factor in holding back the evil which had blasted so much of the country. It was a hard way to follow, for, as I had seen from my rock perch in the Heights, it was very broken, sharp ridges dividing narrow ravines, so that it seemed to me we were eternally climbing, or descending to climb again. Yet Kaththea appeared to be in no way baffled at direction and unhesitatingly took the lead, always bearing to the left. Now I could see the Heights themselves as proof she was right.

We stopped at last beside one of the pools of sweet water. I ate one of the few remaining roots Orsya had given me, though I could have finished them all. But again Kaththea would have no food, seating herself with her back against a great rock, staring downstream. I was well aware that all about us scouts of that company behind watched us.

"We must find a place for night camp." I tried to find a normal subject to discuss with this stranger I found it hard to believe was my sister.

"We shall find one and—" her thoughts were silent. Then she added, "If all goes well, we shall discover thereabouts what is most needed. But there is no time to linger now."

Already she was on her feet, striding away up the cut above the pool. As I tramped after her I suddenly saw, in the soft earth of the bank, the print of wedge-shaped feet, the toes only marked by faint indentations. As I had learned to know them—Krogan! They led from the pool, away from water, which puzzled me.

Orsya? But I could not be sure of that. If the Krogan had allied themselves with the Shadow as they may well have done by now, then any one of them could be among that company now ranging behind us. Only, *why away from water?* That was the one thing they dreaded more than anything else. I saw no other prints to suggest that this wayfarer had been a prisoner, nor even if he or she had been hunted, and thus forced into dry country.

The marks were to be seen now and again in patches of dry soil, smudged but still unmistakable. A Krogan, apparently deliberately, climbing the same way, against all nature and custom. Twice I knelt to examine them more closely, certain I must be mistaken. Once I touched sword point into one to see if the runes would tell me anything. This might be an illusion meant to deceive. But the runes did not light.

It was growing fast into twilight when we came into a narrow dark cut leading upward and Kaththea went into it without faltering. I saw the prints here also, but something made me believe that the maker now walked with difficulty. Was there water ahead? If so, I trusted that the straggler from the river had managed to reach it.

Then I saw in the deep gloom a tiny spark of white fire. It could be nothing but Orsya's horn-rod, set up as she had before, for protection against the evil roaming here. But Orsya away from water—why?

"Because we have need of her, brother!" Kaththea's thought reached me for the first time in hours. "She gave of her magic in this scarf—and that can be a two-way road. Having put something of herself into it, I could reach her so—now she waits us."

"But she is far from water, and she is Krogan. She must have water!"

"Do not worry; she shall have all she needs when we reach her."

I was aching tired but I ran now, stumbling into rocks which choked this place. Then I came to where stood the unicorn horn with its taper of protection. By it lay Orsya. She moved feebly as I dropped on my knees beside her. Water—but I had no bottle of that precious fluid. Could I take her back, down the broken land, to the pool where I had seen her prints first? It would be almost hopeless to try, but if there were no other way of saving her, that I would do.

"It is not necessary." Kaththea stood there, gazing down at the two of us, "What needs to be done can be done here and now."

"There is no water, and without water she will die."

Kaththea was slowly unwinding the scarf. Orsya's head turned a little on my arm. I had an impulse to life my hand, to cover her eyes so that she could not look upon the monster my sister had become.

"Monster—yes."

I was ashamed that my sister had caught that thought. "But now we have the remedy—that which you can do for me, Kemoc. As I know you will—you will—you will—" She repeated the words in my brain with a beat, and I found myself agreeing that what she wanted would be done.

"Take that good sword of yours, Kemoc, and give me blood—blood to wash away ensorcelment, to be Kaththea again."

"Blood!" I was startled out of my acquiescence.

"Blood!" She leaned closer, stretched out her paws.

"Kill the water wench; let me have her blood! Or would you have me half monster all the rest of my days?"

Then she spoke other words, meant to bind and command, and I raised the sword. On it the runes blazed high and the hilt burned my hand. I looked to Orsya and she gazed at me, though she made no plea for mercy, nor was there any fear in her large eyes, only a kind of patient waiting for what she could not escape.

I cried out, rammed the point of the sword into the earth so it stood quivering between Kaththea and the two of us. And I heard Kaththea cry in answer. This time not with her mind but aloud, it being so terrible I shuddered. In it I heard that moan of one betrayed by him upon whom she had the greatest right in the world to trust. Her anguish cut through the Kaththea who now was, to reveal the Kaththea who had once been. She cowered away from us covering her face with her forearms.

I laid Orsya back on the ground and reached for the sword hilt.

"If you must have blood," I began and raised that blade to my own flesh.

But she did not listen. Instead she laughed, that terrible, lost laughter. Then she ran away from us, back into the dark. But her thoughts still reached me.

"So be it! So be it! I shall make another bargain. But perhaps it will not be so simple, and you shall rue it even more, Kemoc Tregarth!"

XVIII

I would have gone after her, but Orsya caught at my ankle, so that I tripped and fell. She held tightly, and, when I writhed around to free myself by force, she cried out:

"I do this for you, Kemoc, for you! She is no longer what you think her. Now she would lead you straight into their hands. Look upon your sword!"

I was loosening her hold finger by finger. Now I glanced to the sword which had fallen from my hand, and which now lay, point out into the dark. Never had I seen those runes blaze so fiercely.

"It is Kaththea out there!" I loosed the Krogan girl's hold. "And we were followed by forces of the Shadow."

"She is not the Kaththea of your knowing," Orsya repeated weakly. Her eyes closed, and she forced them open again with what was manifestly a great effort. "Think you, Kemoc; would she to whom you have been bound ask you to do what she did?"

"Why—why did she?" I had my hand on the sword hilt. But I was no longer so driven by the need to follow Kaththea. Thought had returned to me.

"Because it is true. Blood if life, Kemoc. Among the half people, hunters drink the blood of the bravest of their kill, that they may have the life force and courage of those they have vanquished. Do not warriors mingle their blood, that henceforth they may be brothers?"

"Among the Sulcarmen they do."

"Wherever your sister has been, she has been marked. She cannot be whole and herself unless blood draws her

235

back entirely to this world again. Kemoc—your hands!" She was staring at my paws. I held them closer to her unicorn candle for her viewing.

"As she is marked, so am I. It is worse for her. To be a fair maid, and then look upon yourself as—*that!* It is enough to drive one mad!"

"Which is also true." Orsya's reply was but a whisper. "She put the drawing spell on me, did she not?"

"Yes."

I looked from my paws to the Krogan girl, roused from my thoughts. Water—Orsya would die if she had no water. If I followed Kaththea, Orsya would die in this desolate place as surely as if I had done as my sister demanded. If I could not kill Orsya by sword stroke, still less could I leave her to die more lingeringly.

"Water . . . ?" I looked dully about me as if I expected to see it gush forth from some rock at my saying of the word.

"The pool—back there," I added, though I thought that was hopeless. Even if I could find my way back in the dark, carrying Orsya, she might well die before we reached there. If we were able to escape being pulled down by that monstrous army . . .

Her thoughts whispered faintly in my mind: "Over Heights—"

I looked up the cut. Such a climb—in the dark. . . .

She struggled feebly, reaching out her hand for the horn. When I would have taken it up for her, she roused to refuse me.

"No . . . if you touch it . . . virtue departs. . . . Hold me . . . to take it."

I supported her until her feeble fingers closed about the horn. Then I fastened the sword to my belt and got to my feet, gathering her up in my arms. The horn lay upon her breast and the light from it was no longer a narrow candle but a radiance which showed something of the path ahead.

That night was our time of fear, despair, struggle, endurance. Somehow Orsya held to life, and I kept going, carrying her. Now and then the sword would blaze, but I dared not wait to see what followed. The sky was dawn-gray when we came through a pass, blundered through. We looked down into wild lands. Somewhere, farther on, might lie the Valley. But for us both now there was only one need—water.

"Water—" It was not a plaint, that word from Orsya, but, I realized with an inward leap of hope, recognition! "Left, now—"

I wavered to the left, downslope. Brush tore at me and my burden, and I was so weak with weariness that, had I fallen then, I do not believe I could have come again to my numb feet. But when I did stumble forward, it was near a small cup into which fed the merest thread of spring.

Laying Orsya on the ground, I used my paws to splash and throw that precious liquid into her face, along as much of her body as I could. When she stirred I could have shouted aloud my relief. Then I pulled her closer to that small basin, and she plunged her head and as much of her shoulders into it as she could, lying there unmoving as she soaked it into her skin, regaining so its vitalizing energy.

Then she raised her head and sat up, to put her feet into its freshness. This was an act of magic as great as I had ever seen, for the body which had been so light and withered as I carried it, grew firm and young again under my eyes. I half lay now on the opposite side of the pool, sure she could care for herself, so drugged with fatigue that I could not have kept from sleep if Dinzil himself had appeared before me.

I awoke to a kind of singing in which there were sounds which might be words but which I did not understand. The hum was soothing, and held off any terrors night in these haunted wilds might hold—for it was the dark of night which I saw when I opened my eyes. Orsya, much as she had been when we journeyed into the land of the Dark Tower, sat there, facing her candle-horn, holding out her hands to its light as one warms oneself at a fire.

But when I remembered the Dark Tower, then there returned to mind all else, so the content of those first moments was lost. I sat up abruptly, looking over my shoulder, for we were still in the cup of the pool and behind us the Heights from which we had come, wherein Kaththea might still wander lost.

"There is no going back!" Orsya came to me. As she had done to show me Kofi, she knelt behind me and put her hands upon my temples. So I "saw," that the land behind us was a-crawl with the forces of the Shadow, that they were uniting for some great thrust. I knew without her telling that the thrust would be at the Valley. My allegiances, so long divided, I still could not reconcile. I was torn two ways—Kaththea and those to be warned.

"This is not the moment, nor the hour, nor the day, on which you can stand battle for Kaththea. If you return into that caldron of danger, then you shall have wasted your strength and what gifts you have for naught. Indeed, you may do worse; did not Dinzil hint that in you he might find yet another tool? Will he not be more inclined to try that since he can no longer control Kaththea? You might be a rich prize—" Orsya reasoned.

"How know you what Dinzil said to me?" I interrupted.

"While you slept you dreamed, and while you dreamed, I learned much," she returned simply. "Be assured, Kemoc, your sister has stepped beyond the limits where you can call to her."

"There are powers; they can be sought." I closed my mind, or tried to, to that fear.

"But not by you. You know too little to be properly on guard; you might lose too much. Now must be your choice: Throw away all by going back, or take your warning to the Valley."

She was right, but that did not make her words any easier to accept. I had failed, and for the rest of my life I must live with that failure. But, matters now going as they seemed to be, that life would probably not be long. Best spend it doing all I could to withstand the Shadow.

We had to keep to water, which made us vulnerable. Yet I would not do as Orsya urged and leave her to follow alone. I knew too well what might happen to her. I had lost Kaththea through ignorance—for I might have given her my own blood and so won her back—but I was not going to be responsible for Orsya's loss also.

She kept the horn tight against her. It glowed still and gave us light. And, she told me, it had other properties for our protection. But I disliked using it, for power draws power, even if they are of opposite natures.

At dawn we huddled in a niche between two large boulders. The thin rill we had followed from the pool linked here with a larger stream and first Orsya lay long beneath its surface, drawing restoration into her. Once we roused from uneasy dozing, hearing a ring of hooves on stone. I pushed into a crack from which I could see below. Men rode there—not on Keplians, but on Renthans. They might be a scouting party from the Valley, was my first thought, until I saw their banner and read the device on it as one borne by a follower of Dinzil.

But they would be welcome in the Valley, thus opening a door for their fellows. . . . In me now was born a need for speed, to deliver the warning. Orsya's hand touched my paw.

"They ride from, not to, the Valley," she said. "But it is true that time grows short for all of us!"

How short we realized as we moved on. Twice we crouched in hiding as parties of the enemy went by. Once some shadowy things which glowed and left a putrescent odor on the air; then, three Gray Ones who loped with a fast, ground covering stride.

Orsya found food for us, things which she routed from under stream rocks and which I crammed hastily into my mouth and tried neither to think on or taste, as I manfully chewed and swallowed. We kept to the stream which luckily ran in the right direction. Shortly before sundown Orsya pointed to a vee of ripples.

"Kofi?"

"No, but another of his people. Perhaps he has news for us."

She trilled and twittered as she had with Kofi, and then turned to me with a slight frown.

"The forces of the Shadow are spread widely between us and the Valley. They await some word for attack."

"Can we pass them?"

"I do not know. You swim, but not well enough to take the deep ways."

"If I have to, then I shall. Show them to me," I told her grimly.

She seemed very doubtful. But after further twitter

speech with the Merfay, she shrugged. "If it must be, it must—"

But we were not to reach her "deep ways." From nowhere, there converged on us shortly after what looked to be, by the troubling of the water, a large school of Merfays. They treaded water about Orsya. I heard their small cries which must have been delivered with great vigor to reach my ears.

"What is it?"

"My people are coming—"

"They have joined the Shadow, then?"

"No. They still believe they can make peace and go their own way, if they pay a price to those they fear the most. That price is you and I. They know we travel the river and their magic I cannot hope to elude."

"You can hide. Surely the Merfays will show you where. I can take to the land again." I was impatient to get on. There was an urgency which burned me as a fever.

Orsya did not appear to hear me. She had turned back to those splashes and ripples and was once more twittering. "Come—" She moved downstream, the invisible Merfays, judging by the disturbance, falling in on either hand as an escort.

"But why? You said—"

"Not far. There is a side way, partly underground . . ."

"Through the tomb caverns?"

"Perhaps it is an outer section of those. But not the portion we saw before. It is one my people do not know."

We did not go much further before the Merfay ripples darted ahead; Orsya paused and held out her hand to grasp that beastly paw which now marked me.

"They go to mislead the others. My people do not know this country and they will come slowly. Also they will listen to the Merfays. Now—we go this way!"

She dropped her hold and used that hand to sweep aside some bushes which trailed in great drooping fronds, the tips floating in the water. Behind that screen was another waterway, shallow as a brook, running through a narrow slit.

Part of that way we went on hands and knees, hidden by the walls of the slit. By luck it was largely overgrown with the trailing branched bushes and, while sometimes those lashed at us stingingly, we could make our way under them. The brook ended in a pool and Orsya halted there.

"The entrance is below; we must dive for it."

"How long underwater?"

"Long for you, but it is the only way."

I made the sword fast to me. Then I pulled off that warm jacket Kaththea had spun out of reeds and illusion. I rolled it into a ball and thrust it beneath the roots of one of the bushes, only to see it dissolve into a frayed bunch of yellowed reeds. I filled my lungs and dived.

Once more that nightmare, wherein I pinned my hopes on Orsya's guiding touch on my shoulder, to steer me. I had reached the point where my lungs were bursting when my head broke water and I could breathe again. There was dark, but out of it came Orsya's touch and voice.

"Thus—" She urged me forward and I swung clumsily, the weight of the sword pulling me down. It is hard to judge distances in the dark and I do not know how long we swam. But I was tiring as we came out, as if through a door, into a gray place and saw in the wall not too far above our heads crevices through which the light came.

Those were not difficult to reach, and then we were out among rocks, looking down at the last of the sunlight on a plain. There mustered an army. It would seem that our side path had led us directly to the enemy.

I did not recognize the land beyond. If this was before one of the ramparts of the Valley, it was a section I did not know. I said as much to Orsya.

"I do not think they move against the Valley yet. Look—"

My gaze followed the pointing of her finger. To our right and not too far away was a ledge and on that stood a group of people. I caught a glimpse of a green swathed head.

"Kaththea!"

"And Dinzil." Orsya indicated a cloaked man, looming tall beside my sister. "There is also one of the Captains of the Sarn Riders, and others who must be of note. And—do you not feel it, Kemoc? They dabble in power."

She was right. There was a tingling in the air, a tension, a kind of ingathering of force. I had felt it once before, on that night when the Wise Women of Estcarp had made ready their blow of doom against the army of Kartsen coming through the southern mountains. It sucked at one's life forces, gathered, gathered. . . .

"They will try such a blow, and then, with those of the Valley still reeling under it, move in."

But I did not need Orsya's explanation. I had guessed it for myself. Worst of all—I caught one strong element in that brewing of evil. Kaththea was mind calling—not me, but Kyllan! She was now so utterly of the Shadow that she turned that which was born in us to summon my brother, to use him as a key to the Valley.

Then I knew the true meaning of Loskeetha's fates, that Kaththea was indeed better dead. And that it was laid upon me to kill her. If she could use such calling, than could I also.

"Stay you here!" I ordered Orsya, and I began to creep along the heights so I could find a place above and behind that ledge. It did not take me long to reach it. I think they were so oblivious of anything besides what they did that they would not have seen me had I marched down to them.

I found a place where I could stand in the open. Then I drew the sword and pointed its tip at my sister. All the wisdom I knew went into the call I sent in one lightning thrust.

She swayed, her hands to her swathed head. Then she turned and began to run across the ledge, scramble up to me. They were still so intent upon their convergence of wills and forces that they did not understand for a moment, long enough for her to start the climb. Then Dinzil followed her. She could not reach me; she would not have time. So I did what I had seen myself once do in Loskeetha's sand bowl; I hurled the sword at her, willing her death.

It turned in the air and its hilt struck between her eyes. She dropped and would have fallen back to the ledge, but her body caught against a point of rock and lay there, the sword in the earth, standing upright.

Dinzil, seeing her fall, halted. He looked up at me and began to laugh; it was the laughter I had heard from Kaththea, only more lost and evil. He raised his hand to me in salute as one salutes a clever bit of weapon-play.

But I was already sliding down beside Kaththea. I took up the sword and then her also, setting her body back in the slit between spur and cliff.

"The hero," he called. "Too little, too late, warrior from overmountain!"

He made a gesture and suddenly the sword slipped

from my grip. Nor could I make that misshapen paw grasp it again.

"And now harmless—" he laughed. He stood there, laughing with the rest of that company of the Shadow gathering behind him, watching me with their eyes or whatever organs served them for sight. These might not be of the Great Ones of evil, but they did now strive to reach such heights. I think even the Witches of Estcarp would not have willingly matched strength with them.

"You have found one talisman." Dinzil glanced to the sword. "If you had only known how to use it, you would have done better, my young friend. Now—"

What he meant for me I do not know. But that it was wholly of the dark I understood. Even death does not close some doors. But there was a slide of earth and small stones as Orsya came down in my wake. She held her right hand against her breast, and in it, point out, was the unicorn horn.

Whether by some magic of her own she mystified Dinzil, for the necessary moment or two, I do not know. But she was beside me and he still stood there. Then she plunged the point of the horn into her other hand so the blood welled up about it. As that flowed she reached out and caught my now useless paw, smearing it with the scarlet fluid. There was a tingle of returning life. I saw that foul toad flesh slough away and out of it emerge my fingers. Then I threw myself to the left and reached the sword.

The enemy was moving, not with weapons, but with their knowledge. As one might use a blacksmith's sledge to crush an ant, they were turning on me, on us, the weight of what they had been about to send against the Valley. To meet this I had nothing left but my weapon of despair.

I stumbled to my feet, sweeping Orsya behind me with my sister's body. This was indeed the last throw of fate. The sword I held up, not in a position of defense, but as one saluting an overlord. And I spoke the *words*. . . .

It had been sunset when we had come upon that gathering of attackers. Twilight had crept in as a part of their indrawing of dark force. Now it was instant day, with so brilliant a flash that I was blinded. I felt some of the substance of that light strike the sword blade, run through it and me—then out again. I was deaf; I was blind. Yet I heard the *answer*—and I saw. . . .

No, I can summon no words to describe what I saw, or think I saw, then. There had been many kinds of power loosed in Escore during the ancient struggles, and keys to some long forgot. Just as Dinzil had striven to find one of those keys, so had I, by chance and desperation, found another.

I was a channel for the power which *answered* my summons, and it used me. I was not a man, nor human, but a door through which it came into our space and time.

What it did there neither did I see. But it was gone as suddenly as it had come. I lay helpless against the earth while the heavens were filled with a storm such as I had never seen, and only lightning flashes broke the dark. I could not move. It was as if all the life which had been mine to command was now exhausted. I breathed, I could see the lightning, feel the lash of icy rain over me: that was all.

Sometimes I lapsed from consciousness, then I roused again. Weakly my thoughts moved as my body could not. After what seemed a long time, I called:

"Orsya?"

At first there was no answer, but I persisted, and that

became the one tie which held me to the world about me. I felt that if I ceased to call I would slip away into some nothingness and never come forth again.

"Orsya?"

"Kemoc—"

My name in her thoughts! It acted upon me as water upon a man dying of thirst. I struggled to rise and found that I could move a little, though I lay partly covered by a mass of earth and small stones. My numbed body began to feel pain.

"Orsya, where are you?"

"Here—"

I crawled—hardly rising from my belly, I crawled. Then my searching hand touched flesh and in turn was gripped eagerly by her webbed fingers. We drew together while about us the rain poured less heavily. The lightning ceased to beat along the ridges. Gradually the storm died, while we lay together, not speaking, content that both had survived.

Morning came. We were on the ledge where Dinzil had tried to bring power to move the world. There had been a slide down the mountain, half entrapping us. But the enemy I did no longer see.

"Kaththea!" Memory returned to sear me.

"There—" Already Orsya crawled to a body half hidden in a pile of earth. The green scarf was still twisted about my sister's head. I put out my hand to touch it. Then looked at the fingers Orsya had given back to me. Furiously I began to dig free Kaththea's body with those fingers.

When she lay straight upon the ledge, I set her paw hands upon her breast. Perhaps I could hide those so none would ever know why and what she had become.

But, under my hand I felt a faint beating—she was not dead!

"Orsya"—I turned to my companion—"you—you gave me back my hands. Can I give Kaththea back hers, and her face?"

She moved away from me, looking about as if she searched for something among the debris. "The horn—" Tears gathered in her eyes, ran down her slightly hollowed cheeks. "It is gone."

But I had seen something else—a glint of metal. Now I dug there, though my nails broke. Once more my hand was able to close about the hilt of the talisman sword. I jerked it free. But of the blade there remained now but a single small shard and that was not golden but black and dull. I tried it on the ball of my thumb. It was sharp enough and it was all I had.

I went back to Kaththea and tore off that much faded scarf, looked down at the monster head. Then I did as Orsya had done before me, I cut my flesh with that broken sword and allowed the blood to drip, first upon the head, and then upon the paws. As it had for me, but more slowly, the change came. The red skin and flesh melted; my sister's own face, her slender hands, were free of their horrible disguise. I gathered her into my arms and I wept—until she stirred in my hold and her eyes slowly opened. There was no recognition in them, only puzzlement. When I tried to reach her by mind call, I met first amazement and then terror. She fought to free herself from my hold as if I were some nightmare thing.

Orsya caught her hands, held them firmly but gently. "It is well, sister. We are your friends."

Kaththea clung to her, but still looked doubtfully at me.

The Krogan girl came to me a little later where I stood looking down at the havoc the storm had wrought. There were bodies in that wrack, but no man nor creature moved under the rising sun of a fine day.

"How is it with her?" I asked.

"Well, as to her body. But—Kemoc—she has forgotten who and what she was. What power she had is now gone from her!"

"For all time?" I could not imagine Kaththea so drained.

"That I cannot tell. She is as she might have been had she never been born a Witch—a maid, sweet of temper, gentle, and now very much in need of your strength and aid. But do not try to recall to her the past."

So it was that while Orsya and I brought Kaththea back to the Valley, we did not bring back the Kaththea who had been. And if she will ever be that again, no man nor witch can say. But the forces of the Shadow suffered a second defeat, and for a space we could ride Escore more boldly, though the darkness was far from cleansed. And our tale of three was not yet ended.

ANDRE NORTON

☐	78745-2	**STORM OVER WARLOCK**	$2.25
☐	63825-2	**ORDEAL IN OTHERWHERE**	$2.25
☐	24623-0	**FOREFUNNER FORAY**	$2.50
☐	27231-2	**GALACTIC DERELICT**	$2.25
☐	14236-2	**THE DEFIANT AGENTS**	$1.95
☐	81253-8	**THE TIME TRADERS**	$1.95
☐	43675-7	**KEY OUT OF TIME**	$2.25
☐	78434-8	**THE STARS ARE OURS**	$1.95
☐	78016-4	**STAR BORN**	$2.25